Shadows of BRIERLEY

The Wanderer

VOLUME ONE

OTHER BOOKS AND AUDIO BOOKS
BY ANITA STANSFIELD:

First Love and Forever
First Love, Second Chances
Now and Forever
By Love and Grace
A Promise of Forever
When Forever Comes
For Love Alone
The Three Gifts of Christmas
Towers of Brierley
Where the Heart Leads
When Hearts Meet
Someone to Hold
Reflections: A Collection of Personal Essays
Gables of Legacy Series, Six Volumes
Timeless Waltz
A Time to Dance
Dancing in the Light
A Dance to Remember
The Barrington Family Saga, Four Volumes
Emma: Woman of Faith
The Sound of Rain
A Distant Thunder
Winds of Hope
Shelter from the Storm
The Silence of Snow
The Best of Times
A Far, Far Better Place
A Loving Heart
Tranquil Light
Every Graceful Fancy

Shadows of BRIERLEY

The Wanderer

VOLUME ONE

a novel

ANITA STANSFIELD

Covenant Communications, Inc.

Cover: *By Candlelight* © Daniel F. Gerhartz. For more information go to www.danielgerhartz.com.

Published by Covenant Communications, Inc.
American Fork, Utah

Printed in the United States of America
First Printing: February 2011

17 16 15 14 13 12 11   10 9 8 7 6 5 4 3 2 1

ISBN: 978-1-60861-209-3

For Gabriel.
Welcome to the world.

Chapter One
Northward

London—1838

The coldness of the cobblestone alleyway crept through Ian's coat, luring him reluctantly into consciousness. Distant noises attempted to find recognition in his clouded brain. Peering through heavy eyelids, he saw a glimmer of faint light that felt frightening. Once his senses had evaluated his surroundings, Ian gasped and bolted to a sitting position, looking around himself frantically. He was alone. He was alive. The first was a relief; the latter a miracle. He felt beneath his coat for the haversack he wore hidden, and his relief deepened to find it there. At least his few remaining possessions had not been stolen while he'd been unconscious from his latest drunken escapade. Fearing he might have jumped too quickly to such a conclusion, he opened his coat and did a frenzied search inside the bag. He felt more than saw its contents, and let out a long, ragged sigh when he found everything there. Even the money was where he'd tucked it. Without what little he had left, he had no hope of ever seeing another day.

Ian finally pulled together enough presence of mind to get to his feet. He hung his head and groaned from the way it protested at being upright. When he finally gained some equilibrium, the pounding relented enough to make him believe that he could find his way out of this deserted alley and get his bearings. And then what? He couldn't keep going like this. If he didn't end up as a dead victim of thugs who might take advantage of his frequent drunken state, he would likely end up starving in a gutter somewhere, with no motivation or reason to keep living.

Ian felt almost capable of appearing normal by the time he'd walked to the end of the alley. Glancing in both directions, he was able to get a sense of where he was. Shopkeepers were just beginning to set out their wares, so he knew it was still early morning. He found a water pump and splashed cool water on his heavily stubbled face, then he ran his wet fingers through his thick, dark hair that was sorely in need of a trim. The mass of loose curls had completely lost any hope of control. The combination of the cool air and the colder water made him feel more awake. By then the market was coming to life with more noise and bustle, and he purchased a cup of steaming coffee from one vendor and a round of bread from another. He ate some of the bread and tucked the rest into the haversack beneath his coat.

He wandered aimlessly for the better part of the morning, resisting the temptation to slink into a pub and spend good money on a drink. When it occurred to him that his resistance wasn't likely to last through the day, he was struck more strongly than he ever had been that this path to self-destruction was quickly coming to a dead end. It was far from the first time that he'd considered the appalling futility of the way he was living. But for some reason, today it pierced something deep within him, something that reached beyond the pain and fear, something that wanted peace, something that had come to accept he would never find it by wandering and hiding. But where to begin? Thoughts of home tugged at his heart, but even these thoughts were enmeshed so thoroughly into the pain and fear that he doubted they could *ever* be untangled.

"Help me, God," he muttered under his breath, then noticed that he was headed in a general northward direction, as if some intangible magnetic force was pulling him toward home, even while an equal force seemed to drag him the other way. He continued north instinctively, as if the force of the North Star had some power over him, even in daylight.

A small crowd gathering at the end of the street caught his attention, and he moved in that direction, curious and desperately needing a diversion—any diversion that might keep him from ending up in a pub. As he neared the edge of the crowd, Ian could hear a loud voice preaching some kind of sermon. He bristled from the inside out. The very thought of God encouraged his guilt and tempted him to turn back to the pub where he could purchase the means to drown out the taunting voices of shame that had taken up comfortable residence in his tortured mind. He listened for a minute longer and was about to leave when the voice increased in volume with words that seized Ian's heart, preventing him from taking another step.

"Wherefore, redemption cometh in and through the Holy Messiah; for he is full of grace and truth. Behold, he offereth himself a sacrifice for sin, to answer the ends of the law, unto all those who have a broken heart and a contrite spirit; and unto none else can the ends of the law be answered."

Ian hesitated and turned again toward the crowd. He tried to get a look at the man who was speaking, but even as tall as Ian was, the volume of the crowd and the angle of his position made it impossible. He pressed carefully through the people gathered there—a cross-section of social status and backgrounds. When he finally came to a vantage point where he could see the speaker, he was surprised to see two men: one was holding up a book in his hand with a certain triumph while he spoke to the crowd of the unwavering love of Jesus Christ for all men and women, and the possibility of redemption no matter the sins or mistakes that had been made in this mortal state.

If only it were true, Ian thought and took notice of the other man standing beside the speaker, glowing with silent agreement with the words being spoken. Both men looked clean and groomed, but their manner of dress clearly signified poverty. And yet, there was something similar in the countenance of both men, something indescribably warm that caught Ian's attention and kept him standing there. He glanced at the people gathered around him, most of whom were mesmerized and eerily silent while they listened.

Ian turned his attention back to the preachers as the other one began to speak, reading out of that book his partner had been holding. Ian's heart began to pound for reasons beyond his own comprehension when he heard the words, "Awake, my sons; put on the armor of righteousness. Shake off the chains with which ye are bound, and come forth out of obscurity, and arise from the dust. Rebel no more against your brother . . ."

Ian didn't hear the rest; he didn't need to. It was as if the words had been spoken directly from God to his own heart. He felt almost heady with the effect. He *was* bound with chains, as surely as he was existing in obscurity. And he'd never rebelled against his brothers, but their differences had certainly contributed to his reasons for leaving home—or perhaps more accurately, his reasons for not returning.

Ian was startled when he realized the sermon was apparently over, and the two preachers were milling among the crowd. His heart quickened with a strange excitement when he realized they were selling copies of the book they'd been reading from. He had no idea what it was, but he felt as compelled to own a copy as he had been earlier to go into the pub and drown himself in liquor. He waited patiently for the crowd to thin while his thoughts wandered through memories and possibilities. Could he really go home? Was it possible to go back? To mend bridges that felt unmendable? Again he was startled when he realized that one of the men he'd heard speaking was standing in front of him, a smile on his face, his hand outstretched. He introduced himself, but Ian didn't have the presence of mind to remember his name. He did take the proffered handshake, and the tightness of this man's grip roused Ian to his senses.

"And you are?" the man asked.

"MacBrier," he said. "Ian MacBrier."

"Might I guess you're from Scotland?" the man asked.

Ian wasn't sure if it was the name or the accent that gave it away, but he nodded in response.

"You're a long way from home, then," the man said with an American accent.

"Not nearly as far as you are," Ian said, trying to ignore the sting that had been induced by this man's comment.

"All for a good cause," the man said. "If you've got some time, we would like to share a message with you about the—"

"Could I just . . . buy one of those books?" Ian asked. The man's face lit up, as if he knew the book might hold some secret that could change Ian's life. Ian handed over the money without even thinking about how much liquor he could have purchased with that amount.

The man started telling Ian about the origins of the book, but Ian didn't hear him. He thumbed through the pages, half wondering what he'd been thinking, and half wondering if it actually *might* hold some secret that could change his life. He absently thanked the man and left him standing there as he hurried away, tucking the book into his haversack and moving with more purpose in a general northward direction.

It occurred to Ian that if he actually intended to travel, he should get more bread, and perhaps some cheese—whatever his bag would hold. While he was making his purchases, he discreetly counted his remaining money and determined that he could get home a lot faster by carriage, but he wasn't sure he could afford that *and* food. But then, he would need less food if he was traveling more quickly. A heartbeat later his decision was made. He needed that ticket home as desperately as he'd needed that book. He considered it a miracle that he had enough money to get to Edinburgh. It would still be a long walk from there, but at least it would get him within a reasonable walking distance. He didn't think about how hungry he might be before he arrived. He could only think of going home, and he didn't bother to wonder why he'd been too terrified to even consider the possibility before today. And now he couldn't imagine any *other* possibility.

* * * * *

The Book of Mormon. Ian stared at the title with a sense of bewilderment that was likely rooted in his absolute exhaustion. He'd spent the first several hours of the journey in a seat on top of the carriage, since that's what he'd been able to afford. He'd been pelted with rain, and his skin felt windburned. But his mind had been filled with his destination and the possibilities of what might happen once he arrived. Had his loved ones changed? Or rather, had they changed the way they felt about him?

Now Ian was inside the carriage, since most of the other passengers had arrived at their destinations, and the space had opened up. Ian sat across from an elderly couple with kind smiles. Now that he was inside and out of the wind, Ian had tried to sleep. He'd dozed off for a while—he had no idea how long—but now he felt restless. He ate just enough of the bread and cheese from his bag to stop the growling in his stomach. Then he noticed the book he'd purchased and he took it out to look it over. He wondered now why he'd even purchased it. In retrospect, the decision seemed a little crazy. He wondered if his decision to go home was equally crazy. But it was too late to turn back now. Once he got to Edinburgh, home was the only place to go without first dying of starvation.

Ian thumbed through the book a bit, then put it away. Again he tried to rest with his head against the side of the carriage. His height made it awkward, and his neck kinked painfully until he stretched out a bit, grateful that no one was sitting next to him. As he began to relax, more pleasant memories of home filled his mind, offering some measure of comfort and a small dose of peace. He had come to believe that it was good for him to be going home. Home to Brierley.

Brierley. The enormous house called *Brierley* rested in all its magnificence in the highlands of Scotland, like a sentry guarding the huge estate and its tenant farmers. A tower stood at each of the four corners of the house, and Ian imagined standing on a nearby hill where he knew he could see the crowning stones at the top of each of those towers. From a distance they appeared identical, but he knew that one side of the house was built so tightly against the forest that it was impossible to actually walk around its entire perimeter. The other side of Brierley was banked by neatly manicured lawns and gardens of groomed shrubberies and luscious flowers. Ian thought of his brothers. He recalled the way they'd played in the gardens, and he had equally pleasurable memories of them venturing into the forest for great games of imagination and elaborate games of hide-and-seek among the trees. As the brothers matured, they had enjoyed riding through the trees—sometimes at a dangerous pace—or hunting game. Or sometimes they would just escape to the forest to lie back on the cool, shaded ground and talk, basking in the pleasant comfort of being brothers *and* friends.

Ian wondered what his brothers were doing now. James was likely flirting with some woman he shouldn't be flirting with. For all of his grand qualities, Ian's oldest brother was shameless in his philandering ways. Their parents had always declared that it would be his undoing. They had boldly taught their children that intimacy should be saved for marriage, and they had lectured, and exhorted, and pleaded with all the energy they possessed for James to not live his life in this deplorable way. Ian hoped it hadn't been James's undoing in the nearly two years that he had been gone.

Ian thought of his brother Donnan. He was Ian's elder by barely a year, and their mother had called them "the twins of separate births," due to their closeness in age and their inseparable nature. They were as close as brothers could be. There had been the natural brawls and bantering that occurred between growing boys, but all disputes had been mended quickly, and they could hardly bear being apart. Even living in a house as huge as Brierley, with numberless rooms available, they had chosen to share a bedroom so that they could talk to each other as they fell asleep and throw pillows at each other in the mornings, making the space between their beds an imaginary moat of evil that had to be crossed through dangerous endeavors in order to begin their day together.

Ian smiled to himself and settled more deeply into the carriage seat, his arms folded over his chest. He thought of his sister, Gillian, and wondered how she was doing. She'd been married more than a year prior to Ian's flight from home. She was now living in a home even larger than Brierley with her husband's family, more than a day's drive by carriage from Brierley. Ian had only seen her once following her marriage, when she'd announced that she was pregnant. He wondered if everything had gone all right with the birth. He wondered how old the child was now. Thoughts of Gillian saddened him, and the sadness deepened with thoughts of his parents. Of everyone in his family, he knew he'd hurt them most of all. Facing them would be the most difficult. But he had to do it. Too much time had passed. It had already gone on too long.

Gavin and Anya MacBrier were surely the kindest, greatest people in this world. Ian had spent the early years of his childhood believing that all parents were this way and that all children grew up loved and secure. It had been a rude, ugly awakening when he'd realized that wasn't true. If anything, the way that Ian's parents lived their lives was more unusual than it was common. Ian had always felt an inner sense of gratitude for being born into such a family, but that didn't mean he hadn't taken it for granted. Now he longed for the opportunity to express such feelings to his parents. Of all the people he'd hurt, he knew they would be the most forgiving. He didn't have to wonder if they'd be happy to see him. But facing them was the most difficult, simply because he knew how much he had disappointed them. He could face the anger of his brothers with more courage than he could face any form of sadness or disappointment in the eyes of his parents, knowing he was the cause.

Outside of his family circle, there was only one other person he feared facing—and he feared that most of all. *Ailsa Wren Docherty.* To him she was simply Wren. She detested being called Ailsa, and far preferred the middle name her father had insisted on at her birth. He'd never had any particular fascination with the birds of the same name; he'd just liked the name. And Ian couldn't deny that it suited her.

Perhaps Wren would be married by now. Perhaps she would have forgotten all about him, or at the very least become indifferent over his well-being or his desire to apologize for how he'd hurt her in ways too numerous to count. Only when he thought of *her* did tears sting his eyes with too much force to be held back by his closed eyelids. He took a quick peek to see if his traveling companions had noticed the tears on his face. Relieved to see that they were both resting with their eyes closed, he hurried to wipe the tears away and shifted his position so he would lean less conspicuously against the other side of the carriage. He finally drifted toward oblivion while images of Wren's rich, dark hair and eyes of a green so dark they were almost black rose to haunt him. He imagined those eyes burning a hole in his heart and shuddered before he settled into a tormented sleep.

Ian started from sleep to find the carriage moving into the crowded streets of Edinburgh. It felt good to get out and stretch his legs, then the reality descended over him that he had a long walk ahead of him. He dug out his last few remaining coins and purchased more bread, realizing that he had very little left. Then he headed in the direction of the highlands, toward the home of his youth, toward Brierley.

Evening came on quickly as the noise of the city receded far behind him. Before darkness fell, he found a place in a meadow with tall grasses where he could rest far from the road and be hidden from any possible passersby. He ate a bit more, then tried to find some measure of a comfortable position. He pulled his coat more tightly around him, but he still felt cold. Exhausted as he was, he searched the starlit sky as if he might find a star to guide him back to Brierley. Or perhaps he was hoping to find some kind of comfort in facing what he knew would meet him when he arrived. Focusing on a particular star that caught his attention, he allowed its light to accompany him to sleep. Dreams of the comfort of home merged into nightmares of how tainted it had become prior to his leaving. He came awake to the light of dawn, relieved to find himself alone and in a place where there was no threat to his safety. He was also freezing. Walking seemed the best way to warm up, so he jumped to his feet and pressed on.

Ian focused entirely on putting one foot in front of the other, ignoring the hunger that had nothing to satisfy it. Hours later, he was actually startled to look up and see the village of his destination in the evening light. He knew the streets and the shops. He knew the people and everything about them. And they also knew him. They knew his mistakes. And they knew the ugly rumors that had surely blazed in the wake of his leaving. Would these people believe that Greer's death had been his fault? How could they not when Ian believed it himself? He couldn't remember exactly what had happened. But he knew the results. Greer had been his closest friend from childhood, as good as a brother. And now he was dead. Ian should have had the presence of mind to get him out of the fire. But he'd been too drunk to do anything but get his own sorry carcass to safety.

Ian forced his mind to the present and willed himself to move on. He would never know what the townspeople thought of him if he didn't just face them and find out for himself. But facing them was insignificant in light of the hearts he'd broken. And before he could face his family, he needed to face the woman he'd hurt most. Or perhaps he was deluding himself to think that she was hurt at all. Maybe she'd quickly moved on. Maybe he should give her credit for being smart enough to realize that he wasn't the right man for her, and never had been.

Knowing he'd never get any answers just standing there, Ian gathered courage and wrapped it tightly around his heart before he took the final steps toward facing the past he'd left behind.

* * * * *

Wren neatly folded the tailored items that would be picked up tomorrow by anxious customers. She glanced at the clock, glad for evidence that the day was coming to a close. She relished the peacefulness of these nighttime hours that only concluded when exhaustion forced her to end her reprieve with sleep. Even though she generally needed to work on sewing one thing or another every waking minute when she was not occupied with other tasks, she loved the hours when no one was making demands on her and no one needed her care.

"Wren!" her father called from the other room, reminding her that those who needed her were never far away.

Wren went through the curtained doorway that separated the Docherty Tailor Shop from the four tiny rooms where she lived with her father and sister. She found her father sitting on the edge of his bed, looking as if he might cry. He was staring down at his feet—one with only a stocking, and the other still shoed. Angus Docherty said in a voice that was almost childlike, "The lace is knotted; I can't do it."

"It's all right, Pa," Wren said and went to her knees to untangle the knot with little effort.

Angus gave her an appreciative smile, and Wren tried to ignore the silent apology that accompanied it. Her father's arthritis had worsened suddenly over the last several months, until his hands were so stiff and sore that he could no longer do the intricate needlework that he was famous for in this village. His inability to work and provide for his daughters had broken his heart, and no amount of reassurance would soothe his constant discouragement over that fact. Angus was largely able to care for himself, and he even managed to help with some cooking and laundry. He had no trouble interacting with customers in the shop to take orders or deliver them. But his hands couldn't manage anything that required the more complex use of his fingers. Wren's sister Bethia had cleverly modified their father's clothing so that his breeches could be fastened with a drawstring and his shirts could be pulled over his head. With no buttons or hooks, he needed no help with any task that would cause him any personal embarrassment. But there were moments such as this when he had need of help from one of his girls, and such moments never failed to enhance Angus's feelings of humiliation and uselessness. Wren knew from experience there was nothing she could say to soothe him, so she just smiled and kissed his brow as she came to her feet.

"Did ye get yer medicine?" she asked.

"I did," he said. "Thank ye, m' dear."

"Sleep well," she said and left the room, knowing that he would be sleeping deeply in less than half an hour—thankfully aided by the medicinal liquid that the local physician had prescribed to ease the arthritis pain. Angus only took it at night because it made him so sleepy, and during the days he just endured the pain and tried not to grumble too much. In Wren's opinion, her father's definition of not grumbling *too much* was far different from her own. As she saw it, all he did was grumble. But she had no way to understand his pain, and she tried to be kind in return. Still, the fact that he often went quickly to bed after supper and slept late into the morning was a blessing she would not dispute.

Wren walked through the little kitchen on her way back to the shop, noting with gratitude that her father had washed the dishes from supper and everything looked tidy. Bethia was sitting at the table, leaning toward a lamp, sewing diligently on a fine waistcoat that had been ordered just today. Wren did well enough with the basic skills of her father's trade, but Bethia had a knack for it that Wren couldn't quite master. Therefore, Bethia was always responsible for the creation of the intricate pieces and orders that came from especially fussy customers. No one was ever displeased with Bethia's work, even though most of their customers still gave credit to Angus for most of the fine tailoring work that came out of the shop. Since Angus had hardly stepped beyond the shop since his arthritis had crippled him, few people knew the truth. They just assumed that he was in the back room sewing away while his daughters ran the shop and did a few stitches here and there. Wren didn't care what people thought, as long as they kept purchasing enough goods to keep her and her loved ones fed.

"It's getting late," Wren said to her sister, pressing a loving hand over the dark blonde hair that hung down her back.

"I'll go t' bed soon," she said. "Or perhaps I'll read. Reading makes me feel better."

"Are ye feeling poorly?" Wren asked, sitting across from her.

Bethia looked up with an expression that Wren knew well. It was the look Bethia gave her several times a day that was as good as saying, *Ye know the truth about me. We both know I'm crazy, but I'm doing m' best not to cause any trouble for ye.*

Bethia returned to her sewing, and Wren asked, "Is it worse than usual today?"

Bethia sighed and tipped her head to better see her work. "Jinty was very agitated today, but Selma kept her calm."

"Where are Jinty and Selma now?" Wren had become accustomed to talking about them as if they were real people. To Bethia they *were* real, except that a part of her understood—sometimes—that they were a product of her ailing mind.

"In the cellar . . . sleeping, I hope."

"I hope so too," Wren said. "And I hope they let ye get a good night's sleep." She paused and asked, "Do ye want t' sleep in my room tonight instead of in the cellar?" It took courage to offer; dealing with the nighttime panic that sometimes overtook Bethia was never easy. But she hated the thought of her sister secluded in the little cellar, all alone while she dealt with her personal demons.

"I feel safe in the cellar," Bethia said without missing a stitch. "Greer takes care of me."

Wren bristled as she always did at such a mention of Greer. He was Bethia's husband, but he'd been dead for nearly two years. Wren had become accustomed to the imaginary people that existed in her sister's mind, and rarely was there a problem caused by them that Wren couldn't handle. But when Bethia spoke of her husband as if he were still alive and well, it caused a different kind of concern for Wren. But she just kissed the top of her sister's head and said, "I'll close up the shop."

Wren walked back through the curtain that divided the shop from their living quarters. She turned the sign in the window so that it read *Closed* instead of *Open*. Then, out of habit, she moved around the perimeter of the little shop, making certain that all of the fabrics and notions were dust-free and perfectly displayed for tomorrow's potential customers. Locking the door was always the very last thing that she did. Her sister had once noticed the order of her habits, and her explanation had been that she might be hoping for one final customer that might bring in more business. But the truth was that she secretly hoped for someone in particular to come through that door; someone she missed, someone she worried about every hour of her life.

* * * * *

Ian walked through the dark, familiar streets, naturally gravitating toward the tailor's shop that was almost a second home to him. He stopped for a moment when it came into view. A faint, yellow glow emitted from the large window where samples of fine clothing were displayed. It gleamed like a beacon to him, urging him forward. When he was close enough to reach out and open the door, he stopped again, his heart thudding in his chest as he saw Wren with her back to the door, fussing meticulously over the wares for sale. He took a deep breath, made certain all of the courage he'd gathered was still in place, and took hold of the knob to turn it.

A little bell over the door tinkled as he opened the door and closed it again. The familiarity of the sound startled something inside him, bringing him to the realization that he'd finally come back to everything he'd left behind, everything he'd willfully avoided.

"We're closed," Wren said without turning around, and her voice had the same effect on him as the bell. She wore a dark, well-worn dress. Typical. Her hair was loosely knotted at the back of her head, although much of it had strayed from its confinement throughout the course of a long day. Also typical.

"The door wasn't locked," he said.

"But the sign clearly states that we're closed."

"I didn't come for business," he said and saw her freeze. Had it taken that many words for her to recognize his voice? "I came to see you, and I've come a very long way."

Wren squeezed her eyes closed tightly, as if doing so might allow her ears to focus more intently and convince her mind that she was not imagining that he was really here—the way her sister imagined things. There was a long moment where she almost feared that the problem was hereditary; she feared that she wanted so desperately for it to be him that perhaps she had conjured him up as a hallucination. It took an act of bravery for her to turn around. If he wasn't really there, she wondered if she could find anything more to hope for, anything that might prod her to keep going.

Ian could hardly draw breath when Wren turned abruptly to look at him. Her dark eyes burned into his heart, just as he'd predicted. His regret over leaving deepened in exact proportion to his relief at coming back. They stared at each other while Ian imagined crossing the room and taking her into his arms. He imagined kissing her boldly and touching her face and hair with all the seeming madness he felt after being away from her so long. But he just stood there, not knowing what to say, not capable of moving.

"Ian," she said, his name easing through her lips on the labored breath that she let out slowly. "Tell me ye are real."

"I'm real," he said. She crossed the room abruptly, and he held his breath. She stopped directly in front of him, looking up into his eyes as if to further gauge the answer to her question. Then, with no warning, she slapped him hard across the face.

Ian put his hand over the sting, taking a moment to steady his breath before he turned back to look at her. "I suppose I earned that."

"Aye, indeed!" she rumbled. Again they stared at each other, while he felt that hole in his heart burning deeper. Then, with as little warning as the slap, she threw her arms around his neck and buried her face in the folds of his coat, oblivious to how many days it had been since he'd had access to warm water sufficient to shave or clean up.

It took Ian a moment to accept the fact of her embrace. He wrapped her in his arms and forced great self-restraint to keep from bawling like a baby. He managed to harness his emotion back to a little sting of moisture in his eyes, and she held on to him long enough that he was even able to blink that away.

"Wren," he whispered, and she looked up at him. He saw tears in her eyes when she took his face into her hands and once again searched his eyes. "I don't know what to say," he said and looked down, unable to bear the eye contact any longer.

Wren let go and took a step back; she didn't know what to say either. The details of his physical condition jumped past the reality of his presence, and she felt alarmed. He was cold and exhausted; dirty and likely hungry. He looked gaunt and haggard.

"Ye've not been home yet," she said. "Ye've not seen yer family."

He shook his head. "No. I . . ."

"Was it because ye wanted t' see me first, or because ye didn't want them t' see ye like *this?*" She motioned toward him with her hand.

Ian extracted a strange comfort from her saucy tone of voice. He didn't feel scolded as much as he felt comfortable. Her forthright honesty had always made it so easy to be completely honest in return. He was glad to know she'd not changed in that regard.

"Both," he said.

Wren looked him up and down. "Ye can at least wash up and shave," she said, "but it's far too late for ye t' be going home tonight. If ye're walking, ye won't get there until the middle of the night."

"I don't suspect your father will be terribly pleased to see me," Ian said. "I don't want to cause trouble for you, or—"

"My father is sound asleep and will be far int' the morning. I've got no place for ye t' sleep but the floor, although . . ." She looked him over again. "I suspect ye've slept in worse places."

Ian didn't answer. She was right, but he didn't want to admit it.

"Come along," she said, and they stepped through the curtain into the kitchen. Bethia looked up from her sewing.

"Ian!" she said, sounding more afraid than surprised. She rose to her feet as if she might be wanting to run.

"Hello, Bethia," he said.

Bethia's eyes moved slowly and cautiously toward her sister, and she asked in a timid voice, "Is he real?"

Something felt strange to Ian, and an uneasiness in his gut encouraged the feeling. Wren had asked him the same question, but this was different. Bethia really meant it.

"What does she mean?" Ian asked, feeling Bethia's frightened eyes on him again.

"Aye, he's real," Wren said to her sister, who immediately relaxed. Wren turned toward him and whispered, "I'll explain later." More loudly to her sister, she said, "Ian is going t' get cleaned up and sleep here on the floor t'night. Will that alarm ye?"

"No, of course not," Bethia said. "I feel safe with Ian."

"Good, I'm glad," Wren said, lighting the stove where a pot of water was already sitting, ready for morning. She looked Ian up and down. "I don't suppose ye have a change of clothes."

"I do," he said, "but they're dirty as well."

"I'm sure ye could borrow some of Greer's clothes," Bethia said. Ian's heart quickened at the mention of his friend, now dead and buried. While he'd been wandering for nearly two years, attempting to come to terms with that fact, he'd often wondered how Greer's wife and sister-in-law had dealt with the loss. Now he was looking into Bethia's eyes, and he saw no sign of grief at the mention of her dead husband. His heart quickened for different reasons when she added, "I'm sure he won't miss them for a day or two, but ye must promise t' bring them back before he needs them."

Ian caught a discreet glance from Wren that seemed some kind of warning. He looked firmly at Bethia and said, "Of course. I'll have them back in a day or two; I promise."

Bethia smiled and went through the door that Ian knew led to the cellar. Alone with Wren, he turned to look at her, not even knowing how to ask about her sister's behavior.

Wren focused on reheating the stew that had been left over from supper, even though she could feel Ian's eyes burning into her back with a question she didn't want to answer. But he needed to know, and Bethia would be back in a minute. Without looking at him, she said, "It's gotten much worse since . . ."

"Since what?" he asked, unable to keep from sounding angry, even though he kept his voice down. "Since Greer died?"

Wren looked at him. "Aye. Since Greer died."

"It seems *everything* has gotten worse since Greer died," Ian said. "But I don't even know what you're talking about. Is there something I'm supposed to already know that would explain why Bethia believes her husband is going to need his clothes?"

Ian's uneasiness increased dramatically at the evidence of Wren's astonishment. "Surely ye knew."

"Knew *what*?" he demanded quietly.

Wren glanced over her shoulder to make certain that Bethia had not returned. "I can't believe Greer didn't tell ye."

"Tell me *what*?"

"It came on slowly . . . there were signs of it even before they were married . . . but he married her anyway. He took very good care of her. He really loved her."

It suddenly came back to him. Ian shoved down the guilt. "I know he did, Wren."

He stopped when they heard Bethia coming up the stairs from the cellar. She gave Ian a little stack of neatly folded clothing. "Ye're close enough t' Greer's size," she said. "That should be everything ye need."

"Thank you," Ian said.

Bethia looked up at him, smiled with tenderness, and touched his face. "It's good t' see ye well, Ian. Greer will be pleased t' know that ye've come back." She turned toward Wren, and the sisters exchanged a kiss on the cheek. "Good night," she said.

"Sleep well," Wren said, and Bethia went down the cellar stairs, closing the door behind her. Ian could only stare at the door and try not to collapse. The exhaustion and hunger consumed him. But they were nothing in light of his sorrow, his guilt, his unfathomable regret. Greer's death was his fault. And Greer's wife had completely lost her mind in his absence. He wanted to run away again, as fast and as far as he could go. But he didn't have the strength to do anything but turn to look at Wren and wish that she would slap him again. He'd certainly earned it.

Chapter Two
The Prodigal

Wren saved Ian from the dissolution that was threatening him when she shifted to practicality. "Sit down and eat something before ye fall over." She took the clothes from him and set them aside before she practically pushed him into a chair.

"Has anyone ever told you that you're little better than a bully in a skirt?"

Wren stopped for a moment in her attempt to dish up a large bowl of stew. His words stirred up a bucketful of memories, but the good ones quickly drained out of the holes caused by the tragedies that had preceded his leaving, and mostly by his leaving.

"Can you ever forgive me?" he asked, as if he'd known exactly what she'd been thinking. But then, what else would she be thinking?

Wren set the bowl and a spoon in front of him. "Eat," she ordered. "Ye're starving and I know it. There's no need t' be polite and pretend otherwise."

Ian looked at the food in front of him and almost wanted to cry. He was *so* hungry that he wanted to just bury his face in the bowl like some kind of animal. He picked up the spoon, feeling the need to avoid behaving like a savage. Wren then set a thick slice of dark bread in front of him, along with an empty tin cup and a pitcher of water.

"Don't go too quickly and make yerself sick," she said, then she left him alone, going into the room where he knew she slept. He'd spent a great deal of time in her home—and in the shop—but he'd never once been in *that* room. She'd always shared the room with her sister, and he wondered what reason there was for Bethia to now be sleeping in the cellar—a place that he knew to be tiny and dark and even a little creepy. He had a hundred questions he wanted to ask about Bethia, and even more that he wanted to know about how Wren had managed during the time he'd been gone. But the aroma of the stew steered his entire attention to eating. He took a spoonful and savored it slowly, then the next spoonful came into his mouth more quickly. He reminded himself of Wren's advice—to not eat too quickly. But the stark emptiness of his stomach, and the human need for sustenance, drove him to eat with near madness. He was grateful to be alone, certain he'd try to exercise more discipline if Wren were in the room. The bread added a sustaining complement to the stew, and the water felt refreshing and almost cleansing as he gulped it down with hearty appreciation.

Wren returned when he only had a few bites left, and he was able to finish off his meal in a gentlemanly manner. She was holding a towel and a basin which she set on the table. He noticed soap and a shaving blade in the basin.

"I dare say," she said, "that ye could sneak in the back door of Brierley and get t' yer room t' change clothes before ye have t' face anyone, but ye can't get a bucket of water in that place without the whole world knowing it."

"Precisely," he said.

She sat across the small table from him. He glanced toward her, then had to look again. Her desire to hide the fact that she'd been crying was evident, but the redness around her eyes was equally evident.

"Tears?" he asked, setting down his spoon.

Wren looked away, almost hating him for his perception, the same way she'd tried to hate him all this time for leaving the way he had. But his absence had only proven that no amount of anger could change the way she felt about him. She wasn't ready to tell him how desperately she'd missed him, and how much she'd needed him as life had steadily worsened in the months following Greer's death. She didn't want to tell him how much she'd needed his listening ear and his shoulder to cry on. They'd been friends long before this deeper attraction had risen unexpectedly between them. As honest as they'd always been with each other, those feelings had never been openly acknowledged. Of course, it had all been complicated in ways that had yet to be sorted out, complicated long before Greer's death had catapulted Ian into some kind of painful, desperate fog that Wren had never been able to understand. And then he'd left. Gone, with nothing but a cursory note as an explanation.

Wren summoned enough courage to meet his eyes again, wishing she could tell him that the feelings that had only begun to blossom two years ago had grown each day of his absence, which had broken her heart a little more every day. She felt angry with him for that, but too relieved by his presence to address it—at least for now.

"Did ye get enough t' eat?"

"Yes, thank you. I *was* hungry, I admit. You're not going to tell me why you were crying?"

Wren had no intention of spilling her broken heart at his feet. She wanted to tell him to mind his manners *and* his business. She wanted to shout at him and tell him every detail of the sorrow and fear he'd left her to face without a friend in the world. She wanted to call him a selfish coward, and tell him that he had a lot of nerve crawling back to her, half-starved and rueful. For all the words circling in her brain, begging to be voiced, she could only stare at him, uncharacteristically silent.

Ian tried to assess whether she was glad to have him here or whether she was wishing he would have never come back. The slap she'd given him, followed by the embrace, added to his confusion. But perhaps she was as confused as he, and the only way to clear up confusion was to resolve it. And that would never happen while they sat there and stared at each other. He hated the question that was most prominent on his mind, but since he was unable to stop thinking it, he figured it might be a good place to start untangling this mess.

"Have you been seeing James?" he asked, and she looked insulted, perhaps angry.

"Why would I be seeing James?" she snapped in that saucy tone, and Ian questioned his judgment in even bringing it up. But he needed to know.

"Are you going to pretend that I wasn't the person you cried to—over and over, I might point out—about my brother's insensitivity to your feelings for him? Do I need to remind you of how it was your deepest wish that he would put a stop to his philandering ways and choose *you* to settle down with?"

"That was a long time ago. Some things change."

"And some things don't."

Wren tried not to read too deeply into the implications of Ian's accusations. She just took a deep breath and stated the simplest truth. "My infatuation with James ended a long time ago. Ye should know that I had realized ye'd been right all along . . . that love dies quickly in the light of bad behavior and lack of commitment."

"Why should I know that?"

Wren's eyes sparked green fury; her expression darkened with barely disguised defensiveness. "Because it should have been evident I'd come t' my senses long before ye left."

Ian's voice was more quiet. "It wasn't *so* long . . . and I could only suspect. You never actually said it." His pause implied some hope for a comment from her. She only turned her green fury toward the wall. "Funny how a woman who can hardly bite her tongue enough to keep from being brutally honest could avoid telling her best friend such a thing."

The green fury found its way back to glare at him, even more furious. "Some friend ye turned out t' be! Yer leaving here was pathetically craven! That was yer solution t' the problem? Breaking hearts that were already broken? Leaving us t' pick up pieces that were too shattered t' gather?"

Ian took her anger with dignity. He knew he deserved it. Silence echoed her taunting, and he looked away, unable to face her as he said, "There is no apology sufficient for what I did, Wren. I beg your forgiveness, but I'm not sure I'll ever be worthy of it." He looked back at her, surprised to see the fire of fury being extinguished by pools of moisture that magnified the green of her eyes.

The pot of water on the stove began to boil with a noisy bubbling. Wren rose to close the vent on the stove that would prevent any air from feeding the fire. With her back to him she said, "Ye know where t' get cold water t' cool off the hot. I'm going t' bed so ye don't have t' worry about having some privacy t' get cleaned up."

She walked out of the room while Ian tried to muster the ambition to follow her suggestion. When she came back only a moment later, he had the urge to just fall at her feet and beg her forgiveness. He wanted to tell her how he'd thought about her every waking moment, and how she had even invaded his dreams. He wanted to pledge his undying love to her and hear her proclaim the same in return. But he was exhausted to the core and too weary to confront whatever her response to such dramatic declarations might be.

Wren set two blankets and a pillow on the chair where she'd been sitting. "I assume ye have what ye need."

"Yes, thank you," he said. "Thank you for everything."

Wren nodded slightly to accept his gratitude and turned toward her room. She turned back from the doorway and said, "I'm glad ye're safe, Ian."

She closed the door, and Ian sat there, unable to move for interminable minutes. His body felt incapable of moving, while his mind roiled with everything that had been said between them since he'd walked through the door; everything that he'd experienced since he'd last seen her; every unanswered question regarding what *she* had experienced. He finally roused himself enough to get cleaned up and shave. He put on Greer's clothes, which were slightly too big around the middle and too short in the legs and arms. But at least they were clean. He stuffed his own dirty clothes into his haversack and cleaned up after himself before he crawled into his makeshift bed on the floor. The hardness of the wood slats beneath him was certainly no worse than the alleyways of London on the countless nights he'd fallen asleep there. Tumultuous thoughts of Wren merged into the realization that tomorrow he would have a whole new battle to wage. Tomorrow he needed to face his family.

* * * * *

Wren doubted she could sleep *at all,* knowing that Ian MacBrier was sleeping on her kitchen floor. Or perhaps it was presumptuous to think that he was sleeping. Perhaps he was as wide awake as she, full of questions and regrets. She suspected their regrets were for different reasons, but probably equal in self-torment. A part of her wanted to be as brutally honest as he'd accused her of being and just spill her every thought and feeling. But he'd broken her trust the day he'd walked away. He would have to earn it back before she could fully open her heart again. And perhaps such a thing wasn't even possible. Perhaps they'd both changed too much for such a thing to even be wished for.

After more than an hour of pondering and stewing, the tears she'd managed to hide from Ian earlier came again in torrents. She had to fight for silence in freeing her emotion, knowing the walls were thin and Ian was not so far from the other side of the door. She cried and cried, wishing the tears would stop, wishing she had any idea where she *really* stood with Ian. Prior to Greer's death, Ian had been her best and closest friend. They'd been together through events that had an eerie echo of destiny in her memories. Her only vexation had stemmed from his habit of getting ridiculously drunk on occasion. The few times she'd been around him when he was in that condition, he'd made a complete fool of himself and she'd been furious with him. But then, Greer and Ian's brothers—and even her father—had the same habits; worse in some cases. In fact, there was hardly a man in this village who didn't occasionally make a point of getting senselessly drunk, as if it might relieve all their worries and strains of life. Wren couldn't understand how the hangover the next day made the temporary reprieve anywhere near worth it. But what did she know about men and their silly rituals when they gathered in the pubs? And as for Ian, that had been a very long time ago. Now he was sober and changed—and here. It would take time to discover exactly *how* he had changed, and perhaps it would be even more of a challenge to assess how *she* had changed in his absence.

Wren was surprised to wake up and find the room growing faintly light—surprised mostly because she hadn't expected to be able to sleep at all. She heard subtle noises from the kitchen and knew that Ian was up and moving about. Inexplicably, tears overtook her again, but she was determined to get them under control before she opened the door to face him.

* * * * *

Ian dreamt that Wren was there beside him, whispering in his ear that everything would be all right, that they would be together forever, that she loved him as he loved her. He woke to see the room glowing with the faint light that preceded dawn, and he came to his feet with the same urgency he'd felt when waking up in dark alleys, fearing for his life. He carefully folded the blankets and set them with the pillow on the chair where Wren had left them. He looked around to be certain he hadn't left any other signs of his presence, then he sat down to pull on his boots, glad they would cover the fact that his legs were longer than Greer's. Tugging on the second boot, he was startled by Wren opening her bedroom door. Her face showed telltale signs of tears *and* not enough sleep. She wrapped her robe more tightly around her and leaned against the doorjamb.

"I'm sorry if I woke you." He kept his voice down to avoid waking her father.

"Ye didn't. I never would have heard ye if I hadn't already been awake. Did ye get any sleep?"

"Some. You?"

"Some," she said, wondering what had reduced them to such trivial exchanges. "Ye look better," Wren added, noting his clean-shaven face that made him look more like himself. And he didn't look quite so gaunt and exhausted. The clean clothes aided his appearance as well.

"I probably smell better, too," he said wryly and came to his feet.

He reached for his coat, and she felt a little panicked. Was she afraid he wouldn't return? Or was there something in her that simply felt more safe and secure in his presence? Both, perhaps.

"Ye're leaving already?" she asked, taking a step toward him.

"Do you really want your father to find me here?"

Wren tipped her head. "Perhaps he's softened toward ye over time."

"And perhaps he hasn't. Either way, I have enough drama to face today without creating any more of it here."

Her silence implied that she understood. Ian didn't *want* to leave. He wanted to stay here with her and forever avoid facing his family. He wanted to ask her to come with him, to stand by his side and hold his hand, as if that might somehow soften the inevitable difficulties. Instead he just gave her a wan smile and said, "Thank you, Wren. I'll make it up to you."

"There's no need for that," she said. "I'm glad t' be here for ye."

Ian took that in with a quickened heartbeat, wondering if there was a deeper implication, wishing that there was.

"Will I see ye soon?"

"Of course," he said. He put a hand to the shirt he was wearing. "I'll need to return Greer's clothes . . . before he needs them." He tried to make the comment sound light, but it came out sounding somewhat ironic and a bit callous. Not wanting her to think that he needed an *excuse* to see her, he hurried to add, "Of course I'll see you; often, I hope."

She smiled, but he wasn't sure if she agreed. He reached for his haversack, and she looked as if she'd forgotten something. She hurried to wrap some bread in a napkin and handed it to him. "It's a long walk t' Brierley. Ye mustn't go without a little something for breakfast."

"Thank you," he said.

Another idea occurred to her, and she said, "I'm certain Blane would loan ye a horse so—"

"I'd rather not," he said, knowing Blane was an older man who owned the livery near the tailor's shop. He'd always been kind to Wren and her family, and Ian knew him well as a result. "Truthfully, I need to face my family before I have to face . . . everyone else."

Wren felt deeper meaning in the comment. "Do ye think the people of this town will . . . what? Blame ye for the fire? For Greer's death?"

Ian heard some measure of how ludicrous that sounded, but at the same time it pierced him with echoes of the countless times those very words had coursed through his mind. "Perhaps," was all he said.

"There's only one person who held ye responsible, Ian. *One person.* There's only one person ye have to face on that count."

"Who?" he snapped, imagining some bloody fist fight in the streets.

"It is only *ye,* Ian," she said, and it stunned him. *"No one* placed any blame at yer feet except *yerself.* It's a terrible irony, isn't it? That with all yer trying t' run from the guilt, ye couldn't put any distance between ye and yerself."

Ian found himself stuck again, staring at her while she stared at him. Prior to his leaving, he'd believed there could be nothing worse than the shame and guilt he'd felt over Greer's death. Now he knew that wasn't true. The shame and guilt he felt over running away had long ago surpassed it. But it hadn't eradicated it, only exacerbated it. Now he *still* had to face up to inner demons that were only more inflamed than they'd been when he'd left. And he had to also face up to the hurt he'd left behind. Knowing that the need to face it would not go away, he sighed and said, "I should go. Thank you."

Wren nodded and watched him go out the back door from the kitchen. She stood in the doorway, watching him go past the wood pile and the water pump, past the clothesline and out the gate. She leaned in the open doorway and watched until he'd turned the corner and was out of sight.

"I love ye, Ian MacBrier," she said into the cool morning air before she closed the door and talked herself into facing another day.

* * * * *

Ian stood at the crest of the hill and took in the magnificence of the towers of Brierley. He'd walked a route that he'd sometimes taken by horseback when he'd preferred a more tranquil ride, since it was far from the road where he might cross paths with anyone coming or going. The view was all so strange and so familiar.

Ian sat down on the wet grass for a long while, acknowledging the need to be honest with himself in his reasons for leaving—and for coming back. It was more the former that concerned him. For as long as he could remember, he'd been afflicted with a deep desire to leave his home and to wander to other lands beyond this valley. As a child he had fantasized about going to strange places and had spoken of it often. In his youth, his sights had always been set on some distant place with no name and no form in his mind, but he'd felt certain that when he became old enough to leave, he would surely find it. He'd always felt odd and out of place. Not one of his friends or family members had any such feelings, and he'd often wondered if there was something wrong with him. These same feelings had contributed to Ian's rash decision to leave. After having pondered it for so many years, the pain of Greer's death had smothered all logic, and all he'd been able to see was the possibility of escaping to some fantastic euphoria that existed anywhere but here.

Ian knew now that his strange desire to leave had been nothing more than a curse. It had plagued him and driven him away. But now he felt cured. He had no desire to ever leave here again and imagined himself growing old among loved ones in these familiar surroundings. With that image firm in his mind, Ian stood up and brushed off the back of his coat before he started down the hill. While he dreaded facing up to the consequences of his absence, he suddenly felt desperate to be with his loved ones, and he resisted the temptation to run the remaining distance. On foot, the final stretch took longer than expected. The house was so big that it had seemed closer than it actually was. The closer he got, the more the familiarity settled in. His heart quickened when he made his way discreetly around the back of the stables and to a side door that was rarely used. In his youth he had most often used this door to go in and out, and to bring friends to his home. The front door was traditionally formal, and there were other entrances commonly used by the servants.

When Ian was close enough to the house to touch it, he had to just stop and do so. The stones of Brierley felt cold beneath his hand, but a warmth burned inside of him that beckoned him impatiently inside. He stood for a moment in the dim hallway, considering the time of day and where he might find his parents. While he was thinking about it, he decided to see if he could actually make it to his own room without being detected, as Wren had suggested. Wearing his own clothes might boost his confidence. He dashed up one of the back staircases, peered around the corner, and arrived at his room unnoticed. When he opened the door, he was glad that he and Donnan had long ago graduated to separate rooms. He didn't want to run into him now; he needed to see his parents first. And thankfully it wasn't mealtime, when they all might be gathered together.

Ian breathed in the familiar surroundings, thinking of the hundreds of times he'd wondered if he would ever know such comforts again. He tossed his coat onto the bed and opened the wardrobe to see his clothes exactly as he had left them. He threw the haversack into the bottom of the wardrobe, then traded Greer's shirt and breeches for some of his own. Their loose fit was evidence that he'd lost weight, but they still fit better than Greer's clothes. While buttoning a waistcoat, Ian looked at himself in a long mirror for the first time in many, many months. He pushed his hands through his long, tangled curls, knowing it would take more than a good brushing to achieve any improvement. He pressed a hand to one side of his face, then the other. The tiny mirror he'd used last night to shave hadn't betrayed the changes in his face. He felt as if he were looking at a stranger. He looked older than his years, he thought, then he finished buttoning the waistcoat and tugged on it as he pulled back his shoulders. Hoping that his mother would be in her sitting room—whether alone or with his father—he left the room and headed in that direction.

Ian came to the door and took a deep breath before he lifted his hand to knock. He knew *someone* was in there, because the door would be open otherwise.

"Come in," his mother called. Ian closed his eyes just to take in the sound of her voice. *He was home.* He pushed the door open and managed to get a glimpse of her as she bent over her needlework. Her simply styled blonde hair framed her face in the sunlight from the window near where she sat. Her countenance was even sweeter than he'd remembered.

Ian closed the door and leaned against it, but she still didn't look up. She was probably thinking a servant had come into the room to do one thing or another. His heart threatened to jump out of his throat while he waited for his mother to look up and realize who had come into the room, and he wondered what her reaction would be. He'd always believed that of all the people he'd left behind, his mother would be the most pleased to see him, but he had a tiny second of wondering if the opposite might be true. Maybe she was angry. Perhaps this reunion would not be as pleasant as he'd anticipated.

Anya MacBrier finally looked up to investigate the silence. Time slowed down, and the seconds seemed to triple in length. The first second was disbelief. The second was astonishment. The third brought a sound from her mouth that was difficult to distinguish, some kind of joy mixed with sorrow. The fourth sent her to her feet, with her needlework falling unheeded to the floor. In the fifth she took a step forward, and he crossed the room toward her.

"Hello, Mother," he said just before she wrapped him in her arms as if he were still a child. The fact that he was a head taller than Anya seemed irrelevant. She held to him as if he'd returned from war. And he held her equally tightly, his eyes closed against any memories or fears, just cherishing the moment before conversation might be required. When he realized she was crying, it was difficult to hold back his own tears. Then it became impossible. He let the tears come. After all, this was his mother.

She finally relinquished her embrace, but only in a seeming desperation to see his face. She held it in her hands and wept openly, at the same time wiping her thumbs over the moisture on his own cheeks.

"Ian," she muttered. "My precious Ian. I have prayed for you night and day."

Ian tried to smile. "That surely must be what brought me home."

"And now I will pray night and day to thank God for bringing you back to me."

Ian turned his eyes down, but his mother didn't let go of his face. He drew courage to look at her again. "Mother, I . . . am so sorry." His voice broke and his chin quivered. Again he felt like a child. If not for looking *down* at his mother, he might have believed he'd regressed many years. "I . . . I'm not sure I have any reasonable explanation for my leaving . . . or my coming home. I just . . ."

Anya put her fingers over his lips. "It doesn't matter, Ian."

"I'm not certain everyone else will agree with you."

"It won't matter to your father, Ian, and whatever anyone else thinks or believes doesn't count. So long as you make peace with yourself."

Ian looked away again. Since she was no longer holding his face, it was easier to do so. "I'm not certain that's possible."

"Anything is possible, my darling,"she said. He met her warm gaze, wanting to believe her. She smiled, then laughed, then laughed again through more tears. "Oh, my boy! You're really here!"

"I really am."

"We must find your father. He won't stand for having you home for more than a minute without seeing you." She drew a dainty handkerchief from the cuff of her lacy blouse and dried her tears while she stepped toward the door with Ian following. Then she stopped and turned as if she'd remembered something. Her expression darkened, and he knew she was going to tell him something that she didn't want to say—and that he didn't want to hear. Still clutching the handkerchief, she said, "Ian . . . before we see your father . . . you need to know that . . ."

"What, Mother?" he insisted when she hesitated.

He saw her gather courage, and he was immediately covered in cold sweat. "He's not well, Ian."

"What's happened?" he asked in a husky whisper.

"We . . . don't know what happened . . . how it happened." New tears rose in her eyes. "It's a lung condition; something called emphysema. We've seen many doctors. They all concur. It's most common among men who heavily smoke, and your father's never been prone to the habit; therefore, it's somewhat of a mystery. It's not contagious, but . . . he struggles to breathe sometimes, and . . ." she bit her trembling lip, then forced a smile that didn't convince him. "There's no way of knowing how fast or how slow it might overtake him. We've been told he could hang on for years . . . or . . ." She didn't finish, and Ian suddenly understood the implication. He wondered in that moment how it might have felt to come home and learn that his father—or any of his loved ones—had died in his absence. He felt nauseated and had to consciously steady himself. His gratitude for being home deepened. Facing any possible judgment or criticism didn't seem quite so crucial in light of being able to see his father.

Anya dabbed at her eyes again and tucked the handkerchief back in her cuff before she donned a smile. "Come along," she said, taking hold of his arm.

Ian heard the familiar rustle of his mother's skirts as he walked with her down the stairs and to his father's study. He was conscious of her hand on his arm, and he put his hand over it to hold it there, loving the actual physical connection with someone who loved him. At the door to the study, his mother said in a whisper, "Wait here just a moment."

Ian nodded and waited in the hall. She entered and left the door open. He stood back at an angle where he could see Gavin MacBrier seated behind the big desk, reading a book. Ian noted the comfortable way he slouched into the chair, catching the angle of the sunlight. The gray showing at the temples of his thick, dark hair was only slightly more prominent than it had been the last time he'd seen him. The image was all so perfectly familiar, like a painting that he'd passed by every day of his youth. He was relieved to see that his father didn't *look* ill. Perhaps he *would* live for years yet. Ian hoped so, he *prayed* so. He couldn't imagine life without either one of his parents, then it occurred to him that he had selfishly sentenced them to life without *him.* He wondered what had possessed him to believe that everything would be better for his family if he just went away.

He watched his mother move around the desk, while his father watched her with a sparkle in his eyes. She laughed softly and said, "I have a wonderful surprise for you."

"What kind of surprise?" he asked, infected with her laughter.

"If I told you that, it might give it away. Close your eyes."

"They're closed," he said. "Will you give me a hint?"

"The most wonderful surprise you could possibly imagine," she said, standing behind his chair.

Ian saw his mother nod toward him, his cue to enter the room. He moved quietly and stood in front of his father, who said as if he'd also been cued, "If it's *that* wonderful of a surprise, it must have something to do with one of our children."

"Do you care to guess?" Anya asked, putting her hands over Gavin's eyes.

"Either my Gillian has come for a visit, or my Ian has come home."

"How clever you are!" Anya said and moved her hands. "Ta-dah!"

The stretching out of seconds occurred again when Gavin's eyes met with Ian's. The expectation on Gavin's face melted into relief, sorrow merged into joy, and tears pooled in his eyes, then fell on his cheeks. "Oh, my boy!" he muttered and showed no sign of physical ailment with the speed in which he rose to his feet and closed the distance between them, taking Ian in his arms as if he'd feared a thousand times that he might never be able to do so again. Perhaps he had.

Their embrace ended when Gavin put his hands on Ian's shoulders, smiling wide while looking him over from head to toe. "You don't appear to be too much the worse for wear."

"I heartily disagree," Anya said. "He looks too thin and not at all well."

"I'm fine, Mother; really," Ian said.

Gavin stepped back and put an arm around his wife. They stood together to admire Ian, as if he'd just been born and they were examining him to see if he were breathing properly and had all of his fingers and toes.

"You *will* be fine," Anya said, "once you've let me take care of you long enough to make up for all this lost time."

"I think it's evident he can take care of himself, my dear," Gavin said to her.

"Or maybe not," Ian said in a tone that was supposed to lighten the mood, but it had the opposite effect.

"Perhaps we should sit down and talk about where you've been," Gavin said, "and what you've been doing."

"I'm certain we should," Ian said, wanting to put it off and glad for an excuse to do so. "But I'm certain I could use a bath and a haircut. If Duff is still in our employ, I should be able to remedy the latter."

"He's here and faithful as always," Gavin said. "I think he missed you as much as any of us."

"Everyone will be thrilled to have you back!" Anya insisted.

"I suppose we'll see about that," Ian said, and their attention turned to voices in the hall, a man and woman talking as they drew closer. Ian's heart quickened as he recognized Donnan's voice, and a moment later he appeared in the doorway with a woman Ian had never seen before. Donnan looked the same. He was as blonde as Ian was dark. They were close in height and build, but differing in features enough that they didn't necessarily look like brothers. The woman at Donnan's side was lovely in appearance, with reddish-blonde hair and an air of elegance; her eyes were kind.

Everything froze, as if a cold wind and a harsh rain had rushed through the room simultaneously, leaving each of them completely immobile. Ian's gaze connected with his brother's and held fast. Ian wished he had any idea of how Donnan felt or what he was thinking. He wished that one of his parents might say something to ease the tension. Movement occurred when the woman with Donnan put a hand on his arm, as if she feared that this stranger might do her harm and she was seeking protection.

Anya finally spoke. "Say hello to your brother, Donnan."

"Hello, Ian," Donnan said, still holding his gaze steady.

"This is Ian?" the woman said, sounding pleased.

Donnan stepped forward, and the woman let go of his arm. "Hello, little brother," he said.

"Hello, Donnan," Ian said, still not certain if his brother was glad to see him—or otherwise. Donnan extended a hand. Ian felt some relief as he looked at it, then took it. They shared a hearty handshake, then a brief embrace that felt reserved to Ian. Donnan stepped back, looked at Ian squarely, then threw a fist that connected with Ian's face. He stumbled backward, dizzy from the blow and stunned by the confusing greeting. He thought of Wren's slap, followed by her embrace, and decided he preferred it in that order.

"Donnan!" their mother scolded, and the other woman in the room gasped. Gavin stepped between his sons as if he feared a full-fledged brawl might break out.

Ian steadied his footing and touched the blood on his lip before he looked hard at his brother. There was no wondering now how Donnan felt. His anger was evident.

"If you've got something to say to me," Ian said, "then just say it and be done with it." Donnan didn't speak, and Ian opened his arms. "Or if you prefer to just hit me again, do it. Do whatever it takes . . . whatever you believe I deserve."

"No!" Gavin said firmly, his eyes on Donnan. "Say what you need to say, but I'll not have you fighting with your brother."

"Fine, I'll say it," Donnan said. "I will *never* understand how you could do something so selfish and irresponsible. And you will *never* know the grief you left behind." He motioned toward their mother. "She's too kind to tell you." Then to their father. "They're both too kind to tell you, but I'm not opposed to letting you know the truth. There's no counting the tears they cried for you . . . that we all cried for you . . . while you ran off with hardly a word . . . and left the rest of us to try to understand . . . to try to keep believing that you'd come back in one piece."

When Donnan seemed done, Ian said what he'd been prepared to say long before his arrival here. "You have every right in the world to be angry with me, and I know it's not possible to ever undo what I've done. There are no words to sufficiently express how sorry I am, and I'm not expecting you to forgive me, but—"

"*I* expect you to forgive him," Anya said, stepping forward. "There will be no casting stones in this family, because I won't stand for it."

"Nor will I," Gavin added, "so the two of you need to take some time and figure out a way to be tolerant of each other."

Donnan turned to leave, and Anya asked, "Where are you going?"

"I'm taking some time," he said and rushed from the room.

The silence of his absence was brutal. The woman Ian didn't know finally spoke to ease it. "He'll come around. I'm certain he's very glad to see you."

"And you are?" Ian asked in a kind voice that didn't allow him to take out his foul mood on her.

"This is Lilias," Anya said.

"Just Lilias?" Ian asked, touching his lip again to find it still bleeding.

"Lilias MacBrier," she said, startling Ian to a realization that hadn't even occurred to him. She smiled as if she understood his inability to comment. "I'm very glad to meet you at last; I'll look forward to getting to know you better."

"Likewise," Ian said, and Lilias left the room, presumably to try to calm down her husband.

Anya took the lace handkerchief again from her cuff and dabbed it to Ian's lip. "Are you all right?"

"I'm fine, Mother," he said. "But I . . . I need to get cleaned up and . . . I'm tired. If it's all right, I'll see you at supper."

"Of course," Anya said, and Ian headed toward the door.

"Ian," Gavin said, and Ian turned to see his parents looking at him again as if they'd never seen him before. "It's good to have you home, son."

"It's good to be here," he said and meant it. He would be a fool to think that he could come back here and not face some measure of anger and disdain. He just wished that he could go back to that senseless day that he'd left here and do it all differently. He couldn't go back; he could only go forward. He offered a smile toward his concerned parents and assured them, "I'm fine, really. I'll see you later."

Ian hurried up to the refuge of his room, glad to have gotten this far. But he still had to contend with Donnan's anger, and he had yet to face James. Thankfully, his sister lived far enough away that she'd likely hear of his return through a letter and he wouldn't have to face *her* contempt toward him. But contempt was something he'd expected, and he was going to have to learn to live with it.

Chapter Three
Jealousy

A couple of hours after Donnan had used his fist as a manner of greeting, Ian was thoroughly clean from head to toe, and Duff had trimmed Ian's hair to its more typical length—not too short, which would make the curls stand on end, but short enough that he was able to feel like a gentleman again. A hearty lunch had been brought to his room, and he'd eaten every morsel with immense gratitude.

With his stomach contentedly full, Ian gave in to the cumulative exhaustion of his body and succumbed to the comfort and safety of his surroundings. He crawled into the bed and relished the familiar luxury. Then he slept, and slept deeply.

Ian awoke disoriented. It took several minutes for his mind to recount the steps that had brought him home—and given him an aching jaw. His thoughts hovered with Wren. Pleasant thoughts of being reunited with his parents, and less pleasant thoughts of his encounter with Donnan, couldn't keep his mind away from Wren for long.

A knock at the door startled him. He knew it was his brother by the unique rhythm of the knock. He swung his legs over the edge of the bed so he was at least facing the door before he called, "Come in."

Donnan came into the room, looking more like himself than he had earlier when he'd stormed out of their father's study. He closed the door and leaned against it.

"Did you get some rest?" Donnan asked as if he'd not belted him in the jaw the last time they'd seen each other.

"I did, thank you." When neither brother said anything more, Ian confronted the hovering tension. "Did you come to finish me off? A good left hook could make both sides of my face equally swollen."

"Sorry about that," Donnan said.

"No, you're not," Ian countered, only partly joking.

Donnan chuckled, and the tension eased somewhat. "Not entirely, no. After thinking about hitting you every day for nearly two years, I don't suppose I could have resisted."

"I'm sure I deserved it."

"Probably, but . . . now that I've gotten it out of my system, I want you to know that . . . I'm glad you're back. I've missed you."

Ian smiled at his brother. "I've missed you too."

Donnan moved to a chair and sat down. "It wasn't the same without you, brother. I had to go and find a wife to ease my loneliness."

"I dare say you would have found a wife whether I'd been here or not."

"Yes, surely. I just spared *you* having to be lonely without *me* when I got married."

"Oh, I *was* lonely without you," Ian said.

When Donnan asked Ian about his adventures, he simply said that his time away could never qualify as an adventure and guided the conversation toward Donnan's courtship and marriage to Lilias. Ian might have felt some jealousy at his brother being settled with the love of his life, if not for having some hope that perhaps he might yet find a way to convince Wren Docherty of his love for her.

A maid came to the room to tell them that the family was gathering for supper. Donnan told her to have them go ahead and eat, and the brothers talked a while longer. Ian combed his hair and put on his boots while they talked, and they walked downstairs together. Entering the dining room, Ian first noticed that the meal hadn't yet been served. His parents and Lilias were sitting at the table chatting comfortably. A man at the other end of the table was reading a newspaper. Ian knew it was James.

"We sent a message for you to go ahead," Donnan said, greeting his wife with a kiss.

"Oh, we would have if you'd not come in the next few minutes," Anya said. "But we wanted to eat all together."

Ian remained on his feet, waiting for James to put down the paper, knowing that his brother was well aware of his presence in the house—and in the room. The paper folded down just a little, and Ian saw his brother's blonde hair and a mischievous sparkle in his eyes. Ian was reminded of how much James and Donnan looked alike. They both strongly favored their mother, in features and coloring, whereas Ian's looks definitely favored their father.

"Well, hello there, little brother," James said as if they'd seen each other yesterday.

"Hello, James," Ian said.

James set the paper aside and gave up the ruse. He stood up to give Ian a hearty embrace, then laughed and gave him another one, saying close to his ear, "It's *very* good to have you back."

"It's very good to *be* back," Ian said while James looked him up and down, nodding with approval.

"A few weeks of Brierley cooking ought to put some meat back on those bones and get you looking back to normal."

"I'm certain it will," Ian said, and they were seated.

The first course had barely been served when a maid whose name he couldn't remember came into the room, looked directly at Ian, and said, "You have a visitor, sir."

Ian could think of only one possibility, and it made his heart quicken. "Who is it?" he asked to be sure, coming to his feet.

"Miss Docherty, sir," the maid reported. "She said that she would wait in the—"

"Oh, no," Anya said, "you must tell her to come and join us."

"Yes, Fiona," Gavin added, "please have another place set, and ask Miss Docherty to come here."

"Yes, sir," Fiona said and curtsied.

Ian stood there for a long moment, thinking of the list of reasons that this was not a good idea and trying to decide which of those reasons to present to his parents. "Um . . . perhaps . . . Miss Docherty might feel . . . awkward, to be . . . joining us this way . . . on such short notice."

Anya smiled and said, "Surely she knows us all well enough to know that there's no need to feel that way."

Ian was relieved when Gavin added, "Why don't you go and speak to her, son, and invite her to join us."

"Go ahead and eat," Ian said, hurrying from the room. "Don't wait for me." He hurried down the hall to the kitchen, knowing she would be there. Over the years, she'd become acquainted with some of the kitchen staff during her frequent visits, and she felt comfortable there. Ian had *always* found her there when she'd come to see him. He entered the kitchen just after Fiona had delivered the message; he could tell by the look on Wren's face. Her sweet face! He was so glad to see her that he almost forgot the purpose of his coming to speak with her.

"Thank you, Fiona," he said and took Wren's hand, leading her into the hall. Once they were alone, he said to her, "My parents would like you to join us for dinner."

"I'm not dressed for such a thing," Wren insisted.

"It doesn't matter; you *know* it doesn't matter."

"I didn't intend t' arrive at supper time, Ian; I thought ye'd be finished by now. I—"

"We were late starting, but it doesn't matter," he repeated. "Just . . . come and have dinner with us and . . . we can talk afterward." He tugged on her hand to lead her up the hall.

"Is James in there?"

"Does it matter?" he asked and stopped walking.

"Not t' me, it doesn't," she said in that saucy voice.

"Do you think it matters to me?"

"Does it?" she asked, then she proposed an idea that made such perfect sense that he felt stupid for not seeing it himself. "Knowing yer parents as I do, I can't help but wonder if they think it might be good for me t' be in the same room with ye *and* James—at the same time."

Ian felt a little angry over the idea, but he didn't know who to be angry with. Since the most likely candidate was himself, he just guided Wren into the dining room. Anya and Gavin rose to greet her.

"Miss Docherty," Gavin said, kissing her hand. "It's been far too long since you've graced our home."

"Ye're too kind, sir," Wren said.

Gavin let go of her hand only to have Anya take it and press a kiss to Wren's cheek. "It's delightful to see you here," Anya said.

"Thank ye, Lady MacBrier," Wren said and turned to find that Donnan had also come to his feet.

"Hello, Wren," he said with a familiar nod.

"Hello, Donnan," she replied.

He motioned toward Lilias. "Have you met my wife?"

"I heard that ye'd married, but I've not had the privilege." Wren nodded respectfully. "A pleasure, Mrs. MacBrier."

"I've heard much about you, Miss Docherty," Lilias said, and Wren smiled. Ian could see that she was fighting to cover her nerves, but he was proud of her for the way she could so naturally be a lady. If not for her attire, no one would ever guess that she'd been raised by a tailor. Wren would tell him that it was *his* influence that had taught her such things, but he knew for a fact that it was something innately a part of her and he'd had little to do with it.

When Gavin, Anya, and Donnan sat back down, it drew attention to the fact that James had remained sitting. Ian saw him smirk at Wren in a way that made Ian want to pass along the greeting that Donnan had given him earlier. A bloody lip seemed proper payment for such a gaze, especially under the circumstances.

"Ailsa Wren," James said in a capricious tone that elevated Ian's temptation.

"Hello, James," Wren said and turned her attention to Ian as he helped her with her chair, then sat down across from her.

Wren was grateful that the majority of the conversation was not directed at her, or even at Ian. It was as if his family had enough sensitivity not to put either of them on the spot. Before dessert Wren was asked how her father and sister were doing. Wren lied and told them that they were fine. She could only hope that in her absence Bethia hadn't gone into one of her fits, and that her father had taken his medicine and gone to bed according to her instructions.

In Ian's absence, Wren had not once been to Brierley—except for a few times when she had borrowed one of Blane's horses just to ride to the crest of the hill and wonder how things might be if Ian had not left. Being here again now, with Ian's family, she was pleasantly reminded of their kind and gracious nature. Unless someone had encountered them personally, no one would believe that the sixth Earl of Brierley and his wife were not at all concerned about typical social convention, and that they were likely some of the kindest, most decent people in the county.

After supper was over, everyone went to the parlor for coffee. Following all of the dinner-table conversation that had seemed to overtly avoid Ian's absence, James finally asked, "So, tell us where you've been, little brother. What *have* you been doing all this time?"

"I spent most of my time in London," Ian said as if he'd memorized how to answer this question. "But there isn't much to tell."

"Surely, there's *something* to tell," Anya said. "You've been gone a very long time."

"Forgive me, Mother, but I'm afraid it was all just one big misadventure. I've been wandering around trying to find myself, while everything that mattered to me was here at home." He cleared his throat and added, "So, Gillian is doing well?"

They talked about Ian's sister for a few minutes, then Anya commented on how good it was to see her sons all together again. Everyone heartily agreed. Then Gavin said how blessed he was to have three fine sons. He teased James a little about losing his inheritance if he didn't stop stealing his father's favorite biscuits from some secret hiding place. This made everyone laugh except for Lilias and Wren, who shared a wry smile at the fact that they were left out of the family joke. Wren knew that for all of James's philandering ways, he was a good man when it came to the management of the estate and the care of the tenant farmers. He took his responsibility seriously, and he was well prepared to inherit as the eldest son. The other children would be well provided for; money and power were not an issue in the family. They were grateful for their comforts, but they didn't take them for granted.

The brothers teased each other about who might inherit an ugly painting in the upstairs hall. Gavin and Anya were both laughing until Gavin started to cough and couldn't get control of it. Wren saw concern on Ian's face that matched that of his brothers. She also saw that they knew something she didn't know. Gavin gracefully left the room, with Anya accompanying him. Following a heavy moment of silence, James said, "I pray to God that I don't inherit *anything* for many years to come."

"Amen," the others said in haphazard unison.

"I believe I should go." Ian stood, and Wren did as well. "It's getting late. I should see that Miss Docherty gets home safely."

Wren wanted to tell him there was no need for that, but she was glad for an escape with any excuse. She'd come wanting to talk with

Ian. While dinner and visiting had been pleasant, she'd likely already been gone far too long. They all shared polite farewells before Ian escorted Wren toward the back of the house where she'd come in.

"How did you get here, anyway?" he asked.

"I borrowed a horse from Blane, of course."

"Of course," he said. "Well, I'm riding back with you to make certain you're all right."

Wren didn't argue. She did feel an urgent need to check on Bethia and her father. Perhaps she and Ian could talk then, once she knew all was well.

While she was watching Ian saddle a horse, she sensed that his mood was sour. Assuming it had to do with his father's health, she asked about it. He repeated what he'd been told earlier in the day, and expressed his deep concern. Then he helped her onto the horse that had been left tethered in the stable. He mounted his own and they rode toward town. They said little as they rode, but Wren just enjoyed sharing such a simple moment with him again.

When they arrived, Ian helped her return Blane's horse to the livery and made certain it was cared for. Blane trusted Wren to bring his horses back and didn't need to be disturbed. They walked the short distance to Wren's home with Ian leading his horse.

"Something's still bothering ye," she pointed out.

Ian wondered how she could still discern his moods so perfectly when they hadn't seen each other in nearly two years—and he'd believed he'd been doing well at keeping his difficult thoughts from showing. He hated the way he couldn't stop thinking of Wren and his brother. That look James had given her in the dining room was haunting him. He'd kept himself from making a scene over it, but it was still eating at him. He really didn't want to talk to Wren about it, but perhaps it was best if they did so and got it over with.

Ian tethered his horse to the fence surrounding the little yard behind Wren's home. "Why don't you make certain all is well, and then we'll talk."

Wren nodded. "Wait here for just a minute."

Ian was glad for that minute until it had passed, and he still didn't know how to bring it up without sounding like a fool—or making her angry. Or both.

Wren returned to report, "Father's snoring, and the cellar door is closed, so Bethia is fine, I'm sure." She guided Ian out of the cool night air into the kitchen where he'd slept the night before. "Are ye going t' tell me what ye're thinking so darkly about?" she asked, taking a seat. Ian remained standing.

"Assuming you want me to be completely honest, I was a little unnerved by the way that James looked at you."

Wren appeared to be surprised but not angry . . . yet. "Am I t' be held responsible for the way yer brother looks at me? He looks at practically *every* woman like that."

"Yes, but not *every* woman has once spilled their heart and soul to him."

"Do ye think I don't regret that?"

"I believe you do," he said. "But I wonder what exactly it is that you regret." When she looked mostly confused, he had to clarify. "It's unnerving to think of you sharing . . . your affection . . . with my brother."

"My affection?" she asked, now starting to sound angry. "If you mean that I made a fool of myself declaring my undying love, then yes I shared my affection with him."

Ian considered where his thoughts had been all evening and couldn't force himself to drop it now; he needed to know. He needed to know *everything!*

"Do you mean to tell me—and expect me to believe—that *nothing* ever happened between you and James?"

"That is *exactly* what I mean t' tell ye, and I expect ye t' believe it because it's true."

"He's shared a bed with half the women in the county. And most of them were not nearly as in love with him as you were. Why would I think he wouldn't take advantage of that?"

"Why would ye think that *I* would *allow* him t' take advantage of *that*?" Her glare echoed the question before she added, "Did James *tell* ye that something had happened between us?"

"No," Ian said, calmed by his own sheepishness, "I just . . . assumed, because . . ."

"Because you believed I might be some kind of tramp?"

"No, of course not!"

"Ye're contradicting yerself, Ian MacBrier. Make yer mind up. Or maybe ye need t' go ask yer brother and see what he says. Unless ye think he would lie t' ye for the sake of—"

"James would never lie to me."

"It's a pity, then, that ye can't trust *me* as much as ye trust *him*."

Ian heard the accusation come hurtling toward him, much like the slap she'd given him yesterday. He swallowed his pride and admitted, "I know you would never lie to me, Wren; forgive me. I just had to know."

She almost smiled and said, "If I didn't know better, Ian MacBrier, I'd think ye were jealous."

"What makes you think you know better?" he asked and saw her smile deepen.

Since Ian was still on his feet, he wondered if he should just say good night and head home. In spite of his nap he felt tired. It had been a long day.

Wren stood, and he felt sure she would usher him to the door, but she said, "Ye haven't even asked me why I went t' yer house this evening."

"Why *did* you?" he asked, wondering why it hadn't occurred to him that there might be some actual purpose beyond a social call. He saw her foraging for courage and wondered what was coming. He too found the need for a new batch of courage.

"Because . . . every day that ye were gone," he heard a mild quavering in her voice, "there was something I wished I would have said t' ye. I prayed that ye would come back . . . that I might have the chance t' say it. I realized after ye left this morning that I would never be able to sleep one more night without saying it."

Ian prepared himself for another blow. He thought of a dozen possibilities of things she could say that would send him reeling. Rather than letting his imagination run crazy, he just said, "Then you'd better say it."

Wren turned away and tightened her shawl around her arms. "Do ye remember the morning ye woke up in my kitchen, because ye'd passed out drunk on the floor the night before?"

"The morning your father woke me with a bucket of water and a hefty kick? Oh, I remember!"

"But ye don't remember what happened *while* ye were drunk that night, or what ye said."

Ian didn't like where this was going. "Liquor can make fools out of men. They say and do all kinds of stupid things."

"That is true," she said. "But it's also true that . . . sometimes liquor removes inhibitions and makes a man say what he might be afraid t' say otherwise." She turned to look at him. "Ye were drunk, yes, but I know ye well enough to recognize sincerity when I hear it."

Ian's heart quickened, and his throat went dry. "What did I say?"

"What ye said changed everything, but I never got a chance t' talk t' ye about it before Greer died. And it's . . . haunted me ever since."

"What did I say?" he repeated.

Wren looked at the floor. "Ye said that James was a fool, that he could never deserve me. And ye said that *I* was a fool if I believed that he would ever be what I wanted him t' be; ye said that I could never change him." Ian felt some relief; he'd said as much to her sober more than once. Then she added, "And ye said that I was blind if I couldn't see *real* love when it was right in front of my face." She looked at him then, and he could hardly breathe. "I didn't sleep a minute that night. First I cried over the truth of what ye'd said about James; I think it finally sunk in that night. And I cried over what a fool I'd made of myself. Then I had to ask myself if what ye'd said about yerself was true. I tried t' convince myself that it was just drunken nonsense, but I could look back over the years and see the evidence otherwise." She turned more toward him. "Did ye mean it, Ian?"

Ian felt as if he were looking at this moment from a distance, as if he were watching himself in a dream. Then her words echoed in his mind and reminded him that this was real, this was now, he was here—with her.

"Are you asking me if I love you?" he asked, not willing to drag this out one moment longer than necessary. He too had wished every day of his absence that he had told her the truth about his feelings. Apparently he already had, but he wasn't willing to leave any room for doubt.

"I just have t' know if—"

"Yes," he said.

"What?"

"I love you."

In the time it took him to draw a breath, she bridged the river of murky waters of doubt between them and took his face into her hands. She lifted her lips to his with a kiss that he'd dreamt of in a thousand dreams. When it lasted longer than a moment, he took her into his arms, kissing her the way he'd always wanted to. It was everything he'd ever imagined it could be. Ethereal and warm. Intensely consuming. All of his time away from her flashed through his consciousness with its senselessness amplified. "Wren," he murmured against her lips, attempting some self-restraint.

"Ye don't remember, do ye?"

"Remember what?" he asked in a dreamy voice, a result of his keen awareness of the weakness in his knees and the pounding of his heart. And all were a result of this, the sweetest moment of his life.

"Ye kissed me that night," Wren said and saw his eyes widen.

"I thought I'd dreamt it," he said and kissed her again, until he really *did* have to exercise some self-restraint. He eased her head to his shoulder if only to avoid the urge to keep kissing her. "I'm so sorry, Wren."

"That ye kissed me?"

"That I didn't remember. And I'm sorry that I left you."

"Don't ever leave me again," she murmured.

"Never," he said, but she looked up at him with sparks of green.

"I always trusted ye, Ian. Always. But ye broke that trust when ye left me like that. Do ye have any notion of how deeply it hurt me . . . how hard it's been?"

Ian had to dig into the deepest part of his heart to find the strength to face what she was saying. This, more than anything or anyone he'd faced thus far since his return, had frightened him most. He was glad to be facing it and to know that he would no longer need to dread it. But he had trouble finding his voice. He forced it past the huge stone of regret in his throat and said with an uneasy tremor, "I know I betrayed your trust, Wren, and it's weighed on my heart every hour since I left. I was a fool; I was wrong. And I can never apologize enough. But . . . no, Wren. I *don't* have any idea how deeply it hurt you, or how hard it's been. I'm going to find out, however. And I'm going to make it up to you . . . if it takes me the rest of my life."

The sparks in Wren's eyes were extinguished by green pools of relief and tears that trickled down her face. "Don't ye *ever* leave me again!" she repeated, her plea mingled with a quiet fierceness.

"Never!" he said with the same intensity.

"Promise me!" she rumbled, and a sob followed on its wake.

"I promise!" he said with studied conviction, not wanting her to wonder if he meant it.

Wren searched his eyes for sincerity. When she found it she put her head again to his shoulder, slumping into his arms with all the relief of her body and spirit.

"I promise," he repeated and pressed his lips into her hair. With all the years they'd been friends, all they had shared, he had never been so close to her. He'd wondered countless times through his wanderings what it might be like. And now it was happening. He allowed her nearness to saturate him with hope and healing. He'd come home. With Wren in his arms, he'd truly come home. And he would keep his promises to her. He knew then that doing right by Wren had become his greatest purpose in life, even before he'd walked through the door of the tailor's shop the previous evening.

Ian found it difficult to say goodnight; he found some comfort in noting that Wren did too. But it was late and they were both tired. He promised to see her tomorrow evening, thinking he should spend some time with his family first. And she agreed. After another ardent kiss, he finally watched her close the door before he turned and walked toward where he'd left the horse tethered. He barely had time to think that he might have heard a noise behind him when he was hit over the back of his head, and he saw the ground coming toward his face before he blacked out.

* * * * *

Three Years Earlier

Ian carried the picnic hamper; his brothers each carried a blanket. Between them they had all the perfect makings of a perfect picnic on a perfect day. The meadow was soft and green, speckled with occasional wildflowers. The breeze gently contradicted the warmth of the sun, creating an ideal balance. Most perfect of all were the lovely young ladies walking just ahead of the three MacBrier brothers, scouting out the perfect spot to stop and enjoy their lunch. Wren and Bethia Docherty had become as comfortable as sisters to the three boys; perhaps more so. None of the brothers was as comfortable with their own sister. Gillian was nice enough, but not prone to conversation that interested any one of them.

Ian could hardly remember exactly how the brothers of one family had become so attached to the sisters of another—and the other way around. He only knew it had been years since repeated visits to the tailor's shop and a couple of chance meetings in the town square had evolved into purposefully arranging to be at the same place at the same time. And that had in turn evolved into spending time in each other's homes, although Angus Docherty had gradually become less fond of the MacBrier boys loitering at his house. Perhaps as they'd all gotten older he'd become more suspicious of their motives—a problem that was furthered by James's growing reputation of being a philandering cad, a rumor that Ian could not dispute. The problem was also heightened by the times that Angus had seen Ian pathetically drunk. Ian figured there was a touch of hypocrisy in *that* problem, because he had also seen Angus pathetically drunk on more than one occasion. Angus didn't have a problem with Donnan, except that Donnan was always with Ian or James—or both. And occasionally Greer McMillan—Ian's friend since childhood—also joined the crowd. He too was guilty by association, but less guilty simply because he wasn't "one o' those MacBrier boys" *and* because he was socially from the same class as the Docherty family, being the son of the head gardener at Brierley. Ian felt sure that Angus would *not* be impressed with Greer's occasional inclination toward gambling. But since Greer tried to keep it a secret and he'd sworn Ian to that secrecy, Angus was oblivious to the problem.

Greer and Ian had gravitated to each other for as many years as either of them could remember. Greer had started out as a scrawny, freckle-faced kid with hair the color of dirty carrots just pulled out of the ground. He'd grown brawny and more capable of making Ian laugh than any other human being. His swarthy red hair most often looked like a mop on top of his head, and yet he had a certain charm about him that drew the attention of women. But unlike James, Greer only had eyes for *one* woman. And that was Bethia. Ian felt sure that Bethia was aware of Greer's attraction to her, and in a subtle, indefinable way, she seemed to return that attraction. Beyond their comfort in belonging to the same circle of friends, they'd not progressed much further than making eyes at each other on occasion, but Ian wondered if something would come of it. They seemed well matched in an odd sort of way. Bethia had a certain strangeness about her sometimes—a nervousness, perhaps, that made her easily distracted. And sometimes she would say the strangest things for no apparent reason. But Greer was the one who always managed to alleviate any tension created by one of her odd moments. He seemed to understand her at a level that no one else grasped—with the exception of her sister.

Ian's favorite day of the week was the day that Angus gave his daughters the day off. He manned the shop himself and let the girls do whatever they pleased. In the months of pleasant weather, that usually meant a day for a picnic—as long as rain didn't ruin their plans. On such days, Ian's mother insisted that they provide the array of food that the kitchen staff always loaded into the hamper. Anya said it was only proper since the male gender should be in charge of such things for any such outing. More quietly she had told Ian that she suspected the Docherty family might not be able to afford to feed her three boys who "ate more than the average ten people," according to the head cook at Brierley.

Today as they spread out the blankets, giving sufficient room for everyone to stretch out and eat, Ian had his eye keenly on James. He was always flirting with Wren and Bethia, because he flirted with almost every woman he encountered. The girls had always responded with indifferent teasing, well aware of James's reputation. Until recently—when Ian had realized that Wren was responding to his brother's dallying with a distinct lack of indifference. He felt sure she believed she was being discreet. But he'd spent too much time in her company to not see the difference. Wren was falling for James, and Ian felt far from indifferent. He cared far too much for Wren and her sister to want either one of them to be hurt by his brother. James was a good man in every other respect, but Ian knew more than anyone the string of broken hearts he'd left behind—because it was Ian that James most always confided in regarding his caddish ways. And only Ian and his parents and brother knew about the regular funds that were being secretly given to support more than one illegitimate child. Since there *was* more than one, James's parents could hardly insist that he marry the woman and make it right. In fact, the three situations came to light at almost exactly the same time, and Ian had never seen his parents so distraught and disappointed. The family had been in an uproar for weeks, and had only settled back into some semblance of normality when everyone who loved James had come to accept that he wasn't going to change, and they could only love him for who he was; no one could hope to control his conduct. But Ian would break his brother's nose before he would let him hurt one of these precious women—specifically the one who had suddenly seemed to lose her mind when it came to matters of the heart. Wren knew the truth about James. But the sparkle in her eyes when she looked at him implied some insane belief that James might change for *her.* And Ian knew he never would.

Pleasant summer days were swallowed up by the brisk colors of autumn. Then with no warning, the harsh hand of winter wiped all of the color away. Wren and Bethia were able to get away occasionally and borrow Blane's horses in order to come to Brierley where there was plenty of space indoors to lounge about, share a meal or two, and indulge in the winter version of meadow picnics. They read books from the library of Brierley, or talked about what they'd read. Sometimes they played rousing games of cards if they had the correct number of people. Very rarely did they number six, but most often five. If five of them were together, a game of cards never worked very well, nor did it with three. But occasionally one or two were busy elsewhere, and the other four would have it out with equal attitudes of ruthlessness over triumphing as the winner.

Ian always enjoyed his time with his brothers—and Greer when he was able to join them. And he enjoyed his time with the Docherty sisters. He especially enjoyed times when they were all together—except for the growing evidence that Wren was entirely smitten with James. And James thoroughly enjoyed flirting with her. Wren was blind to the fact that James had no more interest in her than any other woman—in spite of Ian privately telling her so more than once. And in spite of James continuing to have dalliances with other women, of which Wren was fully aware. Ian puzzled over it with his own surprising lack of indifference, until it would often give him a headache. Wren was an intelligent and wise young woman. She was clever and funny and not afraid to speak her mind. She would not stand for dishonesty or bad behavior. But when it came to James, she could apparently see nothing but her own feelings. All practicality and common sense fled in the face of whatever insanity had overtaken her on that one count.

The winter days became especially cold and dark while Ian worried about Wren, knowing that James was spending time with her—just the two of them. Ian had actually taken to threatening James to mind his manners with Wren. James just laughed it off and assured Ian that if he couldn't trust his brother, who could he trust? Ian *did* trust his brother—except when it came to women. In addition to his concerns for Wren, Ian was finding it more and more difficult to ignore that strange and inconsolable feeling inside of him, that bizarre something that pumped through his veins and continually nagged at the back of his brain, luring him to the belief that he didn't fit in, that his life was all wrong, that he needed to leave this place to find who he was and where he belonged. The lack of logic in his thinking was as strong as the compulsion. He loved his home, and he loved his family. His parents were good people who had raised him well. He had *no* practical reason for wanting to leave this house, this valley, these circumstances of his life. But the impulse to leave lingered inside of him like some kind of sickness that distorted his thoughts and feelings. And he couldn't remember a time when he *hadn't* felt that way. Sometimes he feared what rash thing it might make him do. Sometimes he feared it so much that drinking enough to completely dull the feeling was the only pleasurable and comforting thing he could do.

On a particularly difficult evening, Ian's plans to go into town with his brothers were foiled by especially foul weather. He'd been looking forward to one drink leading to another, gradually fogging his mind, knowing that his brothers would make certain he made it home safely—because they always drank less than he did. But now he was stuck at home, where getting drunk didn't hold as much appeal—or perhaps it inspired more guilt. It was easier to drink when surrounded by other men doing the same.

Ian poured a glass of scotch and swirled the liquid around in the glass, thinking about drinking it. There in the dimly lit parlor, the family had been having coffee an hour earlier. Now everyone had gone their separate ways in this very large house, and he was alone. He took a long, slow sip, ignoring the burn, while he debated just taking the bottle to his room. He set the glass down and filled it again. A noise in the room indicated that he was not alone. He turned to see his mother standing just inside the door. He looked at her, then at the drink in his hand. He questioned his reasoning as he swallowed its contents, as if the drink might help smooth over his guilt for being caught with the drink.

"I wish you wouldn't drink so much," Anya said. She wasn't one to nag, or even to scold—at least since her children had become adults. But she never held back in expressing her opinion. Now that she'd expressed her wish, she expressed her confusion. "You didn't learn this from your parents, Ian." Then she expressed her concern. "Help me understand why you do this." She stepped farther into the room and sat down, making it clear that she intended to have a conversation. He wondered now if she'd been watching and waiting for the *right* moment to have this conversation. It was so like her.

Ian had never been a rebellious child. In fact, he'd always had a strong desire to do the right thing. He wanted his parents to be proud of him. He knew they would always love him, no matter how foolish or stupid he might be. But he also wanted their approval. It meant more to him than possibly anything else. He also wanted God's approval. The love of God had been taught passively in their home. There had never been formal lectures or frequent harsh reminders meant to instill the fear of God. But they had always attended church on the Sabbath as a family. And God was spoken of in their home almost as if He were a distant relative who had a vested interest in their lives, and that He could be called on in times of need—or just anytime. Given that Ian had never felt a desire to earn the disapproval of God *or* his parents, he couldn't quite figure out why he eagerly finished off his drink and poured another one before he sat on the same sofa as his mother. It was easier to avoid eye contact that way.

"Are you concerned about Wren?" she asked, and he turned to look at her, needing firm eye contact. There was nothing facetious or cursory about the question. She'd not meant it as a way to casually open the conversation. She really wanted to know.

Ian looked straight ahead and took a long sip. "Is there a reason I should feel personally responsible for Wren's ridiculous infatuation with my philandering brother?" Only after he'd finished the sentence did he hear how snippy and defensive it had sounded.

"*Is* there a reason?" Anya asked with a gentle forcefulness she was known to use when she really wanted to drive home a point. Ian glanced at her briefly but didn't answer—*couldn't* answer. Since he'd never bothered to ask the question, it would be impossible to offer an answer without thinking long and hard about it. And right now he was trying *not* to think at all.

Ian took another sip of his drink, and his mother said, "If it's not Wren you're trying to drown with liquor, it must be . . . that feeling."

Again Ian glanced at his mother. And again he glanced away. He swore sometimes that mothers were given some measure of psychic ability on behalf of their children. This was proven when she said in a voice that implied her perfect understanding of his own confusion, "Tell me why, Ian . . . why would you want to leave here? We have *everything* here."

"I know, Mother," he said and went on with the same rationale he always gave her. "I know there isn't a logical explanation for this. I just . . . can't help how I feel . . . and I don't know what to do about it. My feeling this way is not some kind of . . . betrayal of my home and family." He took a sip of scotch and softened his voice. "At least it's not intended to be."

"I know that," she said softly. "I just . . . don't want to lose you . . . to your drinking *or* to your need to wander." She scooted a little closer and put a hand on his arm. "I pray for you, Ian. I pray that you will find whatever it is you need to find . . . and that when you find it, you will be happy." Ian looked at her then, and didn't turn away. "Above all else, I want you to be happy. Wherever you might go . . . whatever you might become . . . that is most important to me."

"You are too precious, Mother . . . and far too patient with me, I'm certain."

She smiled and put a hand to one side of his face, and a kiss to the other. "Perhaps we should get some sleep. It's getting late."

"Perhaps we should," he said and immediately stood, needing solitude with a sudden desperation—as if the things she'd said might suffocate him if he could not remove them from this room and sort them out in other surroundings. "Good night, Mother," he said, heading toward the door, glass still in hand.

"You mustn't worry about Wren," Anya said. Ian turned around and once again wondered over her probable psychic abilities. "She's stronger than you think she is, but . . . you should tell her how you feel."

"I *have* told her how I feel," he said in a voice not in keeping with the tone of the conversation. More calmly he said, "I've clearly expressed my concerns about her having *any* involvement with James. She knows that—"

"I'm not talking about James," she said. "You should tell her how *you* feel. It has nothing to do with James . . . except for the jealousy, perhaps."

"Jealousy?" he countered in a voice completely inappropriate for a MacBrier boy to use when speaking to his mother. If his father had been in the room, Ian would have received a harsh glare if not a sharp reprimand. He wanted to apologize. He wanted to justify his response. Too clouded by the liquor and his feelings to do either, he stepped back into the room long enough to grab the bottle of scotch before he left too quickly for her to say anything else.

Chapter Four
Home Again

Jealousy? The very idea was ludicrous and Ian knew it. He knew it with every drink he took, and he knew it when he felt the headiness completely overtake him. He knew it when he came awake with the inevitable pounding head. The issue at hand was *not* jealousy. His mother was rarely wrong. But *this time,* she *was* wrong! And what was all that about telling Wren how he *felt*? As he had clearly pointed out to his mother, he *had* told her how he felt. He was *worried* about her. And that was *all*!

For months Ian continued to convince himself that he was *not* jealous; he was merely concerned. For months he watched Greer and Bethia fall in love, certain beyond any doubt that he had no comprehension of the nature of what they felt for each other. He could see it in their eyes and in the way they took such good care of each other. He stood up with Greer at the wedding while Wren stood beside her sister, holding the bouquet during the ceremony. Since Greer had no remaining family, the presence of Ian's family meant a great deal to him. When Ian discovered himself watching Wren more than thinking about the vows his friends were exchanging, a quickening of his heart brought back his mother's words, like lightning flashing in his brain. The words echoed again, like thunder coming seconds after the flash. *You should tell her how you feel.* Another flash followed the first and was again echoed by the rumbling of some kind of internal thunder that was more in his chest than his head. *How* do *you feel, Ian?* It had taken him months to get up the courage to ask the question. Now the answer was making his knees weak and his heart pound. Then a knot twisted in his stomach.

Wren was glancing discreetly toward James, who was sitting back two pews. Ian glanced at his brother just in time to see him wink at Wren. She smiled and looked coyly down. Ian wanted to give his brother a bloody nose. He *was* jealous. His mother *had* been right.

Greer and Bethia had returned from their honeymoon before Ian could fully admit to himself that he was hopeless and helpless in his love for Wren. He didn't know when he'd started loving her. It seemed he always had. But he didn't know what to do about it. If not for James in the middle of everything, it would have been easy to just find the right moment to carefully express to Wren that his feelings for her had evolved into something deeper, something more real and consuming, something that soothed the restlessness in him. But Wren could see nothing but James, and Ian was afraid of saying *anything* for fear of betraying his own seething jealousy. He became a very good actor as he and his brothers spent time with Wren to help her adjust to the absence of her sister. According to all outward appearances, they had a wonderful time and everything was completely normal. But Ian knew that James was spending time with Wren, and he could hardly sleep a minute while he stewed and stewed over this ridiculous quandary. The *only* way he could get any decent sleep at all was to drink, and he became more and more dependent on sneaking liquor into the house and locking himself in his room to be alone in his brooding. His parents expressed repeated concern. His brothers noticed his change of habits but didn't say much. The difference was that Ian knew his parents were fully aware of the *real* difficulty, while his brothers were just confused over the reasons that Ian's drinking had become a *problem.* During the days, Ian was fine. He interacted with his family and friends as he always had. But once alone at night, he had to drink away his wanderlust and his love for Wren. And every morning he had to contend with the hangover and was slow to get himself up and ready to face another day of acting.

Greer and Bethia settled comfortably into their marriage among the servants of Brierley. Greer continued his work in the gardens during the months they weren't covered with snow—and the other months he spent clearing snow and doing various odd jobs. Bethia continued to do sewing for her father, going into town once or twice a week to see her father and sister and to take her projects back and forth. Wren's visits to Brierley were as they had been before, and the group of friends continued their activities much as they had prior to the marriage. And Ian took pride in how well he'd learned to act as if everything was as it always had been. He was fully aware of James's ongoing flirtations with Wren—as well as any number of other women. But he kept his mouth shut. He knew from experience that Wren would just tell him to mind his business, and James would do the same—although Wren would be saucy about it, and James would just laugh off Ian's concerns as if the problem might be nothing more than a disagreement over their attire for an upcoming social event.

Beyond his concern for Wren, Ian had to admit to some concern over Greer's increasing desire to seek out opportunities for gambling. Occasionally he even used his day off to travel beyond the realms of their comfortable valley, always insisting that Ian should not come along. He assured Ian that Bethia was aware of the problem and that he would keep it under control. Ian hoped and prayed that was the case. He wondered how all those cordial games of cards in the parlor had shifted into this dreadful habit for Greer. It got him into trouble more than once, and Ian knew it was bad when Greer actually asked to borrow money. For Ian the money was irrelevant. The allowance his parents gave him was more than generous in meeting his every need and whim, and far beyond. What concerned Ian was the indication of the growing problem. Greer was a proud man, and asking his best friend for money was entirely out of character for him. After he asked Ian a third time, promising boldly that it would be the *last* time, Ian made him promise to stop, and he insisted that he wouldn't bail Greer out again. He knew well enough that rescuing Greer with money was only feeding a bigger problem, and it had to stop. Ian heard nothing more about the dilemma, and he assumed that Greer had kept his promise. It never occurred to Ian that he might not be the only one capable of being a great actor.

Preoccupied as he was with his own hidden feelings for Wren, Ian settled deeper into a habit of feeling sorry for himself, wondering if it would be best if he just gave into his eternal desire to leave this place and find a new life for himself. The woman he loved was blindly in love with a man who would only hurt her. His best friend was married and generally too busy to spend much if any time with

Ian. And there was an inexplicable distance growing between Ian and Donnan. It was as if adulthood had brought out differences that hadn't existed before. There was no contention between them—only an odd sense of discomfort. Ian asked himself if the rift was of his own making, but it was a question he didn't want to answer. If he answered *that* question, he'd have to confront the possibility of admitting the truth to Donnan about other things that he didn't even want to talk about. Ian and his brothers continued their regular weekly outings with Wren on her day off. Bethia and Greer usually joined them, even though Greer always had some obligation that took him away earlier than the others.

On a day that revealed the first hope of spring after a long, bleak winter, the entire group went out for a brisk afternoon ride through the woods before they all went to the pub to eat an early supper, which James paid for. The atmosphere of the pub was pleasant, with warm fires in every grate and the absence of the crowds of drinking men that would fill it up later. Greer ate quickly and excused himself after kissing his wife goodbye. Bethia looked disappointed, then unusually distracted. It occurred to Ian that if Greer had been going back to Brierley to meet some obligation regarding his work, he would have taken his wife with him. When he asked Bethia about that, she insisted that she wanted to spend time with her sister and Greer knew it, but Ian sensed something erroneous about her explanation. An hour later James left the pub with Wren's hand in his, and Donnan tried to talk Ian into coming home with him. Ian boldly declined, and Donnan took Bethia with him in order to see her home safely.

Ian was glad to be left alone at the pub, even though he knew it was likely stupid. On the second drink he wondered what might happen if he passed out drunk without one of his brothers here to see him home. By the fifth drink, he didn't care. An obscure awareness of the bustling of the busy pub drifted into oblivion in his mind. His next awareness was a drowning splash of cold water that soaked him from the waist up, and a hefty kick from Angus Docherty. Wren's father growled at him and told him to get out of his house and stay away from his daughter. Angus left the house to see to an errand, shaking a finger at Ian and snarling, "Ye'd best not be here when I get back, boy, or I'll have yer hide."

Ian laid there on the kitchen floor of the Docherty home, his hand over his eyes to block out the light, wondering how he'd gotten *here,* praying he'd not caused too much of a ruckus. Since he couldn't remember anything, he had absolutely no idea what kind of trouble he might have inflicted. He attempted to gain willpower over his pounding head enough to get to his feet and heed Angus's threat.

"Are ye hungry?" he heard Wren say and turned his head toward the sound before his eyes cracked open enough to see a hazy image of her sitting near the table, her hands busy at stitching something.

That word *hungry* encouraged a rise of nausea. "No . . . thank you," he said and put all his effort into concentrating on her face. A strange fluttering in his stomach completely dispelled the nausea. He forgot about the headache and his recent rude awakening by Angus Docherty. Wren looked up from her sewing and caught him staring at her, but he didn't turn away. That fluttering increased while their gaze remained locked for a lengthy minute.

Wren set her sewing aside and asked in a tender voice, "Dare I ask if ye remember what happened here last night?"

"What happened?" he asked, the fluttering in his stomach rushing to his heart to make it pound with dread.

Ian saw Wren's expression harden, compounding his dread. "Ye *don't* remember," she stated as fact and stood abruptly, turning her back to him. The way she put her hands on her hips implied anger, until he heard a loud sniffle that told him otherwise.

"What did I do, Wren?" he pleaded, needing to know. Her only response was another sniffle while he managed to get to his feet. "Are you crying?" he asked, but still she didn't answer.

He was considering how to get her to talk to him when she turned abruptly, her tears wiped away, her eyes emitting fire. "I'll tell ye what ye did," she rumbled. "Ye *stumbled* int' my house, drunk out of yer mind, making an absolute fool of yerself, then ye passed out cold on my kitchen floor. Now ye'd best be minding my father's threat or there'll be the devil t' pay."

Ian's nausea returned, and he determined it would be well for him to leave before he had the chance to make a fool of himself any further. He could make it up to her later; later, when her father wasn't due to return—later, when he had his senses about him.

"I'll just . . . go," he said. "My parents will surely be . . . worried, and—"

"Donnan came looking for ye," she said. "They *were* worried, but they know where ye are now." She motioned abruptly toward the door as if she would bodily remove him if she had the strength. "Yer horse is at Blane's."

Ian took a few steps toward the door and hesitated. "May I see you later?"

"Ye know where t' find me," she said and crossed the room, opening the door.

"Thank you," he said, "for . . . letting me stay; for . . ."

"Get out of here, Ian MacBrier, before I do after my father's example and give ye another hefty kick."

"I'm going," he said and hurried outside, hearing the door slam behind him before he was even two steps beyond it. He rode home at a slow pace that would not aggravate the pain in his head any more than necessary. His parents were understandably unhappy with him when he got there. He simply apologized and took a long bath while he considered Wren's anger toward him. He knew that such behavior would never convince her that he was a worthy replacement for James in the bestowing of her affection. But he doubted he could ever convince her anyway. He couldn't even think of any point in trying.

Ian *did* go and see Wren later. He apologized profusely while she kept busy straightening and restraightening every item in the tailor's shop. She accepted his apology, but she did it without even making eye contact with him. Then she insisted that she had a mountain of work to do and he needed to go.

"Is there something you're not telling me, Wren?" he asked, his hand on the doorknob. He pointed out the logic of his inquiry. "You've seen me drunk before, and you've scolded me for my behavior many times, but . . . I get the feeling something else is bothering you."

She finally turned to look at him, her eyes on fire with more than her usual anger. "I've got some advice for ye, Ian MacBrier. If ye want t' know what's taking place in yer life, it would serve ye well not t' get so blind drunk that ye can't remember what went on."

"That's very good advice, Wren; I'll certainly take it to heart. But you didn't answer my question. Whether it was right or not, I *don't* remember what happened last night. But I've apologized and I'm humbly asking you to tell me what's bothering you. There's nothing more I can do to rectify the problem . . . unless you tell me what it is."

Wren turned her attention abruptly back to her straightening. "There's not a problem, Ian. I simply . . . have a great deal on my mind."

"Well, when you decide you want to share it with me, you let me know."

Ian left the shop, resisting the urge to slam the door the way she had done earlier that day.

A week later Ian was appalled to note that he'd made little effort to heed Wren's advice. Her apparent anger toward him only induced him to drink away his feelings more and more. His life became more distinctly a pattern of barely being sober through the course of a day until he started to numb his senses once again, obliterating his memories and deadening his desires.

And then it happened.

Ian came out of a drunken stupor to be told that the fire at the pub he barely remembered had taken the life of his dearest friend. Life from that moment became difficult to live. His grief only accentuated his lifelong desire to leave this place for reasons he could never define or defend. He pondered leaving long before he actually got up the nerve to do so. And when he *did* get up the nerve, he couldn't actually bring himself to face his loved ones with the announcement of his intentions. Instead, he skulked away in the night, leaving nothing but a brief note of explanation for his family, and another for Wren.

* * * * *

Now, it didn't take Ian long to realize that whatever ambiguous haven of peace he might be seeking didn't exist. And then he just wandered. And wandered. And wandered. And now he'd come back. He'd faced his family. He'd faced Wren. And he was facing the ground, surrounded by darkness. He groaned and shifted and recalled being struck on the back of the head. Better than waking up with no memory, he concluded. Until he wondered who . . . and why. He heard a strange mumbling. And footsteps. Pacing. Once he'd assessed that he was physically sound beyond the swollen bump on the back of his head, he rolled to his side and allowed his eyes to adjust to the darkness.

Bethia.

He became aware that he was cold the same moment as he went a little clammy with the realization of what was happening. Wren's sister was shuffling back and forth a short distance away, wearing a long coat that had belonged to Greer, carrying a large skillet, which was apparently heavy enough to knock a man unconscious. She was ranting spurts of sentences in different tones, as if she were an actor on a stage, playing the parts of more than one person, having a conversation filled with anxiety, fear, and determination. She seemed oblivious to his being awake, and he no longer felt any threat of danger to himself. But he wondered what aspect of her madness had convinced her to do him harm. He wondered what her intentions for him might have been if he'd not become conscious.

Ian eased slowly, quietly, carefully to his feet. He was glad to note that the pain in his head was not as severe as a typical hangover. He was considering how to get to the door of the house in order to get Wren to help him with Bethia; however, since Bethia was pacing between him and the door, doing so appeared to be impossible. He only took one step and she spun toward him, holding the skillet up as if she were willing and capable of landing him another blow, perhaps lethal this time.

"It's all right, Bethia," he said in a soothing tone. "It's Ian. You know me. I would never hurt you."

"Jinty thinks ye will," she said, and Ian was glad that he knew about the imaginary people Bethia interacted with. "It was Jinty who told me t' hit ye. She thinks ye'll take Wren away from us. She thinks ye'll abandon us, just as Greer did."

"I won't abandon you, Bethia. And I won't abandon Jinty, either. I won't take Wren away from you. I promise. If I take Wren anywhere, I will take you as well. I promise, Bethia. I promise." She looked as if she were trying to believe him, and he went on. "Think how many years we've all been friends, Bethia. I would never take Wren away from you. The two of you need each other. We all need each other."

"Then why did ye leave?" she demanded.

"I shouldn't have left, Bethia. But I never will again. I promise."

"Greer left." Bethia lowered her cast-iron weapon and immediately started to cry like a child. "He left me."

"I know, Bethia. I know Greer left and I'm sorry for that."

"It's *not* yer fault!" she snapped with an anger that halted her tears immediately. Then just as quickly she started to whimper. "I'm sorry I hit ye, Ian," she said. "Selma told me not t' do it, but . . . Jinty was so angry, and . . ." She sobbed. "Ye think I'm crazy, don't ye!"

Ian wondered how to answer her without inciting more drama. He took a careful step toward her, saying, "I think that you need some sleep. It's late." As an afterthought he said, "I think Jinty and Selma need some sleep, too." He saw Bethia relax a little more, and he was able to get the skillet out of her hand before he put an arm around her, guiding her toward the door. Once inside, he wondered how to get Wren's attention without waking her father. Recalling that Mr. Docherty was reputed to sleep deeply with the aid of a pain tonic, Ian closed the back door just loudly enough that he hoped Wren would hear it. But he didn't know how long he'd been unconscious. She could be sound asleep for all he knew. He set down the skillet and searched for a lamp, but he couldn't find a match until Bethia put one into his hand.

"Selma keeps good track of the matches," she said with such repose that he had trouble not laughing. The same moment the room lightened, Wren opened her bedroom door to investigate the noise. She tightened her robe around her waist, and her eyes widened with question and concern.

"Good. You're awake," Ian said. "I need your help."

"What's happened?" Wren demanded.

Before Ian could get a syllable through his lips, Bethia rushed to her sister's arms, babbling frantically. "I'm sorry I hit him. Jinty told me t' do it. Jinty told me t' do it. I should have listened t' Selma. I should have. And Greer will be so angry with me for doing such a thing. He's so pleased that Ian came back. I shouldn't have hit him. I shouldn't have."

Wren put her arms tightly around Bethia, which had a soothing effect. She looked hard at Ian for answers. Not wanting to upset Bethia any further, he said in little more than a whisper, "Bethia is very tired, I believe. Perhaps you should see her to bed, and then . . . well . . . Jinty and Selma are tired too."

Ian saw Wren give him a smile that was barely discernible. But it was quickly swallowed up in the obvious difficulty of the moment—even if she didn't know exactly what had happened.

Ian sat at the table and watched as Wren soothed her sister and urged her to bed. She offered to let Bethia sleep in the same room with her, the way they used to before she'd married Greer, but Bethia refused. She offered to go down to the cellar with Bethia and make certain all was well, but Bethia refused this offer as well. Bethia finally assured Wren that she was fine and opened the cellar door to go down the steep steps to the tiny space below the house. She turned back for just a moment and said to Ian, "Selma wants ye t' know that she's *so* sorry Jinty hit ye like that."

"It's all right," Ian said, giving her a smile. "Just tell Jinty not to let it happen again."

"I'll tell her," Bethia said and closed the door behind her.

Ian turned to find Wren staring at him with wide eyes. "She *hit* ye?"

Ian factiously picked up the skillet from the table. "Knocked me out cold," he said, and Wren gasped.

"Where?" she asked, putting a hand on the back of his head. He moved her fingers up to the spot that was still throbbing, and she gasped again. "Ye've got a bump there the size of an egg."

"I'm sure I'll be fine," he assured her and took her hand, urging her to his lap. "I'm worried about you, however."

"Me? Why?"

"I don't know how you manage to take care of her, Wren. And your father as well." He tightened his arms around her. "I should have been here for you."

Wren laid her head on his shoulder. "Ye're here now."

Ian encouraged her to tell him more about the situation with both her father and Bethia. She got tears in her eyes more than once in response to his compassion, and he nearly cried himself a time or two.

When they realized how late it had gotten, Ian reluctantly said goodnight to her—again. Again he kissed her at the door, and again he told her that he loved her. Oh, how grand it felt to be able to admit it! Oh, how he wished he'd been able to admit it a long time ago! But he was home, and she knew the truth. He felt as if life were starting over for him, and it was destined to be better than it had ever been—in spite of Jinty having knocked him unconscious.

* * * * *

Ian slept through breakfast but found a note that had been slid beneath his door. It was from his mother, telling him where to find her and that she was so glad to see him sleeping safely in his own bed. He got cleaned up and dressed and went downstairs to pester the kitchen staff into giving him something to eat. Some of them were nearly like family, and he'd grown up having them in the center of his life. More than one of them got tears in their eyes when they saw him, then they laughed from his teasing, and he enjoyed eating his late breakfast right there in the kitchen where he could chat with them. He'd been raised on stories of how his mother had once worked as a maid in this kitchen, and the MacBrier children had been taught to respect the servants and always treat them kindly. In that moment, Ian appreciated the concept more than he ever had. It was good to be home.

Ian found his mother in her sitting room. He closed the door and said, "Did you think I wouldn't know where to find you?"

"I just wanted to be certain," she said as he leaned over to kiss her.

He sat down and stretched out his legs. "And you're . . . what? Sneaking into my room to watch me sleep as if I were a child?"

"You'll always be my little Ian," she said with a guilty smile. "Until you have a wife who can look out for you, I'll not be able to resist." She added a couple of stitches to the needlework in her hands. "You were very late. I assume you and Wren have a great deal to talk about."

"We do, indeed," Ian said. "She also . . . needed some help at the house. Her sister wasn't feeling well."

"I see," Anya said, then added in the same nonchalant tone, "Have you told her how you feel?"

"Would you be disappointed in me if I said that I hadn't?"

"Not disappointed," she said. "I just believe you need to be honest with her. Hiding the way you felt didn't do either of you any good before you left, and now that you're back—"

"I told her, Mother. There's no need to be disappointed *or* concerned. But if you must know . . . if we're going to be completely honest with each other . . . it seems that I *did* tell her before I left; I just didn't remember."

Anya looked confused, then enlightened. "Oh," was all she said.

"Rest assured, Mother, such things will never happen again. I promise that I will never drink enough to get drunk again. Never! And I apologize for all the grief I brought to the family—you especially—because of my drinking."

Anya smiled with tears in her eyes. "You've grown up a great deal in your time away."

"Yes, I suppose I have."

"It must have been very difficult."

Ian looked away. "Yes, it was very difficult. Enough said. I'm home now and nothing else matters."

"And Wren is clearly pleased to have you back."

"Apparently she is. I'm not sure *why*." His facetiousness made his mother laugh softly. "But I'm grateful," he added more seriously, "so I'm not going to question it."

Ian changed the subject by asking his mother about all of the happenings among people they knew outside of the family: the servants, the tenant farmers and their families, the townspeople. He wanted to know all of the news and enjoyed hearing his mother tell about births and deaths and marriages, as well as stories, funny or sad. The conversation continued over lunch with the rest of the family present, and they each contributed to filling Ian in on all that had occurred in his absence.

After lunch, they moved to the parlor and visited a long while more. Ian got to know Lilias a little better, and he was glad to be a part of such comfortable conversation. It almost felt as if he'd never been gone, and he couldn't imagine that only a few days before he'd been lost and alone and trying to convince himself that coming home was all wrong. What a fool he'd been!

The gathering broke up when James asked his brothers if they'd like to go out for a ride. Ian was thrilled with the opportunity, but Donnan declined due to having promised his wife to take her into town for a little shopping. James and Ian rode through the woods along familiar paths, not saying much until they came to a meadow they knew well. They both dismounted and led their horses, walking casually side by side.

After James mentioned once again that it was good to have Ian home, he asked, "How is Wren?" Ian bristled, then had to assure himself that there had been nothing in James's tone or inquiry that warranted such a response.

"She's fine," Ian said.

"And Bethia?"

It had been nearly two years since Ian had engaged in a serious conversation with his brother, so he had to reacquaint himself with the fact that he could trust his brother to keep a confidence. For all of their differences in regard to Wren, Ian had never had any cause to not be at ease with his brother in every other respect. "She's not at all well," Ian said. James lifted his brows, and Ian continued. "Did you know that she's been struggling . . . mentally?"

"She was always a tad strange," James said. "But I've not seen her since . . . well . . . probably once since you left; since she moved back home."

Since Greer's death, Ian added silently. Aloud he said, "Wren doesn't want anyone to know. She's afraid of what people will think . . . how they will treat Bethia." He gave James a brief explanation of Bethia's behavior, and his brother expressed compassion and concern.

"Wren must be having a difficult time with this," James said in a way that implied he'd not spoken to her in a long time.

To test the theory, Ian said, "I've been out of the country. I would think you'd know the answer to that."

"Obviously I don't, or I wouldn't have asked about her."

Ian looked away and swallowed carefully. James added with firm resolve, "All right, little brother, let's get this out of the way, once and for all."

Ian looked at him. "Get *what* out of the way?"

"I know you were fuming at the dinner table last night when she was there, so just say what you need to say."

Ian swallowed again. "There's nothing to say that wasn't said many times before I left."

"You never admitted to how you felt about her," James said, "but it was obvious."

Ian wondered if he had truly been so indiscreet. Or perhaps he'd babbled his feelings to family members while drunk, just as he'd done to Wren. Rather than hashing over the past, he addressed the issue as it applied to the present circumstances. "I'll admit to it now. I love her; I've always loved her." James smiled, and Ian added briskly, "Is that amusing to you?"

"Not at all," James said. "It's just good to hear you say it. She's a good woman. She deserves someone who will take good care of her. I know you will. And just so we're clear, nothing ever happened between us. Nothing. *Well . . .*" he drawled, "I did kiss her a time or two, but that was all. I admit that I enjoyed flirting with her, but more than anything she was like a sister to me. I never would have taken advantage of her. I hope you know that."

"I know it now," Ian said. "I confess that I wondered."

"I know, and I should have made it clear . . . back then. I regret that. But you should know that she's not given me more than a polite greeting since you left here."

Ian took that in, combined with the revelation Wren had shared with him about his drunken confessions prior to Greer's death. If he'd known—or more accurately, if he'd remembered—perhaps he wouldn't have felt the need to leave. Perhaps everything would have been different. But the past was the past. He could do nothing now but try to put the pieces back together.

When James spoke again, Ian was startled by the sound of his voice as well as his words. "I hope you've finally had the good sense to let her know you love her."

"I have," Ian said, and James smiled again.

"What are you going to do about it?"

"There's only one possibility, now isn't there?"

James's smile widened into a grin. "And the sooner you marry her the better, in my opinion. Unless you can think of a good reason to wait."

The mention of marriage quickened Ian's heart, and thinking about it for a minute or two didn't bring up *any* reason he could think of to wait. He was pondering it deeply when James asked, "May I ask how you're doing with . . . with losing Greer?"

Ian bristled more intensely than he had over James's inquiry about Wren. He wanted to tell him no, that he was *not* to ask such a question.

But it was brotherly concern, and Ian could surely answer a simple question. "It's been hard. To be truthful, I'm not sure what to think."

"Think? About what? You have a right to grieve; he was your best friend. But what is there to think about?"

Ian had even more trouble answering *that* question, and a long moment's thought didn't bring to mind any words to do so.

James stopped walking and said with astonishment, "I hope you don't mean that you're still blaming yourself for what happened."

Ian stopped walking to face him. "And why shouldn't I?"

"It's just one of those things that happened," James said. "It was nobody's fault."

"That's a matter of opinion, I suppose," Ian said and walked on.

James said nothing more about Greer *or* Wren, but Ian's mind vacillated back and forth between the two topics throughout the remainder of the day. But then, he'd devoted most of his thinking to one or the other during all of his time away. He tried not to show his distress as he ate dinner with his family, but while he rode toward town to see Wren, he felt too weighed down by thoughts of Greer's death to even think about his brother's suggestion in regard to Wren.

Ian was tethering his horse to the fence at the edge of Wren's yard when she came out of the door, a shawl wrapped tightly around her arms. His heart responded to just seeing her come toward him, the light of dusk giving her an almost phantomlike appearance.

"Hello there, Ian MacBrier," she said as he came through the gate.

"I remember you," he said and greeted her with an embrace. They held tightly to each other a long moment, then he looked down at her. "And I remember everything that happened last night."

"Even the bump on the head?"

"Even that," he said and nodded toward the house. "Is everything all right?"

"Bethia had a difficult day; she was very agitated. But she's better now. Father's asleep."

"Does he even know that I'm back?"

"Aye, I told him. He's pleased, if ye must know. He's hoping ye'll come t'morrow when he's up and about. He'd like t' see ye."

"Truly?"

"Truly."

"Likely to interrogate me about my intentions concerning his daughter."

"Perhaps," she said with an impish smile before she lifted her lips to his. Following a kiss that brought Ian a little closer to the life he wanted to believe was possible, Wren looked up at him and said, "Oh, ye're really home!"

"I really am," he said and kissed her again.

When she looked at him again, he saw her brow furrow and she asked, "What's troubling ye, Ian? Did something happen at home?"

"No, of course not. All is well there."

She took a step back as if to get a better view of his facial expression. "Then what?"

Ian looked at the ground, not wanting to talk about it, but knowing he probably needed to. He looked toward where the sun had recently gone down, then back at Wren.

"Tell me," she urged. "Ye must learn t' tell me the truth of yer feelings, my darling. Ye must."

"I know," he said, wondering if all those months of holding his tongue in regard to his feelings for her had brought on a habit of holding it regarding other things as well. "I just . . . can't stop thinking about Greer. It's nothing new. I thought about him every day while I was gone. But . . . now that I'm back, I can't help but see the results of his absence. If he were here, surely Bethia would not be so lost inside her mind. And surely the—"

Wren put her fingers over his lips. "Come inside and have some tea. It's too chilly out here and it's apparent we need t' talk."

"Yes," Ian said with some reluctance, questioning his own wisdom in having opened the topic so boldly. "Yes, I suppose we do."

Chapter Five
Impetuous and Preposterous

Wren took Ian's hand and led him through the door into the kitchen where a lamp was burning low in the center of the table. She sat down, and he scooted a chair closer so that he could sit to face her. For a long moment Wren couldn't find the words she'd intended to say. Just having him here this way was still difficult for her to comprehend as a reality. She'd dreamt of such moments as this through all the long weeks and months of his absence, praying with all her soul that such simple times might be shared between them again. To have him sitting here in her kitchen could be nothing less than a miracle, a blessing she would never take for granted. To have his heart open and humbled was more than she had ever dared to hope for. A tiny part of her heart still felt hesitant to trust that this blessing would not end, but the largest part of her heart knew that Ian's humility was genuine, and that he would never break his promises to her.

Her greatest concern at the moment was the weight that she knew burdened him, and it was her hope that she could help him find the truth and make peace with Greer's death. Surely he would need to do so in order to move on and put the past into the past, where it belonged.

"Forgive my boldness, Ian, but I have t' ask. We must be completely honest with each other. Are ye still feeling responsible for Greer's death?"

Ian considered the question and the tone in which she'd asked it. Recalling his conversation with James earlier today that had a similar theme, he wondered why the people closest to him were so blind to this situation. "You sound so astonished," he said, "as if my feeling responsible is ridiculous. Why *wouldn't* I feel responsible? I was too drunk to help him. I left him there to die."

Wren took his hand and looked at him as if she were about to deliver devastating news that might knock him flat. "Ian, have ye considered the possibility that the only person responsible for Greer's death is . . . Greer?"

"How could *that* be a possibility?" he snarled, wishing it hadn't sounded so unkind. But there was no topic so sensitive for him as Greer's death.

"I believe ye are so consumed with yer own grief over the matter that ye've never even stopped t' consider the obvious. As I see it, most people have some kind of an Achilles' heel . . . a weak and vulnerable place that could be their undoing if they're not careful. And ye know very well what that place was with Greer."

Ian sighed. He knew the answer to the question, but he still couldn't see how it might possibly have anything to do with Greer's death. Wren's expression made it clear she was expecting him to say the word, even though they both knew very well what she was talking about. He sighed again. "Gambling. So, he gambled. I know it got him into trouble now and then, but he—"

"Ye haven't heard everything I have t' say yet," she said, and he held up his hands. "We all have those weak places, Ian, but I've seen some people let those weak places take over everything else in their lives. It's like a disease that festers and grows. Forgive the example, but that's how it is with James. He's a good man in practically every way but one."

"Women."

"That's right. His philandering is so contrary t' his character that it's difficult t' understand, but I fear it will be his undoing."

"That's exactly what my parents have said. It breaks their hearts."

Wren took Ian's hand into hers, as if to prepare him for something he wouldn't want to hear. "Ye must know that Greer's gambling was very much the same. He was in trouble because of it, Ian. He told Bethia that the men he'd gambled with . . . the men trying t' get the money he owed t' them . . . were ruthless."

"*What* men?" he demanded. "Who?"

"Not from around here; that's all I know. He told Bethia that they would never hurt *her,* but that he believed he was . . . better off dead."

Wren saw Ian's eyes widen, then his brow furrowed. He closed his eyes and shook his head.

"I wish I could remember . . . more of what happened."

"What *do* ye remember?" she asked.

Ian struggled to put the images together in his mind, just as he had hundreds of times. But it was all so disconnected and blurred. He'd never actually verbalized them to anyone. Maybe Wren was on to something; maybe she could help him piece it together.

"Everything at the pub was . . . normal . . . typical. Then . . . a fight broke out."

"Who was fighting?"

"I don't know. It was on the far side of the room. I heard things breaking, saw commotion. Something caught fire; the room filled with smoke." Ian struggled futilely to get his brain to retrieve something—anything—beyond that moment. But it just wasn't possible. He had to admit, "The next thing I knew I woke up here . . . and you told me that Greer was dead." Ian pondered a moment. "Are you saying that . . . the fight broke out because of Greer's gambling debts?"

"More than one person there heard the argument start, saw Greer in the middle of the fight, getting the worst of it. There were three men, strangers. Of course, with all the commotion, they got away."

"And left Greer too badly beaten to get out of the fire?"

Wren looked down in silent assent.

"And if I'd not been so blasted drunk, *I* could have gotten him out."

"Maybe, maybe not. That does *not* make his death yer responsibility."

"I suppose that's a matter of opinion."

"And it's possible those men had already killed him, and the fire was set to cover the fact that he was dead."

Ian couldn't speak. His mind was swimming with the possibilities in light of this new information. When Wren spoke again, he looked at her as if she could save him from this dark vortex where he'd been drowning since Greer's death.

"I'm asking ye t' consider the possibility that Greer knew he would never be safe from these people, and that . . . perhaps he knew he was going t' die that night."

Ian's heart quickened. He hated the way this was actually starting to make sense. Recalling his final conversations with Greer, Ian wondered now if there had been hints that he had missed, confirming that this was true. He wandered back out of his memories to look hard at Wren. "Did he say something to you?"

"No."

"To Bethia?"

"Aye."

"What?"

"He told her she would be safer with him gone, that he'd brought this on himself and he knew there was no way t' escape this. He knew they would kill him, Ian, and perhaps if ye'd intervened, they would have killed ye as well. And don't tell me it might have been better if they had!"

Ian touched her face. "I wouldn't."

"Before ye left here ye would have."

"Yes, I probably would have, but . . . I'm grateful to be alive, Wren; truly I am." He kissed her and offered a weak smile. "You need me."

"Aye, I do!" she said and touched his face in return.

Ian's thoughts wandered again through the conversation while Wren absently toyed with his hair. The very idea of Greer being so deep into gambling that it cost him his life made Ian sick. But the notion that Ian could let go of this weight of responsibility was as astounding as it was liberating. He'd been in such a stupor of grief prior to leaving here that he'd shielded himself from seeing or hearing anything but what he'd believed to be true. Now he could see that he'd wasted nearly two years of his life believing that he could have done something to prevent Greer from dying. But even if that were true, the past could not be changed. He couldn't bring him back to life. No amount of holding on to such feelings would help him or anyone else. He looked at Wren, and his thoughts shifted abruptly. Suddenly and completely, an idea that made his heart quicken and his insides tingle overtook his mind. He wondered for only a moment if he should give the matter some time. He'd already wasted far too much of it. The best thing he could do to compensate for Greer's death was to be certain that his widow was cared for. There were many ways he could accomplish *that.* But the best thing he could do for the sake of his own future would be to stop wasting time and do what he should have done a long time ago. He wondered how to go about it, what to say, and how Wren might respond to the idea.

In the midst of his racing thoughts, Wren stated, "Ye know what yer own Achilles' heel is."

"Why don't you tell me," he said.

"Ye already know the answer."

"I need you to say it."

"Why?" she asked, defensive.

"Just say it."

The way she averted her gaze and bit her lip was exactly what he'd expected.

"It frightens you," he declared, glad she'd brought it up, needing to get it out of the way. There had already been far too much grief in their lives due to poor communication.

"Of course it frightens me!" Wren stood abruptly and turned her back to him, planting her hands firmly on her hips. "It frightened me for years before ye left . . . and then I worried every hour that . . . that . . ." Her words faded into tears.

Ian stood up and put his hands on her shoulders, saying gently, "That my weakness had become my undoing?"

"Precisely!" she snapped, then sniffled and wiped her face with her sleeve.

"I don't ever intend to get drunk again, Wren."

"I'm certain Greer said the same thing many times about his gambling; it's like a sickness. And James . . ."

"I'm not sure if James has ever *wanted* to curb his . . . passions. But you keep bringing him up."

She turned to glare at him, any hint of tears completely absent. "Only for the sake of making a point."

"I just have to be sure."

"Sure of what?"

Ian remained unaffected by her testiness over the topic. "Sure that you're not still in love with him."

"I was *never* in love with him! I thought I'd already made that clear."

Ian actually laughed. "As I recall, you frequently declared your love for him, and I—"

"I was young and foolish. I was infatuated. Ye already know this."

"I just have to be sure. You can't blame me for that."

"No." She looked down, and her voice became quiet. "I can't blame ye for that. But I've not given a romantic notion t' him since the day ye . . ." She looked up at him as if she didn't want him to have any doubt over what she had to say. "Since the day ye made me realize what a fool I had been. I love *ye,* Ian. *I do.*"

He smiled. "In that case . . . I'll make a deal with you."

"What kind of deal?" Suspicion sparked in her eyes.

"Marry me, Wren," he said, and she gasped. "Marry me and I'll never get drunk again."

Wren opened her mouth to speak, but no sound came out, and she closed it again. She'd secretly wished for this very thing since the night he'd made his drunken confessions. Every day of his absence she had wondered what it would be like to have him return, declare his love anew, and make her his wife. It was her greatest dream come true! Perhaps that was the very reason it seemed too good to be true. And for all of her wishing and hoping, she felt the need to point out that she could see far too many impediments to his proposal.

"I could count the hours since ye've come back here, Ian MacBrier. Yer proposing marriage is impetuous and preposterous."

"I disagree, Ailsa Wren. I believe my proposing marriage is long overdue. You told me that you love me, and you know that *I* love *you.* What other course did you think we might take with the way we feel about each other? We've been friends for years, Wren. I know you better than anyone, and you know me. I'd say that makes my proposal neither impetuous *nor* preposterous."

"I do not necessarily agree."

"Why am I not surprised?" he countered and held out his hands in resignation. "Convince me that we should not be together, Wren." It occurred to him as he said it that perhaps her purpose in this argument—whether she consciously recognized it or not—was a need for *him* to convince *her* that he really meant it, that he wouldn't back down, that he would do whatever it took to have her. And he was prepared to do so. Still, he wasn't prepared for her next blow.

"You're a MacBrier, for one thing," she said, and Ian was shocked at how quickly that made him angry. He moved abruptly closer, and she took a step back.

"I can*not* believe that you would make *that* an issue between us. There has *never* been a lack of equality between us. *Never!* And don't try to tell me that people would talk or judge us for marrying. You know well enough that I've *never* cared what people say or think, and I know that you don't care, either. There is nothing in my being a *MacBrier* that could ever convince me we shouldn't be together. Nothing!"

Ian calmed his own breathing and took note of her complacent expression. He studied her through narrowed eyes. "You were *trying* to get me to say that!"

"Ye can't blame a woman for needing reassurance."

"No, I can't blame you for that."

"I know yer intentions are noble, Ian," she said. "And yer proposal means more t' me than I can say, but under the circumstances, I don't know how I could possibly accept."

"*What* circumstances? If this is still about my drinking, you have to believe me when I tell you that I will never drink enough to get drunk again."

"Ye told me ye'd make me a deal, that if I married ye ye'd never get drunk again. If yer intentions are founded in *me,* then ye're doing it for the wrong reasons."

"My intentions are founded in making a better life for both of us. I vowed the moment I set myself on the path to come home that I would never again drink enough to lose my senses—ever! I cannot deny that my desire to be the kind of man you deserve added to my incentive."

"Before ye came home?"

He took her shoulders into his hands and eased her closer. "You kept me alive, Wren. Through all the confusion and grief; through all the . . . hiding and running. You were there, in my mind, in my heart."

Wren looked up into his eyes and had to steady herself to keep from leaning into him and losing all reason. She looked away and again took a step back, forcing him to let go.

"Do you not believe me?" he asked.

"I believe ye," she said.

"Then what's wrong?"

"I still believe this is impetuous and preposterous. As much as I might *want* to be yer wife, Ian, it's just not practical."

"Why?" Ian demanded, his heart pounding with dread. What would he do if she rejected him now, after all they had been through? "Why, Wren?" he added more softly. "Help me understand why you would refuse me."

Wren found it impossible to look at him again, and she forced the words out before her wavering courage cowered and hid. "Look around yerself, Ian. I'm responsible for my father . . . and for Bethia. I don't know how I could ever bring that burden into yer life."

"I would never consider it a burden, Wren. Did you think it hadn't occurred to me? Of course, I would assume responsibility for your family. It's only right."

"I don't think ye have the slightest notion of what ye would be getting yerself int' here, Ian. Ye cannot just—"

"I've survived being knocked out cold by your sister, Wren. I can assure you that I'm willing to do whatever it takes. And what better way could I honor Greer than to help care for Bethia?"

"Even so, I could never up and move Bethia away from here. The cellar's the only place she feels completely safe. I cannot move her t' Brierley and have her upsetting life for yer family like that. It's preposterous!"

"Then I'll live here . . . with you."

Wren gasped, then she laughed. "That's even *more* preposterous!"

"Why?" Ian leaned toward her, determined to win this argument. "I've lived with little more than I could carry with me for nearly two years. You think I can't make do living here with your family? As long as there's enough room in your bed for a husband, I should think we'll do just fine."

The reference to sharing a bed made Wren go warm in the face before she turned away to hide the fact from Ian. She struggled to come up with some other point of protest to his proposal, but there was none. She wasn't certain herself if she'd been more intent on trying to talk him out of it or hoping that he would talk her into it. Either way, he was very convincing. Most especially the evidence of his love for her was *very* convincing. Without turning back she asked more softly, "Do ye really mean it, Ian? Do ye mean every word of what yer saying? If ye don't, I need t' know now, because I'll hold ye t' yer promises. I will. Mark my words."

"I would expect nothing less. I *do* mean it, Wren. Every word."

Ian took her hand and lifted it to his lips as she turned slowly to face him. Their eyes met, and she invaded his gaze with that searching intensity for which she was renowned. When he saw her countenance softening he took hold of the moment with all the fervor he felt in his desire to make her his wife. Without letting go of her hand he went down on one knee and repeated his plea. "Marry me, Wren." He saw moisture in her eyes reflecting the lamplight. "Marry me soon. We've already waited too long. I should have been more forthright with my feelings years ago."

"We were too young to be married years ago."

"Not *too* young," he said. "We were both in our twenties even then. But perhaps we were too naive, too immature. I've grown up a great deal since Greer's death, Wren. And I know beyond any doubt that this is the best thing I could possibly do with my life. Don't make me beg you."

"*Would* you beg if I made you?" she asked, a hint of a smile creeping into her expression.

"Yes. Yes, I would. I will do whatever it—"

"Enough," she said. "How could I possibly refuse?" Ian let out a laugh of relief but remained on his knee. "I can't imagine my life without ye there. Being without ye has been torture, Ian. I'll not let ye go again."

"Amen to that," he said and came to his feet. He laughed again and wrapped his arms around her, lifting her feet off the floor.

"I was such a fool to leave you," he said, setting her down.

"Finally, something we agree on," she said, and he laughed before he kissed her. He disciplined himself to stop with *one* kiss and sat back down, easing her onto his lap. They talked of their past and their future, and the marvelous experience of the present moment and all they felt for each other in just being together again. When he needed to leave and allow her to get some sleep, their reluctance to be apart strengthened his conviction that they should be married *soon.* He hated the thought of her being alone with Bethia's unpredictability and her father's inability to do much about it, out cold as he was from early in the evening until late morning each and every day.

"I'll come tomorrow after lunch," he promised. "I need to speak with your father and make all of this official." He chuckled tensely. "With a bit of luck he won't boot me out."

"He won't," she said, and he kissed her with the promise of sharing a lifetime together before he said goodnight and rode toward home. With the light of a partial moon illuminating his surroundings, he was struck with the dramatic change in his feelings since he'd gone to see Wren this evening. He'd found some measure of peace over Greer's death, even if the things he'd learned about Greer had been difficult to hear. And he would soon be married. He felt happier than he had in years—perhaps ever—and he wondered what kind of madness had kept him wandering the streets of London, avoiding the very people and places that were now bringing him such joy.

* * * * *

Wren had trouble sleeping as the magic of Ian's return to her life hung in the air around her. She had difficulty believing that her every hope and dream was coming true and that so much had changed in so few days. She turned over in the bed she'd once shared with her sister and tried to imagine how it would be to wake up and find Ian there beside her—each and every day for the rest of their lives. It warmed her so deeply that she couldn't stop smiling. She finally slept with the warmth of his love wrapped around her, and woke to hear that her sister was already awake and in the kitchen. Before Wren took a minute to get dressed or do up her hair, she went to the kitchen to make certain that Bethia was calm and that all was well. She found Bethia humming and stirring the batter for bannocks.

"Good morning, sister," Wren said, hugging her from behind.

"Good morning," Bethia said, apparently more lucid than usual when she added, "I hurt Ian last night."

"It was the night before, actually," Wren said, standing beside her.

Bethia turned to look at her sister. "The night before? Truly?"

"Aye, but it's all right."

"He's not angry with me?"

"No, Bethia. He understands. Truly he does."

"Greer told me he would," Bethia said, reminding Wren that even a lucid moment could be fleeting—that only a part of Bethia might be existing in reality.

"Will ye tell him I'm sorry?" Bethia asked.

"I will if ye want, but he's coming this afternoon, and ye can tell him yerself."

"Oh, he's coming here?" Bethia became mildly panicked.

"It's nothing t' worry about, sister," Wren said. "He's going t' be around a great deal, if ye must know." Bethia's eyes widened, and Wren figured her sister should be the first to know. In spite of Bethia's illness, they were still as close as sisters could be. "He's asked me t' marry him, and I've accepted. I hope ye'll be happy for me."

A delighted laugh from Bethia accompanied her embrace, then she shifted into concern immediately and looked at Wren hard. "He'll take ye away from here. I'll be here alone with Pa, and—"

"No, Bethia. I'll not leave ye and Pa alone. We'll all be t'gether; Ian promised."

Bethia took a step back, her eyes widening with an overt terror that frightened Wren. "I can't leave here. I can't go back to Brierley. I . . . I . . ."

"Ye mustn't worry, sister," Wren said, putting calm hands on Bethia's upper arms. "Ian will be living here with us. All will be well. I promise."

It took a moment for Wren's assurance to calm Bethia. When she was breathing normally again, she gave Wren a forced smile. "I'm fine. Truly. I'm happy for ye, sister. Greer will be pleased." She laughed softly. "He'll say that it's high time Ian made right with his feelings for ye."

"I dare say that's true," Wren said, and Bethia went back to stirring the batter. "Ye get the bannocks cooked while I get dressed, then I'll get the shop opened for the day."

Bethia smiled and nodded. Wren went back to her room to prepare for the day, smiling to think of seeing Ian this afternoon. She hoped that his talk with her father would go well, then it occurred to her that her father might do better with some warning. She thought about how to bring it up to him while she smoothed her hair and wound it up, pinning it with the ease of much practice to the back of her head.

A while later, Wren was scrubbing the skillet used to cook the bannocks—the same one that Bethia had used to knock Ian unconscious. At the table her father ate his bannocks and a piece of the sausage he loved dearly; Wren had made a point of getting it regularly from the butcher across the street. Bethia was sitting in the shop, working at her sewing. If a customer came in, Wren would hear the bell and either she or her father could help the customer. It was Bethia's habit to discreetly scoot out of the shop rather than be around people who might find her behavior odd. But she liked to sew there because the light was good, especially in the mornings.

Wren waited until her father was nearly finished with his breakfast before she sat across from him and said, "There's something I need t' talk t' ye about, Pa."

Angus looked up while shoving the final nugget of sausage into his mouth. Once he'd chewed and swallowed, he said, "I'll wager it's got something t' do with Ian MacBrier."

"He's changed, Pa."

"So ye told me yesterday. What's changed since then, girl? What's so important?"

"He's coming later t'day. He wants t' talk with ye." Wren saw her father take in the implication. He set his fork down but didn't speak. She forged ahead to get it out into the open. "He wants t' marry me, Pa. He's promised t' take care of me."

Angus leaned back in his chair, overcome with thought. For all of his complaining over the pain of his arthritis and his inability to work for a living, he was a good man with a good heart. But Wren still wasn't sure how he would take this. She was prepared to talk to him until he accepted that Ian MacBrier really was going to be his son-in-law. She just hoped it didn't take *too* much talking.

"I take it ye're pleased with this," he said.

"Aye, Pa; I am pleased."

"And who will take care of yer sister?" he asked, as if his own need for care did not exist.

"Ian will take care of all of us, Pa."

"If ye think that we're up and moving to Brierley, then—"

"We're not," Wren said quickly. "Ian will live here with us."

Again Angus assumed a silence that dragged on and left Wren nervous. But she waited patiently to hear what he had to say.

"Are ye trying t' tell me that Ian MacBrier would leave behind all those niceties t' live *here*?"

"That's right, Pa. He wants ye and Bethia t' be comfortable, and he doesn't want us t' be apart." She hurried to get to the most important point. "He's coming later, Pa, t' ask for my hand. Promise me ye'll be kind t' him. He's a good man. He deserves t' have ye hear him out."

Angus took a thoughtful moment before responding. "Ye seem t' believe he's changed. For all our sakes, I do hope ye're right."

"He *has* changed."

"Do ye love him, Wren?" Angus asked. "Does he love ye too?"

"Aya, Pa. He loves me, and I love him."

Angus showed a faint smile. "I want my girls t' be happy. If he can make ye happy, I'll not stand in yer way." He stood up and carried his dishes to the sink and started to clean them. "I only hope he can put up with yer ornery old pa."

Wren laughed softly and hugged her father from behind. "He'll learn t' love ye as I do, Pa. I know he will."

Angus dried his hands and put one of them over hers. "Ye're a precious girl, Wren. And I know ye're smart. If he's earned yer love, I'll not put up a fuss."

Wren tightened her arms around her father, happier than she'd ever been, but as the morning proceeded with all its normalcy in the tiny house and shop, Wren's imaginings of Ian living here became tainted by reality. How could he possibly be happy and comfortable in such close quarters with her cantankerous father and fragile sister? Her heart went heavy with the thought, and she knew she needed to speak with Ian right away. Holding on to such fears quietly would not help the matter.

When everything was in order and her sewing for the day completed enough to get by, Wren told her father she wished to borrow a horse from Blane and ride to Brierley before lunch. He agreed to keep a careful eye on Bethia and assured her that all would be well. Riding away from town, she prayed that all *would* be well, at home and with Ian. She loved him and wanted him in her life, but not if it would make him unhappy. Above all else, she wanted him to be happy.

* * * * *

In spite of coming in late, Ian made a point of being present for breakfast with his family. He enjoyed the easy conversation and banter, and he appreciated getting to know Lilias a little better. She was well suited for Donnan, and he could see how they loved each other. How glad he was to have such love in his own life! He thought it ironic that his life and Donnan's would take such different paths in the way they lived. But Ian didn't care. He would see his family often, and he was glad to have *any* life with Wren.

When the meal was finished, Ian said, "Mother, Father . . . I wonder if I might speak to you."

"Of course," Gavin said, coming to his feet. "Let's go into the study." Gavin helped Anya with her chair and took her hand before they walked ahead of Ian out of the dining room, up the hall, around the corner, and into the room where Gavin spent a great deal of his waking hours, handling matters of business in regard to the estate or just reading, as he so enjoyed doing.

Ian closed the door, and they were all seated. He noticed as Gavin settled into his chair that his breathing had become so labored that Ian could hear it from across the room.

"Are you all right?" Ian asked. His mother didn't seem concerned, and he wondered how commonplace such an incident had become.

"It happens when I walk too far . . . too fast," Gavin said, attempting to breathe deeply. Ian was astonished. Had walking from the dining room to the study at a normal pace been considered too far, too fast? "It will calm down in a minute."

Ian tried to take his word for it, but he knew he couldn't begin his intended conversation until he saw evidence for himself that his father was all right. While Anya commented on the weather, as if to purposely draw attention away from her husband's strained breathing, Ian noticed that it *was* calming down, and Ian was able to breathe more easily himself.

"What is it, son?" Gavin asked when he could ask it in a normal voice. "Is something wrong?"

"No, not at all," Ian said. "I'm very glad to be home."

"No more glad than we are to *have* you home," Anya said, and they exchanged a smile.

In response to his parents' expectant expressions, Ian got straight to the point. "I'm going to marry Wren . . . soon." He enjoyed the surprised expressions on their faces.

"Isn't this . . . a bit hasty?" Anya asked. "You've not been home a week."

"I've loved Wren for years, Mother. And she loves me. I need to take care of her . . . and her family. I need to make it official."

"If you're certain," Gavin said, "then of course we'll support you in your decision."

"Thank you," Ian said. "You always do."

"And, of course, we have plenty of room here for her father and her sister," Anya said. "We will gladly—"

"I'm certain the two of you would gladly open your home to them, and I'm grateful for that. But I will need to live with Wren after the marriage . . . at least for now." Before they could ask why, he hurried to explain; he'd been memorizing how to say it just right. "I know you were aware years ago that Bethia is a very sensitive person. She actually has some kind of illness. It's gotten dramatically worse since Greer's death, and it's impossible for her to even leave the house without getting very upset. Wren fears that moving her elsewhere would just be too hard on her. She's also concerned about the townspeople discovering the truth about Bethia. She fears that they would misunderstand and make things more difficult for the family."

The silence told Ian his parents were taking in a great deal of information. Gavin spoke first. "You need to do what you feel is best, son, but do you really intend to raise a family in the little house behind the tailor's shop? It's certainly possible, but perhaps the need to move Bethia to a different location will become necessary eventually anyway."

"Perhaps," Ian said. It had certainly crossed his mind. "All I can say for certain is that for now . . . I need to do it this way."

Ian could tell that his parents weren't pleased about the living arrangements, but they would never be critical or unkind. He found it touching to realize that they would far prefer to take in Wren's cranky, arthritic father and her mentally ill sister than to have him living a few miles away.

"Perhaps," Anya said, her eyes telling him she hoped to change his mind, "Bethia might be safer here . . . if there's concern over the townspeople misunderstanding her condition. She can be more secluded here. We can protect her."

"People can sometimes take their silly superstitions to extremes," Gavin added.

"You would know," Ian said.

"You don't remember my sister, Effie," Gavin said.

"No, but you've told me about her, of course," Ian said.

"Her mind just wasn't right," Gavin continued. "She would sometimes have fits or outbursts that were difficult to deal with. But most of the time she was sweet and loving. She made a great contribution to our family. We never begrudged the challenges."

"I hear what you're saying, Father, but it's different with Bethia."

"Different how?" Gavin asked. "If you're going to marry into this family, perhaps you should educate us on exactly what you're dealing with."

Ian didn't have to wonder if he could trust them to keep this confidential. He just didn't want to talk about it. He couldn't deny that it concerned him; his own ability to take on the care of Bethia concerned him most of all. He reminded himself that he needed his parents' support. He cleared his throat and leaned forward. "There's only one place that Bethia feels completely safe, and that's the cellar of the house. It's where she sleeps, and she won't let anyone else go down there. It's as if *she* is safe there, but she believes if anyone else goes down there, they will be in danger."

"In danger of what?" Anya asked.

Ian sighed. The thought of saying it made it sound all the more strange. "She believes there are three other people living down there with her. Two of them are apparently created from her mind . . . much like when a child has imaginary friends, I suppose. Except that she hears them talking to her; she sees them. She truly believes they're real. Well, I should clarify that about 90 percent of the time she believes they're real. Occasionally she's very lucid and admits that she knows she's not well, and she admits that these people aren't real. When she *does* believe it, she talks to them, argues with them, insists they're telling her to do things, and she has to do them. It would only take about ten minutes out on the street for people to declare her as evil and want to burn her at the stake."

"Now, that's an exaggeration!" Anya insisted.

"No, it's a metaphor," Ian said. "At the very least, I'm certain people would believe—even insist—that Bethia be put into an asylum. Wren has no idea how people would respond to her, but you can be certain it wouldn't be good."

"Probably not," Gavin said.

"Who is the third person?" Anya asked, and Ian looked at her. "You said she believes there are three people living in the cellar. If she—"

"She believes that Greer is with her. She talks about him as if they're still husband and wife."

"Oh, it's just tragic!" Anya said. "That poor girl."

"If you marry Wren, you take on the responsibility of her sister as well." Ian knew that his father's words were not meant to try to talk him out of it. He was just concerned. "And her father is ill as well, is he not? Donnan has spoken to Wren now and then. She told him about the situation."

"He is," Ian said. "I love Wren, and I'm fully prepared to take on the responsibility. I just believe it would be best—for the time being—if we allow Bethia to remain in a place that's comfortable for her. And her father as well. He's not able to do the work he used to do because of his arthritis, but the shop is his life. Perhaps over time, when Bethia's learned to trust me more, we will be able to move her. And perhaps a time will come when Mr. Docherty will also be willing to go. For now, my place is with them. I hope you understand."

"Of course we do," Anya said. "We will miss you, of course."

"I'll see you often, Mother. I'm not so far away."

"For that we are all grateful," Gavin said and smiled at his son.

Chapter Six
Stitches and Buttons

Ian talked with his parents a while longer about possible plans for the wedding and once again expressed his appreciation for their support. When he left the study, he was only partway up the stairs before a maid called after him, telling him that he had a visitor waiting in the drawing room. He knew it was Wren even before the maid told him so. He found the woman he loved looking out the window, the sun illuminating her profile and casting a sheen on her ebony hair. When she turned to look at him, it stole his breath from his lungs. He closed the door and leaned against it until he could draw breath enough to fully embrace the joy of her presence. She loved him. She was going to marry him. It was a miracle too large to hold or even imagine. Then he caught something dark in her eyes, and his breathing tightened for a different reason.

"Is something wrong?" he asked in lieu of a greeting.

Wren turned back to the view out the window, a little unnerved at his ability to sense her emotions so readily. His years away had not diminished his ability to do so. But since she was equally able to sense *his* emotions, she had to consider it fair.

"Nothing, exactly," she said, continuing to focus on the lovely view of the gardens. Memories of hiding and playing among the shrubberies and flowers momentarily distracted her from her purpose.

"What does that mean, *exactly*?" he asked, coming up behind her. He took hold of her shoulders and pressed a kiss to the back of her neck where soft wisps of hair strayed out of the knot wound at the back of her head.

Wren tried to keep her resolve from weakening as a result of the pleasure of his kiss, coupled with the strength she drew from his nearness. It became more difficult when he kissed her again.

"You haven't answered my question," he said behind her ear.

"Nothing's gone wrong, if that's what you mean." She turned abruptly to face him, finding his expression startled. She hurried to say what she needed to say. "But I just have t' be certain, Ian . . . certain that ye're certain."

"About *what*?"

Wren stepped around him to put some distance between them, again turning her back to him. It was easier that way. "I'm not talking about making a waistcoat for ye, Ian. Ye asked me t' marry ye."

"I did," he said, "and you accepted."

"But I have t' be certain."

"And again I ask: about what?"

She turned to face him. "That ye know what ye're getting yerself int' here. That ye really believe ye can share our tiny, little home and be happy there. I don't want our being married t' be a sacrifice for ye. Ye deserve better than that. But it *would* be a sacrifice, Ian. It *would*! I know it's always been equal between us. Ye've always treated me like a lady. But . . . Ian . . . it's marriage we're talking about. I just don't know how ye can leave all of this behind." She made a sweeping motion with her arm. "Just t' be with me."

"Because I love you, Wren. It's not a sacrifice for me to leave here and help you take care of your family. It's a privilege. Do you have any idea of the uselessness of being a *gentleman*?"

"Ye've certainly talked about it before, but I don't see how it applies t' yer walking away from—"

"I'm not walking away from anything. I'm walking toward a new life with purpose and meaning. My parents taught me to work and be responsible. They insisted that we be involved in running the estate and the household. But the fact is that it all runs just fine without me. I need something to do with my time . . . with my life. And I need to be a part of *your* life. I'll see my family often enough, and you and your family will never go without."

Wren lowered her head, but it took Ian a moment to realize she was crying. "What is it?" he asked, lifting her chin to make her face him. She shook her head to indicate that she couldn't speak, and he wrapped her in his arms, urging her head to his shoulder where she wept openly. Ian just held her and allowed her all the time she needed to unloose every tear.

"Speak to me, Wren," he whispered when her weeping subsided. "Tell me what troubles your heart."

Without relinquishing her comfortable place against his shoulder, Wren said, "Every day has been hard since ye left, Ian; every day. I went t' sleep every night imagining what it might be like t' have ye come back, safe and well. I imagined what it might be like t' have ye love me as I love ye, and t' have ye share in my burdens. But even as much as I imagined such things, the biggest part of my heart always believed it was just imaginings, that it could never be." She drew back to look at him. "But it's happened. Ye're here, and it's real. I feel as if God has opened the windows of heaven and poured upon me every possible blessing, and I wonder . . . why . . . of all women . . . why I would be so blessed."

Ian pressed a hand over the side of her face and her sleek dark hair. He smiled and kissed her brow. "It is I who am blessed, Wren. I don't know what life might bring to us . . . what challenges we might face . . . but we will face them together, my love. Always together."

She smiled, and he kissed her quickly.

"If you're here, I assume everything is well at home," he said.

"Pa is watching out for Bethia. I told him why I needed t' talk with ye. He was very understanding."

"Was he?" Ian asked, still nervous about facing Angus Docherty.

"Aye," she said. "Ye mustn't worry. I've told him ye'd be coming t' talk with him. I believe he'd be very unhappy if he had t' leave his home . . . and he knows he couldn't get by without me, even if he'll not admit it. He only expressed concern for Bethia. When I told him it was yer intention t' live with us, he told me that as long as I'm happy, that's all he cares about."

"*Are* you happy, Wren?" he asked, even though he knew it was a rhetorical question.

"Happier than I've ever been," she said with eyes that agreed with her words. "And yerself?"

"The same," he said and took her hand, leading her out the door and down the hall. "Now come. I've given my parents the news, and I'm certain they'd love to see you. With any luck they're still . . ." He opened the door to the study. "Ah, there they are."

Gavin and Anya both stood when Ian entered the room with Wren.

"Oh, my dear," Anya said and rushed toward Wren, wrapping her in a motherly embrace. She looked at Wren and held her shoulders. "We're so pleased!"

"Thank ye much," Wren said and glanced at Ian. "I can assure ye that no one is more pleased than I am."

"That is debatable," Ian said, winking at her.

Gavin took Wren's hand, then he gave her a hug. "We *are* pleased, my dear. I'd say it's about time Ian came to his senses."

"Amen to that," Ian said.

"Ye've always been so kind t' me, and t' my sister," Wren said. "For that and many other reasons, it's a privilege t' think of being a part of yer family."

"The privilege is ours," Anya said, and Ian could see that Wren was trying not to cry.

"We must be going," he said and caught a subtle glance of relief from her at being rescued. "I must speak to her father and make it official."

"Yes, you must do that," Gavin said, and Ian hurried Wren from the room.

"Are you all right?" Ian asked her.

"I'm fine," she said, wiping away the single tear that had escaped. "Ye just have such a fine family, Ian."

"Yes, I do." He squeezed her hand. "And it's soon to become finer."

They rode side by side back toward town, going slowly and talking as they went.

"There's something else I have t' say," Wren said, "before ye speak t' my father."

"I'm listening," Ian said.

"I'm well aware that ye have money enough t' see us comfortable for the rest of our days, but . . . the tailor shop is my father's life, and . . . the sewing keeps Bethia busy—and calm. I don't want yer being there t' make—"

"You mustn't worry," Ian said. "I don't want anything to change, *except* that I don't want you to have to worry—ever again—about having enough to get by. I will make my contributions to the household discreetly, and it will remain between you and me."

Judging by her smile, Ian assumed Wren was pleased with his position on the matter.

"Is there anything else you need to clarify?" Ian asked, returning her smile.

"Not at the moment," she said. "I'll be sure and let ye know if I think of something."

"I'm certain you will."

"And what of yer thoughts, Ian? Do ye have concerns?"

"My only concern is being able to handle the situation with Bethia. I haven't been around her enough to know what to say or do . . . and I fear that my being around all the time might upset her."

"As long as she can stay where she is, I don't think she'll have trouble adjusting. And I'll not be leaving ye alone with her until she *has* adjusted. At least not alone with any skillets lying about."

"Very wise plan," he said.

"How *is* yer head?"

"A little tender, but fine."

A minute or two of silence preceded Wren saying, "I'm guessing yer parents were not pleased with our plans."

"My parents are pleased that I am marrying such a wonderful woman. I'm certain they were aware of my feelings for you . . . long before I was able to admit it, if you must know."

"Truly?"

"Truly," he said and chuckled. "My mother told me long ago that I was jealous of your attention to James, and I was *furious.* I felt certain she had no idea what she was talking about. It took me months to see that she was right, and more months to really admit it to myself."

"I'm glad ye've finally come t' yer senses . . . just as yer father said."

"Yes, indeed."

"Did they have no objection to our marrying, then?"

"None," he said. "Although, I think they would prefer that we live at Brierley. The first words out of my mother's mouth were about having your father and sister come to live with us. But I explained the situation, and, of course, they will keep it confidential."

"Of course."

"I think they're disappointed. I think they would prefer that we live under their roof. I told them that perhaps with time that might be possible, but for now this was best."

"So, ye told them all about Bethia?"

"I did."

"Everything?"

"I summarized the situation. I didn't tell them she knocked me over the head with a skillet, if that's what you mean."

"I was more concerned about how they feel about ye marrying int' such a family."

"*That* is not their concern at all, Wren. They expressed concern over having the space to raise a family in your home, but we'll deal with that as it happens." They shared a smile, and he continued. "Their only other concern was that we might not be able to keep Bethia's problem concealed forever. They think it might be better to move her to Brierley, that once she adjusts to the move, we'll be able to protect her more fully."

"It's a wonderful thought," Wren said. "I cannot believe that yer parents would be willing t' open their home in such a way."

"They just want to help; they want what's best for all of us. I believe they're most concerned about how some people can become so misguided in acting on their superstitions. They have some experience with that, and they don't want to see Bethia—"

"*What* experience?" Wren asked.

"Surely with all the years we've known each other, you know *that* story."

"Apparently not."

"My father's birthmark; his older sister, Effie, whose mind was not normal."

"I have no idea what ye're talking about." Wren's tone scolded him for not telling her before now, and her eyes made it clear that she wouldn't let him get away with leaving the story untold for another minute.

"Don't you need to hurry home?" he asked lightly.

"They'll be fine a while longer. Just tell me."

"My father was not raised as the Earl of Brierley. He was actually raised by a servant girl in the forest tower of Brierley, believing that she was his mother."

Wren was so astonished that she pulled her horse to a halt, and Ian had to do the same. "Surely ye're teasing me."

"I'm not," Ian said. "What he didn't realize until he was an adult was that the birthmark on his shoulder was inherited from the Earl of Brierley, and had in fact been present on *each* earl for generations.

But the Earl had never been involved with this servant girl; he'd never been unfaithful to his wife."

"How did he find out?" Wren asked.

"After he was married to my mother, who had worked as a servant at Brierley, and—"

"I knew about that. And she was actually a blood relation to the Earl, but after his death the remaining family was cruel to her and put her to work."

"That's right," Ian said. "And they were also cruel to Effie MacBrier, the daughter of the Earl, because her mind was not normal and she could sometimes be difficult to handle."

"Yer father's sister? Is that what ye said a minute ago?"

"That's right," he said again and started his horse forward. Wren followed to keep up with him and listen to his story. "My parents took Effie in to protect her from people living at Brierley who were unkind to her. It was then that it became evident she had a birthmark almost identical to my father's. It turned out that a servant to the Earl's wife had been superstitious enough to believe that the birthmark was the reason for Effie's mental challenges—that it was somehow evil. When my father was born with the same mark, she did a horrible thing and manipulated switching the baby with an illegitimate boy born to the servant girl that raised my father. Therefore, my father was raised with no knowledge of his true identity, and someone else was raised to believe he was the Earl of Brierley."

"Astonishing!" Wren said. "And what happened to him?"

"He died in a terrible skirmish that had something to do with the entire thing coming to light. According to my parents, he was a selfish, evil man, and he'd caused a great many people a great deal of grief—most especially my parents. Apparently there were many people who were glad to have the truth of my father's identity become known."

"I can imagine! And what of this birthmark? Is it really true that all of the earls for generations have had it? The very idea is remarkable!"

"It *is* remarkable," Ian said. "But I confess that it's true. My father has the mark on his shoulder, and so do my brothers."

"Both of them?"

"That's right," Ian said.

"But ye don't?"

"No, I don't," Ian said, not admitting to how he'd once believed it was some bizarre validation that he was different from his brothers, and that he didn't belong. He knew now that the very idea was ridiculous, and he'd put away such thinking.

"Remarkable," Wren said again.

"The point of the story being that my parents have some understanding of caring for someone whose mind is not what it should be, and they know the damage that can result when people misunderstand. I'm certain they will be happy to do anything they can to help care for Bethia."

"They're very kind."

"Yes, they are."

They rode in silence for a few minutes before Wren slugged Ian in the shoulder.

"What was that for?" he demanded but couldn't hold back a laugh. It was something she'd often done during their youth.

"I cannot believe ye never told me that story before t'day."

* * * * *

Ian went with Wren to return Blane's horse that she'd used and to see that it was cared for and back in its stall. Blane heard them and came to investigate, expressing joy at Ian's return. Blane was near the age of Angus Docherty but in better health. He was robust and jolly with a bald head and a tooth missing in the front of his mouth. His laughter brought back to Ian all of the years of kindness he'd offered to Wren's family, and his own. He gladly let Ian leave his horse there while he spent the remainder of the day with Wren, just as he'd done countless times over the years.

"Just like old times, eh?" Blane said, as if his thoughts had been the same as Ian's.

"Exactly," Ian said and resisted the urge to tell him that he would soon be marrying Wren. He needed to make it official with Wren's father first. "Thank you, my friend. Perhaps I'll see you later."

"Nah," Blane said with more laughter. "I'll be t' sleep long before ye give up yer time with that sweet one."

"Likely true," Ian said, winking at Wren, who smiled prettily.

Ian and Wren walked hand in hand the short distance to her home. They went around and entered through the shop door. Bethia looked up from her sewing at the sound of the little bell. Ian wondered if she would dash into the back as Wren had said she did at the appearance of customers, but she hastily set her sewing aside and hugged Ian tightly. She seemed like a completely different person. Perhaps because she was, Ian thought ruefully.

"I'm so sorry that I hurt ye, Ian," she said without letting go. "Wren told me that ye understand."

"I *do* understand," Ian said, worming out of her suffocating embrace.

Bethia took his face into her hands and looked at him hard. "And now I hear ye're going t' marry my sister."

"I am, yes," Ian said, and Bethia hugged him again.

She said close to his ear, "Ye'll take good care of her?"

Ian took a step back and held her shoulders. "I will, Bethia. I promise. And I'll take good care of you as well. You have my word."

He saw tears in her eyes. "Ye'll not take her away from me?"

"No, never! I promise."

"Oh!" She smiled and sighed. "Greer will be so pleased t' know that ye're t' be married t' our precious Wren."

"I hoped that he would be," Ian said, certain that going along with her was the best option. "If you see him, tell him that I'm pleased . . . that he's pleased."

"I'll tell him," she said as if nothing were out of the ordinary, then she returned to her sewing with no further comment.

"I'll be nearby if ye need me," Wren said to her sister.

"Well enough," Bethia said without looking up.

Ian followed Wren past the curtain into the kitchen of the house, where Angus Docherty was sitting at the table, wearing eyeglasses to read from a book.

"Ian is here, Pa," Wren said. Angus looked up and removed his glasses, then he came to his feet.

"Hello, lad," Angus said. "It's good t' see ye well."

"And the same to you," Ian said.

Angus motioned Ian to a chair, and the men both sat down.

"I'll leave the two of ye t' chat," Wren said and went back into the shop, although Ian felt certain she would hover close to the curtain and do her best to eavesdrop.

"I worried about ye, ye know," Angus said to Ian's surprise.

"Did you?" Ian asked, determined to be forthright. This man was going to be family. He'd not have any pretentiousness between them. "I would have thought you'd be glad to be rid of me."

"I was not glad t' have ye passed out drunk on m' floor," Angus said, equally forthright. "But if ye stay sober, I'll not have complaint."

"You have my word," Ian said and forged directly into the purpose of this conversation, knowing that Angus was already well aware of that purpose. "I know that Wren spoke to you about my intentions, but I need to make them known between us. I would like to ask for your blessing, Mr. Docherty. I'm making it official. I'm asking for Wren's hand in marriage, and hope that you will approve."

Angus Docherty smiled. It was the first time Ian had seen him do so. "My daughter loves ye, ye know."

"So she tells me."

"She missed ye something dreadful."

"And I missed her, as well."

"Ye'll not be leaving here again, I take it."

"No, sir."

"Ye take good care of my Wren, and ye have my blessing. O' course, ye know that taking care of Wren means taking care of her sister, too. Her mind's not right, I tell ye."

"I understand," Ian said.

"And while I'm not keen on admitting it, I'm not so good off myself these days. I don't want to be a burden to ye, lad."

"I will never consider caring for Wren, or her loved ones, a burden. I don't want to change your life here, Mr. Docherty; I only ask to be a part of it."

"I believe Wren was right about ye."

"How is that, sir?"

"Ye *have* changed since ye left here. I see a man before me now."

"You're very kind."

"Not usually, if ye must know," Angus said with a little chuckle, and Ian smiled.

"We should drink to it," Angus added, standing up to get a bottle from its hiding place.

Knowing it was a common tradition, Ian said, "Just a little one for me."

Angus set two tin cups on the table and poured a small amount into each one. Ian stood, and they tapped their cups together and drank. After setting their cups down, Angus offered Ian his hand and they shook firmly. Ian's theory that Wren would eavesdrop was proven correct when she entered the room at precisely that moment.

Angus smiled at his daughter and said to Ian, "I hope ye'll be as happy with her as I was with her mother."

Wren smiled up at him, but Ian felt a little prick in his heart. Wren's mother died before Ian had even become acquainted with the Docherty family. He couldn't imagine ever losing Wren, and prayed they would both live long and healthy lives.

Ian shared a simple lunch with Wren and her family. The meal started out mildly awkward, and he could imagine Wren believing that he'd change his mind and call it off. But before they were finished eating, the tension had eased and Ian had no trouble seeing himself participating in every meal right here in such simple surroundings. They finished eating and remained at the table, exchanging idle chatter, until Wren had to leave to help a customer, and Bethia picked up her sewing. Angus started clearing the table, and Ian rose to help him. Before Wren returned, Ian and Angus had finished cleaning the dishes and had them nearly put away. She looked surprised, but smiled at Ian, then at her father.

"I've got some shopping t' do, Pa. Will ye be all right watching the shop for a while?" Ian knew that meant also watching out for Bethia.

"O' course I will," he said. "And don't ye be forgetting m' sausages."

"I won't, Pa," she said and kissed her father's cheek before she went out the back door with Ian following her.

"I can't believe ye think ye're going t' live with us that way," Wren said the moment the door was closed behind them.

"I *knew* you were going to say that! I can't believe you think I *wouldn't* want to live under the same roof with you—under any circumstances."

Wren made a disgusted noise that prompted laughter from Ian, but a subsequent glare from Wren stopped him.

It wasn't until an old acquaintance stopped Ian on the street, surprised at seeing him back in town, that Ian recalled he'd been nervous about facing the people of this town, fearing they'd believed all this time that he'd had something to do with Greer's death. A few greetings later, he could see what Wren had seen all along. No one had blamed him for what had happened. All the blame had come from within himself. He could see now how distorted his thinking had become when people were genuinely glad to see him and concerned about his well-being. He'd been such a fool. But with Wren's hand in his, and early spring in the air, he was more prone to looking to the future as opposed to dwelling on the past. He was on the brink of a new life, and he was determined to make it a good one.

Ian spent the remainder of the day at Wren's home. Not only did he want to be with her every possible minute, he also wanted to prove to her that he could fit in and be comfortable. Given that he'd avoided telling her the grueling details of his time in London, she likely didn't comprehend that he considered the safety and comfort of her home to be more than adequate. He did leave early enough, however, so that he could arrive at home before his parents went to bed—something he'd not done since his return. He found them chatting near the dying fire in his mother's sitting room. He sat with them, and they talked long after his parents normally *would* have gone to bed, but they all agreed it was nice to catch up with each other. They were pleased with his plans to marry Wren, but his mother tried again to talk him into moving Wren's family to Brierley. He assured her that he would visit often, and that this was best for now.

* * * * *

News spread quickly that Ian MacBrier was going to marry the tailor's daughter. Ian's brothers were thrilled, and his sister would be coming for the wedding. The tenant farmers and townspeople who knew either or both of them expressed glad tidings over the upcoming event; they even expressed pleasure that such a marriage could take place and strengthen the unity between the social classes of the community. Ian didn't really care about bridging any social gaps. He just wanted to be married to Wren and settle into the life that he could see unfolding before him. Word came that those in the county who were of a higher social status were disgusted by the forthcoming marriage. But Ian didn't care about that, either—and he knew his parents didn't care. They hardly interacted with those kind of people, anyway.

Bethia was busy making Wren's dress for the wedding, and Ian knew that with Bethia's skills it would be magnificent. Bethia became excited about the project, and it was evident that her love for her sister went into every stitch. He didn't really care what Wren wore to be married, as long as it made her feel beautiful and special. To him, she was always beautiful and special, and he told her so often enough that she wouldn't ever doubt his sincerity over the matter. Bethia was also making a dress for herself to wear when she stood beside Wren at the wedding. Wren helped with both dresses, doing the stitching that was simple and less crucial to the beauty and intricacy of the project; Bethia was the expert, and those things were seen to by her. And each day Wren was carefully coaching Bethia on behaving appropriately at the wedding. Since Greer had died, Bethia had hardly stepped into public or interacted with anyone besides those who came into her home, except when she occasionally attended church with Wren and Angus. But Wren wanted her sister to stand by her when she was married, and it was right that she should. Ian was often present for these coaching conversations, and he was amazed to see Wren speaking to Jinty and Selma as if she too accepted them as real.

"I'll behave m'self at the wedding," Bethia said to Wren as she did nearly every time this came up. "I promise. It's Jinty ye should be worried about. Selma tries so hard t' keep her in line, but ye know how Jinty goes off."

Wren put her hands on her hips. "Is Jinty here now?" she asked her sister.

Bethia glanced over her shoulder to the left. "Aye, she's here . . . and not very happy about the way we're talking about her."

"Jinty!" Wren said, looking to Bethia's left. "I've put up with yer antics and I'll continue t' do so. Ye know ye're welcome in my home and we'll always see that ye're safe. In return I insist that while ye're there at my wedding with Bethia, ye must behave yerself. People will not understand if ye make an uproar, and it could put Bethia in a bad situation. Do ye understand?" Wren then looked at Bethia. "Does she understand?'

Bethia looked over her shoulder. "Aye. She promises t' mind herself at the wedding."

"Good, then. Surely all will be well."

"Selma promises too," Bethia said, looking over her other shoulder.

Wren looked that way. "Thank ye, Selma. Ye're always such a good girl."

Bethia smiled at this and returned to her sewing.

Ian began dividing his time evenly between his own home and Wren's. He enjoyed time with his family and wanted them to know that he did, but he also wanted to work himself gently into the routine in the home that would soon be his own. He helped Wren do some rearranging in her bedroom, and he even purchased a new wardrobe that fit nicely on the wall opposite the bed. Between the wardrobe and a small dresser that had belonged to Wren's mother, there was space sufficient for both Wren and Ian to keep their clothing and personal items. As the date for the wedding drew closer, Ian began leaving a few things here and there in Wren's room, so that once they were married he would have all he needed without any big fuss or to-do.

Wren also spent time at Brierley with the full cooperation of her father, who promised to look out for Bethia. This was a much more satisfactory arrangement than Wren sneaking out when she knew her father was sleeping, and hoping that Bethia would mind her manners and stay in the cellar. Ian was pleased to see the bonds deepening between Wren and his family, especially his parents. They took to her and her to them as if they were already family. Ian's mother helped Wren plan the simple wedding celebration that suited her taste. When Anya first offered to have a feast and celebration at Brierley following the wedding, Wren was reluctant, wanting to keep the matter simple. But Anya spoke with Wren about the joy that friends and acquaintances received from taking part in the celebration and assured her that the staff at Brierley would see that everything was perfect, and Wren wouldn't have to worry about a thing. Wren finally agreed, telling Ian privately that perhaps she needed to make concessions in regard to the fact that she was to marry the son of an earl.

"If ye're wiling t' move int' the tailor's house, I should be able t' tolerate a fancy party in that castle where ye were raised."

"I dare say we will both manage just fine with such compromises," Ian said with a little smirk, then he kissed her in a way that made any compromise seem insignificant.

Ian quickly became comfortable among the Docherty household, and Angus warmed up to him with little trouble. Ian enjoyed helping with simple tasks in the kitchen, and it became his specific assignment to fill and empty the water tubs in the tiny room just off the kitchen that was used for laundry or bathing. Because of his strength he could do it without several trips with a bucket as Angus or the women had to do.

With the wedding only days away, Wren drew Ian's attention to a sensitive matter. She asked him if he would be present when she spoke to her father about it, and if he would also be willing to help. He heartily agreed. The following day after lunch, while Bethia was in the shop, busy at her sewing, Wren put a hand over her father's on the table before he could stand up.

"Ye know the wedding will be soon," Wren said to him.

"O' course I know," Angus said.

"I know ye've not wanted t' go out, and it's been a long time, but . . . Pa, I need ye t' walk me down the aisle at the church. I cannot get married without ye there to give me t' my husband."

Angus nodded. "O' course I would be there, but . . . I'll be needing t' wear m' fine suit, and the tie ye made for me . . . the one I wore t' Bethia's wedding."

"That is exactly what I was thinking," Wren said, glad to know that his thoughts had been the same as hers and that she wouldn't need to talk him into wearing the proper attire. But there was still a challenge to be faced. "I'll get them out and see that they're freshened and pressed, but—"

"I'll need help with the buttons," Angus said with humility, but without the self-deprecation that often came with admission of not being able to do the things he used to be able to do. He looked at Ian and asked with the same humility, "Would ye help me with the buttons, lad, so that I can be properly dressed for m' girl's wedding?"

Wren felt an urge to cry on more than one account. Her father's need for help was difficult to observe. But his willingness to reach beyond his pride for her sake touched her deeply. She was also touched by how her father had come to trust Ian. While help with the buttons might seem a simple and insignificant task, Wren knew that for her father it was very much the opposite. Perhaps her father was glad to have a man around who could help him and avoid any possible embarrassment with his daughters. It was just one more thing that made her grateful to have Ian in her life and to see his willingness to become a permanent part of her family.

"I would be glad to," Ian said with a smile, "and no one will be the wiser."

Angus offered a wan smile in return, and Wren changed the subject, talking excitedly about how lovely the wedding would be, and how she felt sure that the weather would be perfect on that day. She predicted pleasant spring warmth and a complete absence of rain.

The following day Ian walked with Wren to do some shopping. She needed things for the household and also a few odds and ends to finish up every detail for the wedding. They returned to the house to find that all was well there. Ian helped Wren make supper and put it on the table. Bethia kept sewing up until the moment she started eating, then she went right back to it, wanting every stitch perfectly in place before the wedding day.

Angus went to his room to get ready for bed, and Wren stepped outside to get some wash down from the line. Ian put away the dishes that he and Wren had just cleaned, then he sat at the table to look over a recent newspaper.

"Greer won't be at the wedding," Bethia said without looking up from her intense attention to her stitching.

"I know," Ian said gently. "I wish that he could be, but I understand."

"Ye stood with him at our wedding; he wishes he could do the same for ye, but he just can't be seen in public." She looked up briefly. "He hopes ye'll forgive him."

"Of course," Ian said. "You tell him that it's all right. My brothers will be there with me."

Bethia returned to her stitching. "I do so like yer brothers, Ian. They're very kind."

"Yes, they are," Ian said, but he felt a little hollow ache in his heart that Greer *wouldn't* be at the wedding, and an even greater ache as he wished that Bethia's husband could still be in her life. But such wishes were futile, and he needed to focus on the joy he'd found with Wren and the good life they would share.

Chapter Seven
Restless

Ian stood with unassuming dignity and fervid peace at the head of the church, near the minister, who wore a pleasant smile. Donnan and James stood close to Ian, and their parents were sitting with Lilias in the front pew. Gillian and her husband were also there with their young daughter. It had been wonderful for Ian to see his sister again, and they'd enjoyed catching up. But right now, his entire focus was on his own wedding. Cheerful rays of morning sun kissed the atmosphere of the church with spring warmth—just as Wren had predicted. Ian met the eyes of both his parents at the same time, making it clear they were both focused on him. They exchanged smiles, and he saw his mother dab happy tears from her eyes with a lace handkerchief. The music began, and Ian's heart quickened. The moment he'd anticipated and longed for had finally come to pass. His heart had loved Wren long before his head had been able to acknowledge it. His foolish selfishness had delayed their being together and given them both much grief. But the joy he felt in that moment eradicated his imprudence, and only a bright future lay before him. Surely God had smiled upon him to leave him so thoroughly blessed. Surely God had been merciful in regard to Ian's ridiculous mistakes and shortcomings to have brought him home to so much love and acceptance, and to such a dear and precious woman who was about to become his wife.

Ian focused on Bethia as she walked slowly up the aisle. The dress of pale pink she'd made for herself was lovely, and her countenance was calm and warm. There was no hint of the uneasiness that was often present. She carried a small bouquet of early spring flowers. He caught her eye, and she smiled at him. He was reminded of the day she'd married Greer in this very church, and he had to force his mind back to the present.

Bethia took her place on the other side of the minister, facing the audience that left few empty seats in the church. The majority of those present were the good common people who mostly interacted and associated with the Docherty family *and* the MacBriers. There were very few of the upper class present; most people of that class were too appalled by the marriage to show their faces. And every MacBrier was fine with that. The sixth Earl of Brierley had never stood for such nonsense, and everyone who knew him knew better than to question it.

Ian lost every awareness and every thought except for Wren when he saw her coming with slow gracefulness up the aisle, on the arm of her father. Angus looked as proud and nostalgic as any father might at such a moment. Wren looked impossibly beautiful with flowers wound into her dark hair, and a gauzy veil flowing down from them. Her gown was truly magnificent! But it paled in comparison to her loveliness. Ian knew that in addition to how lovely she was, her heart was good, her spirit strong, and she loved him as he loved her. He wondered if every man felt such unspeakable joy in crossing this bridge of marriage. He felt vividly sorry for the ones who didn't.

When Wren was standing before him, Ian could only take his eyes from her for the brief moment necessary to make eye contact with her father as he placed Wren's hand into Ian's and stepped back. Wren gave him a smile of perfect serenity while her eyes glowed with complete contentment. Neither of them gave the minister even a cursory glance while the ceremony proceeded. Ian felt nigh to bursting with joy that felt impossible to hold when he slid the ring onto Wren's finger and they were pronounced man and wife—until death. That word *death* cast a pebble into the perfection of the moment, but he hurriedly smoothed away the ripples of any fear or dread, thinking only of a long, full life with Wren—a life overflowing with the sharing of joy and sorrow throughout the course of everyday living.

"Ye may kiss her now," the minister said, and Ian did not hesitate to heed the instruction.

Following a barely sufficient kiss, Ian looked at his wife and grinned. "At last." He kissed her again. "Mrs. MacBrier."

"Indeed!" She laughed softly, and he saw his own happiness reflected in her eyes. It was a memory he would hold close to his heart for a lifetime; forever.

* * * * *

The wedding celebration at Brierley proved to be more delightful than Wren had anticipated. She'd only wanted to get married, and had seen no reason to indulge in such nonsense. But now, surrounded by a pleasant crowd of jovial friends and acquaintances, she could see that Ian's mother had been right in her advice. There was cause for celebration this day! And these were the people that she and Ian would be surrounded by and interact with for the rest of their lives. It only seemed right that they be included in the celebration. And she enjoyed the opportunity to get to know Gillian and her husband a little better. During her youth, Gillian had kept herself mostly separate from her brothers and their friends, and Wren had barely been acquainted with her. Now she showed perfect acceptance of Wren as her sister-in-law, and Wren thought it was too bad that Gillian had to live so far away. They would be leaving to return home early in the morning, and it was impossible to say when they might all see each other again.

Wren was pleased to note that Bethia was remaining docile and calm, and her father appeared to be enjoying himself. She wondered if this might help pull him out of the cave he'd sentenced himself to when his arthritis had overtaken his own sense of self. Beyond his interaction with customers who came into the shop, he'd hardly spoken to anyone for months now. No one would know Angus had difficulty with his hands unless they were watching very closely. It was only the intricate things that he would do at home or in his work that were a problem. Wren smiled to see her father laughing with the butcher and exchanging jokes with Blane. She saw him express compassion to a neighbor whose wife had passed away not long ago, and he cooed pleasantly at the baby of the cobbler who lived down the street from the tailor shop.

At the very moment when Wren began to feel concerned that Bethia might be reaching her limits of appropriate social behavior, James approached and said quietly to Ian, "Would you like me to take Bethia home and watch out for her?"

Wren knew Ian had the same thought she did when he tossed a glance of concern toward his brother. But James chuckled and raised his hands. "No flirting, I promise. I'll just see her home safely."

"That would be wise, I think," Wren said, eyeing her sister warily.

"And I'll see if your father would like to stay longer or if he's ready to go," James added. "I'll be pleased to help him with whatever he needs."

A quick word with Angus made it evident that he too was reaching his limits in pretending that his joints weren't aching. Bethia and Angus offered their farewells and congratulations, and James left with them.

"It would seem we were blessed with a miracle for our wedding day," Ian said to Wren. "Bethia was calm, and your father rather enjoyed himself, I believe."

"A miracle indeed!" Wren said and smiled up at him. "A multitude of them, perhaps."

A few hours later, Ian took his bride away from the festivities. He drove back toward town in the trap that his parents had given them as a wedding gift. Wren held tightly to his arm and rested her head on his shoulder. They left the trap and horse at Blane's livery, since Ian had already made arrangements—and given payment—to store the trap and house his horse. Arm in arm Ian and Wren walked the short distance to the house, where they found James sitting at the kitchen table with his feet propped up on a chair, reading a newspaper that Ian had left there. He reported that he had helped Angus get off to bed, and Bethia had gone down to the cellar, and he'd not heard a peep from either one of them.

"Thank ye, James," Wren said and kissed him on the cheek. Ian was pleased to note that he didn't feel even an inkling of jealousy.

"A pleasure, Mrs. MacBrier," he said, adding more to Ian, "I'll stay the week if the two of you change your minds and go on a real honeymoon."

"Your offer is very kind," Wren said, "but . . ."

"But I'm certain we'll manage to adjust to wedded life just fine right here. It's better this way," Ian added.

James smiled as if he understood and offered a handshake to Ian. "Congratulations, little brother. You deserve every happiness."

"Thank you, James. I would wish the same for you. Perhaps it's time to find the *right* woman and settle down."

"Perhaps," James said and whisked himself away.

Once the door had closed, an unnatural silence penetrated the room. Their eyes met with a mutual realization of what had changed between them this day. Wren wanted to voice her thoughts, her amazement that she was truly his wife, her relief that he didn't have to go home, her gratitude that he would be there for her always. But she knew his thoughts were the same, and words had become trite in their possible threat to dispel the perfect gossamer quality of the very air around them. She took his hand, he picked up the lamp, and together they went into the little room that had become Wren's haven from the difficulties of her life. Now it was theirs to share, and she would never have to be alone again.

* * * * *

Wren awoke in the middle of the night to find a lamp still burning on the little bedside table. A quick glance around the room oriented her to all that had happened prior to falling asleep. There, draped over a chair was her wedding gown, along with Ian's coat and waistcoat. She smiled at the very evidence of having a husband sharing her room, then she turned over to see him sleeping beside her. Gingerly she touched his dark curls, not wanting to wake him, but feeling the need to convince herself that he was not just some visage of her imagination. He shifted slightly but remained asleep, and Wren just watched him, recounting the indelible memories of all that had taken place between them as husband and wife. Never could she have imagined such bliss! The very idea of sharing the rest of her life with him was too large and wondrous for her heart to hold.

Carefully she eased her head to his shoulder. He shifted again and put his arm around her, drawing her close to him. His voice heavy with sleep, he murmured, "Are you all right?"

"Indeed I am," she whispered and fell back to sleep, wrapped in the comfort of his nearness.

When Wren woke again, it was daylight and the lamp had run out of wick and burned itself out. It was evident by the angle of the sun and the ticking of the clock nearby that she had slept late. She became aware of Ian close beside her and turned to find him watching her. He smiled and touched her hair the way she had touched his in the night.

"For years," he said, "I have imagined a moment such as this."

"I hardly *dared* imagine such a moment," she said.

They gazed at each other in thoughtful silence until Wren asked, "What are ye thinking, my darling?"

"Forgive me for bringing him up, but . . . I don't know how James can live the way he lives. I don't know how he can share with a woman what we have shared and just . . . walk away . . . without leaving a piece of his soul behind."

"Perhaps his soul is more broken apart than he lets on," Wren said. "Perhaps even more than he himself realizes."

"I'm sure you're right," he said and kissed her. "I'm glad to say that my soul is intact, Mrs. MacBrier—and my heart belongs to you."

"As it should, Mr. MacBrier." She laughed softly and eased away to get dressed.

"Where *are* you going?" he asked, taking hold of her arm to stop her.

"T' make some breakfast," she said. "I can well imagine Pa and my sister speculating over why we've not shown our faces."

Ian chuckled and pulled her back into bed. "Since they've both been married, I'm certain they have no need to speculate." He kissed her and buried both his hands in her luscious dark hair. "Let them speculate all they want. They're capable of making breakfast without us. *We* are on our honeymoon."

"And we've got t' get something t' eat sooner or later."

"Later," he said and kissed her again.

* * * * *

Two days after Ian MacBrier took up residency in the tailor's house, an elegant carriage came to a graceful halt in front of the tailor's shop. But it was not a prospective customer coming to choose fabric for a new gown. It was the sixth Earl of Brierley and his wife coming to call on their son and daughter-in-law. They sat in the tiny kitchen as comfortably as if they were in their own spacious parlor, visiting with Angus while Wren served scones and tea in mismatched cups. Bethia remained in the shop, busy at her stitching, and Ian brought the extra chair from the bedroom so that they could all sit together. Ian felt proud of his sweet wife for her genteel hospitality toward his parents and for her lack of embarrassment in a situation that some people might find awkward. For a long moment he became lost in admiring Wren openly. She met his eyes, and they shared a familiar smile that emitted the love they shared. Ian turned to find his parents observing them, and then *they* shared a similar smile. He was glad to know that they understood how he felt about Wren and that they were unquestionably supportive of the life he'd chosen.

The following day, Wren and Ian took inventory of the gardening tools available in the little shed behind the house, then they went together to buy seeds and a few other needed items. When Wren questioned Ian's enthusiasm over planting a garden for vegetables and some flowers along the fence, he reminded her that his best friend during all of his growing-up years had been the son of the head gardener at Brierley, and that Ian had learned a great deal by spending time with Greer. Now he would have the chance to try out what he'd learned, and it would also be a way for him to contribute to the household and to have something useful to occupy his time.

While spring melted into summer's warmth, Wren had difficulty comprehending how alone and frightened she had felt the previous year with Bethia's condition worsening and her father's health on the decline. Now she felt safe and secure, and blissfully happy. She marveled at how her father had warmed up so thoroughly to Ian, as if they were father and son. Ian became the son Angus had never had, and he had a way of drawing Angus out of his self-pity and reclusiveness. Little by little Ian had maneuvered Angus into going with him here and there to do an errand where they would naturally meet up with an old acquaintance of Angus's, or occasionally they went to the pub, mostly for the socializing. Wren and Ian had discussed how one of the advantages to Angus becoming a hermit was that he'd not indulged in drinking the way he once had. Therefore, Ian had cleverly gotten Angus to make a pact with him that if they went to the pub they would make certain that the other didn't have more than one drink, so that they could go home sober and not disappoint the woman they both loved.

Occasionally Ian met his brothers at the pub. He enjoyed their company more than he had in years, likely because he stayed sober enough to participate in the conversations and recall them the next morning. He was amazed at how he'd completely lost the temptation to drink away his feelings. The combination of Greer's death and the alleys of London had cured him. He was glad to know that he'd matured beyond the thing that Wren had called his Achilles' heel. Unfortunately, the same could not be said for James. He was continually flirting with the serving maids, and it was never a surprise to see him leave with one of them. Ian and Donnan discussed their concern between themselves, and occasionally one or both of them would express that concern to James. But he was as flippant as ever about the situation. Ian's concern rose dramatically when Donnan told him in confidence that he wasn't as concerned about the maids at the pub as he was the wife of an earl in the next county. Ian was appalled to realize that James's indiscretions had deteriorated to the point where he had become involved with another man's wife. He feared more than ever that it *would* be his brother's undoing, but James had no interest in taking advice from anyone.

Ian could do nothing more for James than he'd already done. He focused instead on the aspects of his life where he *could* make a difference. He was able to help Angus get beyond his efforts to hide his arthritic condition from his neighbors and acquaintances. Ian assured him that it was nothing to be ashamed of, and he pointed out the physical maladies he knew that other men in the community struggled with. Wren pointed out to her husband that she had said the same thing to her father many times to no avail, but for some reason Angus took it better coming from another man. Gradually he was known to actually talk with others in the community about the ailment, and he could express gratitude for his daughters being able to keep the business running with the skills they'd learned, as opposed to feeling ashamed that he could no longer support his family as he would prefer.

On Sundays after church, Ian and Wren made a habit of going to Brierley for a fine meal with the family, and they would generally stay late and visit. After a few Sundays, they talked Angus and Bethia into coming along. The four of them could just manage to squeeze into the trap together. Only once had Wren needed to discreetly escort her sister out of church in order to avoid a scene, but she did marvelously well with Ian's family. Ian suggested to Wren the possibility that Bethia felt instinctively comfortable at Brierley, since she'd lived there as Greer's wife. Wren agreed, but they also had to agree that Bethia had her limitations. She could only be so many hours away from her safe place in the cellar without becoming agitated.

Ian felt a growing warmth and admiration for his parents as he witnessed their genuine kindness and acceptance toward Angus and Bethia. They treated Wren like a daughter in every respect, and Ian couldn't imagine life being any better. Occasionally they brought up the issue of Ian and Wren being able to raise a family in such tiny accommodations behind the tailor's shop. But Ian felt sure that with time everything would work out. Either Bethia would become comfortable enough at Brierley to make the move, or they would find a way to add rooms and remodel the little old house. At one time Wren had been concerned that her father would never let go of his pride enough to leave his tailor shop and rely on others for his livelihood, but Ian had helped him grow beyond that, and she now believed that with time he would be able to accept Ian's full support of the family. For the time being, Bethia kept at her sewing, with Wren doing some seamstressing here and there and running the shop. The men actually did the majority of menial tasks necessary to keep their little household running, and Angus or Wren—or both—enjoyed helping Ian in the garden. Occasionally they all went out for a ride in the trap on a pleasant day, and sometimes they even took a picnic to enjoy in the meadow. Now and then they stopped to visit Greer's grave and leave flowers. Some days Angus would join them for their excursions, and other times he would decline. But Bethia loved the outings; she even seemed to thrive on them. Wren and Ian discussed the possibility that she might do fine going into town with them and that it might be good for her. But Wren always chose caution, fearing that a single outburst from her sister in front of the wrong person could have the townspeople in an uproar, and her sister would then end up in some horrid asylum in a faraway place.

Throughout the summer, the flowers blossomed and the vegetables flourished, all coming to fruition in their own time. The only problem was that once they'd dried or preserved the fruits of their labors for the winter months ahead, Bethia refused to allow anyone else to take them down to the cellar. Instead she gladly hauled everything down the stairs to be stored, and Wren only had to tell her when they needed something from the cellar for a meal, and Bethia would go down and get it.

Wren talked with her husband about her concerns for Bethia in regard to living in the cellar. Of course, now with Ian living in the house, there was nowhere else for her to sleep. But Bethia was still so emotionally drawn to being in the cellar alone with her imaginary companions. She went down long before it was time for bed and often came upstairs long after the rest of the household was awake in the mornings. Wren told Ian that perhaps her biggest concern was that the cellar had always been so damp and dark, and it seemed a terrible place to imagine her sister sleeping and spending so much of her time.

Ian suggested, "If you're concerned, why don't we just take a peek when we know she's not there?"

"She hardly leaves the house for a moment!" Wren said, astonished. "But even if she did, I promised her I would never go down there. She made me promise, and she was adamant. I'll not break my word t' my sister."

"Of course not," Ian said, "but *I* did not make such a promise. While she's busy in the shop, you keep her distracted, and I will—"

"And if a customer comes in, she'll dash int' the kitchen, and possibly want t' go down the stairs and ye'd be caught. She'd never trust ye again. She'd be more upset than I can even imagine."

"Then how about this," Ian said. "I'll do it the next time she takes a bath. She locks herself in the bathing room to soak in there for at least an hour. And she usually bathes after your father has gone to sleep. Once we know she's actually in the tub, it would only take me a few minutes to go down there—quiet as a church mouse—and see what it's like, and make certain all is well. And then *you* can stop worrying."

Wren gnawed at her lower lip a few moments before she admitted, "I like yer plan. Not that I want t' deceive my sister. I just want t' know that there isn't some problem down there she might not be telling me about."

"I understand," Ian said, and Wren knew that he did.

The next time Bethia took a long bath, Wren kept watch in the kitchen, keeping an eye on the door of the bathing room, while Ian carefully opened the door to the cellar and disappeared down the stairs. Wren was glad to note that neither the door nor the stairs creaked or strained enough for sharp ears to hear any evidence of his secret plan. He came back up less than five minutes later and closed the cellar door with a complete absence of sound.

"Well?" Wren asked quietly, and he motioned her out into the yard so there would be no chance of Bethia overhearing.

"It's actually rather nice, if you must know. She's hung lengths of fabric on the walls . . . almost like wallpaper, only more elegant . . . in a way. It's clean and cozy, and it appears relatively comfortable. There's nothing out of the ordinary. It doesn't look much different from our room, except for the absence of any windows." Wren heaved a sigh of deep relief. "And there was no sign of Jinty or Selma," he added facetiously.

"What a relief!" Wren said with mock concern. "And no sign of the ghost of Greer McMillan?"

"Not him, either. I'm not sure why she feels so safe down there, but if such personal, secluded surroundings achieve security for your sister, I don't see anything wrong with that."

"I'm sure ye're right," she said. "Thank ye, Ian. I do feel better."

"A pleasure to be at your service, my lady," he said and bent to kiss her. When their kiss inspired a desire in him that had become warmly familiar through their months of marriage, he pushed an arm around her waist and kissed her again.

"Someone might see," she scolded and eased away with a teasing laugh.

"Oh, how terribly dreadful!" he teased with sarcasm and mimicked the gossip. "That Ian MacBrier is kissing his wife out in the yard again. So scandalous!"

Wren laughed and went back into the house, and Ian followed, determined to kiss her again—in private.

* * * * *

In spite of the minor challenges of day-to-day life, Wren had never felt so content. She saw her own contentment mirrored in her husband as his lifetime need to wander seemed to have vanished completely and his years away had taught him to find joy in a life of simple security. Wren also saw that her father and sister were doing better than they had since Greer's death. Bethia was still prone to her erratic behavior and occasional outbursts, but she had grown to trust Ian, and he had a gentle way of calming her down. Wren reminded him now and then of how his presence in her life and in her home eased her burdens in too many ways to count. He never responded in any other way but an expression of his love for her and for all that she loved. It was no wonder she'd fallen in love with him! Any woman with half a brain would want a man like Ian MacBrier by her side for a lifetime.

Autumn brought the final harvesting of the garden just as the cold of winter was threatening to take over. With no more to do in the garden, Ian became somewhat restless until he asked his father-in-law one morning over breakfast, "Would you teach me your trade, Angus?"

Angus let out a shocked chuckle that expressed Wren's equal surprise when she overheard. "I've not got use o' m' hands enough t' show ye much," Angus said.

"But you can still teach me," Ian insisted. "It's all still in your head. You can tell me what to do, and tell me if I'm doing it wrong."

Angus thought about it a long moment. "I suppose we could try," he said, then turned to Wren, who had been totally unprepared for this conversation. Ian had not mentioned a word of it to her. "Wren can gather what we need when she's got the time."

"Wonderful!" Ian said with enthusiasm, then turned and winked at his wife.

A while later when they were alone out in the yard, Wren said to Ian, "Ye're having my father teach ye t' sew? Do ye really expect me t' believe that ye want t' learn t' make breeches and waistcoats?"

"Not particularly," Ian said, keeping his attention on the potatoes he was digging out of the ground, the last of the season. "What I want is for your father to know that I respect his profession." He looked up at her. "What better way than to have him teach me?"

Wren put a hand to her heart, and tears stung her eyes. "Ye're a good man, Ian MacBrier. I think I'll be keeping ye."

Ian chuckled. "As if you had a choice." He returned to his digging. "It's too late to back out now . . . Mrs. MacBrier."

"As if I would want t' back out," she said, hugging him from behind. He stuck the shovel into the ground and turned to make the most of her embrace.

"I've got something t' tell ye, Ian MacBrier."

Ian turned to look at her sideways; her expression incited suspicion. "Tell me then, madame."

Wren smiled, and her eyes sparkled. "Ye've made me happier than I ever thought possible, that's what."

"That certainly gives us something in common," Ian said, then he returned to his digging, wanting to avoid eye contact with her when an unexpected thought caught him off guard, and he didn't want her to notice his sudden distraction.

Wren returned to the house and Ian kept working while a tiny thought turned to a bigger one, which then devoured his every other thought until he could think of nothing else. His work gained momentum as the overpowering nature of the thought made him thoroughly angry. He'd struggled for most of his life with feelings of restlessness and a desire to wander from his home for reasons he could never understand or make sense of. He'd fought the feelings, analyzed them, talked them through with loved ones, and eventually drowned them out with liquor when there had been no reasonable explanation that could give him peace. He'd finally acted on those feelings with a rash, witless journey that had only created bigger problems and had brought him nothing but heartache. He still could hardly think about his time away, nor the suffering it had inflicted upon his loved ones. But he'd believed that his journey had cured him. He'd seen the world beyond this beautiful valley—at least enough of it to know that this place was close to heaven on earth, with loved ones surrounding him and the comfortableness of his youth at every turn.

Ian dug potatoes ferociously, pushing the thoughts away, fighting the feeling. He went to his knees to work the dirt off the potatoes as much as possible with his hands, then stuffed them into a burlap sack for winter storage. He took advantage of being on his knees and muttered hotly, "Please, God, take this feeling from me. I don't know what I've done to bring this curse upon me, but I beg you . . . take it from me." He stopped working and glanced around quickly to assure himself that he was alone before he pressed his dirty hands to the ground and hung his head. "Please, God. I beg you. I don't want to feel this way. I love my home . . . my family. I don't want to leave here; not ever! Not for any reason! Please take this unrest from my heart."

Ian remained on his knees until they ached, and until Wren opened the door to call him to get cleaned up for supper. "Are ye all right?" she added, noting the way he knelt on the ground.

"I'm fine," he lied and hurried to bag up the remaining potatoes he'd dug, knowing he'd need to finish digging the rest tomorrow. He brushed the dirt from himself the best he could and set the sack inside the back door and near the door of the cellar, assuring himself that it wasn't too heavy for Bethia to carry down the stairs. He went into the bedroom, where his sweet wife had left warm water for him to wash, and had laid out his clean clothes. His life was simple but good. If Wren knew the thoughts of his heart, it would surely break hers.

More than two weeks later, the potatoes were all securely stored in the cellar, and an early snow had snatched away the remaining pleasantry of autumn. While the weather outside turned bitter, Ian's heart grew cold in proportion. He managed to convince his wife that all was well, but his prayers went unanswered. The restlessness inside of him only grew, like some festering disease that would overtake and consume his every other desire. He could find no logic to his longing to leave here. He couldn't even think of where he might want to go. He could find every reason to want to stay. But contentment eluded him. Nothing had changed in the actuality of his life. In every practical way, life was as pleasing as it had been the day he'd married Wren and settled into the happiness of sharing his life with her. But something inside of him that had been dormant had sprung back to life for reasons completely beyond his control or understanding. He wanted to curse and scream and demand that it go away, then he wondered if that's how Bethia felt. If he gave his feeling a name, could he speak to it and tell it to mind its business and leave him in peace?

Wren found Ian sitting on the edge of the bed, where he'd sat down to remove his boots but had lost the motivation to do so. He was staring into the fire when Wren's voice startled him, and he looked up to see her standing in the door frame.

Wren took a long look at her husband, which confirmed what she had been suspecting for days. Something wasn't right, and she needed to know what it was. She closed the door and watched his gaze move back to the embers in the grate.

"Something's troubling ye," she said. "I've given ye more than ample time t' tell me what it is and t' stop pretending. Now, ye're not leaving the room until ye talk t' me."

When Ian said nothing, she sat down, sensing a darkness around his spirit that tightened the knots in her stomach. "What is it, my darling?"

Ian sighed and leaned his forearms on his thighs, hanging his head. He knew she would make good on her threats, and he'd do well to start talking. Clearly he was not as good an actor as he'd believed, but a part of him needed to share his burden. He just wasn't sure how to go about it.

Wren toyed lightly with his dark curls while she waited patiently for him to begin. For all that she'd stewed and speculated over what might be wrong, she had no idea what to expect.

"I think you had me figured wrong, Mrs. MacBrier."

"What do ye mean?" she asked, pushing his hair back from his brow.

"Do you remember when we were younger . . . how I was always talking about wanting to leave here? How I never felt like I fit in, even though I could never explain it?"

"Of course I remember."

Ian looked hard at his wife. "You said that my Achilles' heel was my drinking, but you were wrong, Wren. My Achilles' heel is that feeling inside of me . . . and I know now that I was drinking to try to suppress the feeling." He saw the concern in her eyes turn to fear, but he had to keep talking. "When I came back, I thought that I'd seen enough of the ugliness of the world that the feeling was cured, that it was gone for good. But it's not, Wren; it's not. I don't understand it, and I don't know what to do about it."

"How long have ye felt this way?" she asked with nothing but sadness.

Instead of answering the question, he considered her tone, her expression, the growing fear in her eyes. "What do you think I'm saying, Wren? I'm not going to leave you. I would never leave you!"

She started to cry so quickly that he realized she had truly feared that was the intended point of the conversation. He held her close and muttered gently, "I'm struggling with the way I feel, Wren; I'm trying to understand it. But I would never leave you. *Never!*" He drew back and looked at her. "If I ever leave here again, I'm taking you with me."

"And ye'll end up taking my father and my sister as well?"

"Maybe one day we'll *all* decide we'd like a change."

"Maybe," she said, but he knew she would never be convinced that such a platitude could ever dispel what he was feeling. And she knew that he knew it. But he smiled at her and kissed her, hoping that he could make peace with this feeling inside of him. Still, after all his prayers and all his efforts, it felt like a sickness, like a disease eating away at him. And he didn't know what to do about it.

Chapter Eight
The Bond of Brothers

Ian spent the winter caring for his new family, relishing the joys of marriage, and watching his father's health decline. Gavin did well at hiding his difficulties in public, but his family knew he was struggling, and it was only the cough tonic the doctor had given him that made it possible for him to avoid intense coughing fits. He had to move slowly from one room in the house to another, and then it took him minutes to be able to breathe normally again. But Ian, like the other members of his family, was determined to enjoy each opportunity to spend time with his father and not think too much about the inevitable outcome of his illness.

Ian found a perfect place in the back of his mind to tuck his fears concerning his father, and in that same place he tucked his ongoing feelings of restlessness and the bizarre belief that his spirit somehow needed to leave this place in order to be at peace. With such thoughts and feelings locked carefully away, Ian enjoyed his life and found gratitude each day for the benevolence that surrounded him and the people who loved him.

As spring crowded winter away, Ian could hardly believe it had been nearly a year since his return home. The streets and alleys of London, which he had mostly viewed through a drunken haze, all felt like a very bad dream from which he was glad to have awakened.

On a morning that showed the promise of being the warmest day of the year thus far, Ian sat at the kitchen table, practicing his stitching while Angus looked on and offered advice. Angus joked in good nature about Ian never being able to make a living as a tailor, and Ian told his father-in-law, "I don't know that I could ever make a living at anything. I'm relatively useless."

"Ye take very good care o' m' girls," Angus said. "Yer doing that makes ye more of a gentleman than most, in my opinion."

"Well, thank you, sir," Ian said. "Now, if I could only sew a button on straight, I could—"

A knock at the door interrupted his reply, and Ian set aside his work to answer it, surprised to see Donnan there. "Hello, brother!" Ian said with a pleasant laugh. "Come in."

"Thank you," Donnan said and stepped inside to greet Angus kindly, then he said, "I was actually hoping that you might be able to go out for a while."

"He's got his chores all done," Angus joked, and the brothers laughed.

Wren came in from the shop, having overheard Donnan's voice *and* the conversation. "Of course he can go," she said, giving Donnan a quick hug in greeting, "so long as ye take good care of him and make sure he only has one drink at the pub."

"What makes you think we'll end up at the pub?" Donnan asked.

"How often do men go out t'gether and not end up at the pub?" Wren said.

"True," Ian said, "but I don't need my brother to make certain I only have one drink." He kissed Wren. "I can do that all by myself."

Ian and Donnan ambled slowly around the corner and down the street, talking mostly of trivial things. Before they reached the pub, Ian said, "It's nice to see you, Donnan, and it's always good to catch up with you, but I don't think you came to see me just for a chat."

"You think I wouldn't just want to spend some time with my brother?" Donnan said with false lightness.

"I'm not questioning that," Ian said.

"I do need to talk to you," Donnan said, "but first I want to share some good news with my brother. Lilias is going to have a baby."

"That's *wonderful* news," Ian said, wondering when the same would happen for him and Wren.

"We've known for a while now, but Lilias wanted to keep it to ourselves at first."

"Congratulations, brother," Ian said, and they both stopped a short distance from the door to the pub. "I'm glad to hear the good news, but I can tell something's bothering you. So, before we go in there with all the noise, perhaps you should tell me what it is."

Donnan looked the other way, then he looked down. He shuffled the toe of his boot over the ground. "It's not so noisy in there this time of day," he said. "Come on. Drinks are on me."

"But only one," Ian said, following him through the door.

"Only one," Donnan repeated.

Donnan had been right; the pub was relatively quiet, with very few people there. Once seated across the room from the other customers, with their drinks on the table, Ian looked at his brother and repeated, "Tell me what's bothering you."

Donnan sighed. "It's about James, actually." He took a sip of his drink while Ian just swirled his around in his glass. It was evident that during Ian's absence, James had taken to confiding more in Donnan—which was opposite to the way it used to be. But of course it was natural, since Ian had not been around to confide in.

"Another illegitimate child?" Ian guessed. "More broken hearts?"

"None that I know of specifically," Donnan said, but there was a complete absence of the subtle humor that often accompanied their conversations about their brother. Once they'd accepted there was nothing to be done, humor was the only way they could talk about it and not get angry. James's behavior went so starkly against their beliefs that it was impossible to understand and difficult to accept. But the entire family knew it was impossible to change a person who didn't want to change.

"Then what is it?" Ian probed when Donnan showed unusual hesitancy.

"You know that we've hoped and prayed he would find one woman whom he could love and with whom he could settle down."

"Yes, of course."

"It seems he *has* decided to settle for one woman. He declares to be utterly in love and determined to make her the center of his life. He claims that for her he has given up all of his philandering and she is the only one."

"That's remarkable!" Ian said, not seeing the problem. Donnan sighed, and Ian kept talking, if only to fill the gap. "I take it he's intimately involved with her."

"Indeed, he is. Intimacy *after* marriage never occurred to James, in spite of the way it was grilled into us by our parents. You know that, of course."

"And you know all of this because James confided in you, I'm assuming."

"Yes, he confided in me, and I'm confiding in you."

"Our parents don't know?" Ian asked.

"Not yet, they don't. But they will. It's all going to explode very soon, I'm afraid."

"I don't understand the problem, Donnan. Perhaps you should get to the point."

"This woman that has apparently claimed James's heart . . . is the very wealthy and beautiful wife of the Earl of Kentigern."

"Heaven help us all," Ian muttered and leaned back in his chair, too weak to sit up straight without its support.

"Amen," Donnan said and swallowed the rest of his drink, coughing from the burn of too much at once.

Once the dreadful news had settled in, Ian leaned forward again, glancing around to be certain they were still far from any listening ears. "How can James believe there is any possible outcome to this that's favorable?"

"That's what I told him," Donnan said.

"How can . . . another man's wife be the woman of his dreams?"

"I asked him that as well. But his determination is . . . is . . . it's obsessive, Ian; it's frightening. Of course, the Earl is a difficult man. Anyone in three counties knows that. He treats his wife no differently than he treats his horse or his dogs—and he's not necessarily kind to animals. James has not only fallen for her, he's convinced that he can rescue her from the horror of her marriage, and that they can run away and live happily ever after."

"The Earl won't stand for it!" Ian insisted.

"That's what *I* told him!"

"He'll never tolerate having his pride wounded in such a way, even if he cared nothing for whether or not he actually gave up his wife."

"Yes, yes," Donnan said. "You and I think so much the same it scares me sometimes."

"He would kill James before he'd let his wife go. He would hunt them down mercilessly."

"You and I are in complete agreement on that," Donnan said. "But James has lost his mind over this woman. He's convinced he can get away with it, that he can rescue her, and they will never be found."

"Found?" Ian echoed. "In other words, he means to leave Brierley behind —forever—and live in some faraway, exotic location with someone else's wife?"

"That's exactly right," Donnan said.

Ian's anger grew by the second. "Having sufficient funds to support a wife in another country somewhere is not necessarily sufficient to give her a good life. It's immoral and destined for trouble!" Donnan nodded and took a sip of *Ian's* drink as Ian went on. "His thinking is completely backward. No matter how bad her marriage is, James will only take all that is bad and make it worse; somehow . . . somewhere along the way, there will be a price to pay. And we as his family will surely all contribute to paying that price . . . especially if he intends to leave and never come back."

"Precisely," Donnan said. "*If* he could actually get away and be assured that the Earl would never find them, we would likely never see his face again, and that means that *I* would be left as the next Earl of Brierley. I can assure you that my concern for James *far* outweighs my concern for *that.* However, I do *not* want to be the Earl of Brierley. It doesn't suit me at all. I'm very much wishing that *you* had been born a year before me, rather than the other way around."

"Wish away," Ian said with a strained chuckle. "I'm perfectly content being the youngest son. *I* certainly don't want to be the Earl of Brierley. But we'd do well to keep our feelings about it from ever coming up around our parents. They would be heartbroken to know."

"It's not that I don't respect the position, and I would honor it as our father has—if it were to fall to me. But it's a great deal of responsibility, and I'm not so sure the people would be in good hands if they were reduced to being in mine."

"I disagree. I think you're a good man and you'd do well at running the estate and seeing that all is well. *However,* the problem at hand is our brother's madness. *He* was born to be the Earl, and we must talk some sense into him and see that he fills his position and leaves us both to our lives of leisure."

Ian uttered the final phrase facetiously, and Donnan chuckled. "You are hardly leading a life of leisure."

"I love my life, and I love being able to do simple chores for a good cause. But I know that you keep yourself plenty busy with your own causes. Neither of us is destined for gentlemanly laziness. Our parents wouldn't stand for it. Nevertheless, James needs to understand the responsibility he was born to and accept it, because I'm not going to do it."

"Nor am I," Donnan said, the mood between them lighter now.

Donnan became more serious and added, "Will you help me talk some sense into him? Maybe he'll listen to you."

"I can try," Ian said. "But I don't know that I have any more pull with him than you do."

"You'll try?"

"Of course I'll try. Do you think he'll be home in the morning?"

"He usually is."

"Then I'll be there for breakfast."

"Thank you, brother," Donnan said, then shifted the topic to more pleasant matters. As the crowd thickened, they got in the middle of the town gossip, hearing the same old jokes told among men who had surrounded them as they'd grown up.

When Ian returned home, he found the house dark except for a lamp that had been left burning low in the kitchen to guide him. He picked it up and went quietly into the bedroom where he set it down again.

"Ye don't need t' worry about waking me," Wren said, "because I'm not asleep."

"In that case . . ." He sat on the edge of the bed and bent over to kiss her.

"Did ye have a good time?" she asked, putting a hand to his face.

"Mostly."

"And ye're quite sober, I see."

"Quite," he said and turned to pull off his boots. "I hardly had a sip."

"I love a man who keeps his promises," Wren said while Ian was undressing for bed.

"As long as that man is me, there isn't a problem." He slipped between the covers and eased his arms around her.

"May I ask what Donnan wanted t' talk t' ye about? Or is it a secret?"

"I don't keep secrets from my wife," Ian said. "He had good news and bad news. The good news is that Lilias is going to have a baby."

"Oh, that *is* good news!" Wren said. "What a joy that will be!"

"Yes, it will," Ian agreed.

"And the bad news?"

"He's concerned about James."

Ian shared the gist of the conversation with her, and in return she shared his concern and offered compassion.

The following morning Ian was up early and kissed Wren before he set off for Brierley, arriving in time to make a grand entrance into the dining room and enjoy the delight on his parents' faces when he announced that he would be joining them for breakfast and staying the morning to visit. He felt certain if they had any idea of the plans formulating in James's head, they would not be nearly so chipper.

After a pleasant breakfast, Ian suggested that he would like to go riding with his brothers, something the three of them had not done together in a long time. James agreed but didn't look surprised. If he'd recently confided his plans to Donnan, he surely knew that Ian was aware of them by now.

They rode into the forest that banked one side of Brierley, and then to a meadow where they had commonly gone in their youth. They all dismounted to let the horses graze on spring grasses.

"So, out with it," James said. "I know a conspiracy when I see one. Or should I call it an assault?"

"If your brothers' mutual concern for you is offensive," Donnan said, "then you've *truly* lost your mind."

"I'm grateful for the concern of my brothers," James said, "but if you think that outnumbering me will get me to change my mind, you're both terribly wrong."

"James," Ian said, "do you have any idea of the implications of what you're doing? Regardless of the circumstances of the marriage, this woman *is* married. You have no right—legally *or* ethically—to intrude upon that. If this woman is so unhappy, then she should divorce her husband and leave him legally; you could help her if needs be. But not while you're committing adultery with her. And you can't just think that you can offend the Earl's honor by stealing his wife away and believe that this will have some kind of fairytale ending."

James sighed with the impatience of a child listening to a parent's lecture but not hearing a word of it. "My mind is made up," James said. "She needs me, and that's all there is to it."

For nearly an hour the brothers argued. Ian and Donnan pleaded and reasoned and begged, but James was firm on leaving the country—and soon—with this woman who had gotten hold of his heart. In the end, James told his brothers he loved them and always would. He didn't expect them to agree with his decision, but they were all adults and they had no choice but to accept it.

Donnan responded by saying, "We *do* love you, James, and you're right, we have no choice but to accept it. But we're losing you, and you're trading away everything you have, everything you've been raised to be, for this woman. On top of that, you'll be lucky if the Earl doesn't find you and kill you."

"Not if I kill him first," James said, mounting his horse as if to officially conclude the conversation. "With the way he treats her, he deserves to die."

"That's not your responsibility," Ian said, but James ignored him and rode away. Ian and Donnan had no choice but to mount their horses and ride after him.

James was waiting for them near the stable. They slowed to approach him, and James spoke before his brothers could utter any more argument or criticism. "I'm asking that you not tell Mother and Father until I've had sufficient time to get away."

"You can't truly believe we would keep something like this from them," Donnan said.

"I would hope so if I ask it of you," James countered. "I'll leave a letter for them . . . explaining everything. It will be better this way."

"Better for whom?" Ian demanded. James just rode into the stable and was striding toward the house by the time Ian and Donnan had entered the stable and dismounted.

While one of the stable hands unsaddled James's horse, Ian and Donnan took care of their own. On their way out of the stable, out of hearing range from the stable workers, Ian said to his brother, "I don't know what else we can do. I feel so angry I want to strangle him, but . . . what can we do?"

"Our parents always said that James's philandering ways would be his undoing," Donnan said, "but I never imagined anything like this."

"Nor did I," Ian said, then they both agreed to find their parents and participate in a seemingly normal conversation. In spite of

James's appalling behavior, the bond between the brothers was too strong for them to go tattling on James against his wishes. Just before they entered the study where they could hear their parents talking, Ian whispered to Donnan, "How long do you suppose we should give James to have 'sufficient time to get away?' Isn't that what he said?"

"Oh, I'd say maybe . . . an hour. What do you think?"

"If that," Ian said with chagrin, then he pasted on a grin and they entered the study together to enjoy a nice visit with Gavin and Anya.

Ian had lunch with his family before he returned home, although James was inexplicably absent. Probably packing, Ian thought with dismay.

Ian found Wren in the little room used for bathing and laundry; her sleeves were rolled up and she was busy rubbing something white and lacy up and down the washboard. He leaned in the doorway and said, "Have I ever told you that you're beautiful when you're doing the laundry?"

Wren smiled and focused on her work. "Ye tell me I'm beautiful no matter what I'm doing. Since I don't care if anyone else in the world thinks I'm beautiful or not, I'm prone t' believe ye."

"Your father thinks you're beautiful," Ian said. "I know because he's told me so."

"Besides him," Wren said with a wink while she wrung water out of the camisole she was washing, then tossed it into the basket with other clean items that would go out to the clothesline. Now that spring was returning, they could dry clothes outside instead of draping them all over the house.

"Did ye have a good visit with yer family?" she asked, beginning to wash one of his shirts.

"I did," he said.

"And James?" she asked, glancing over her shoulder.

"It was a disaster. He's determined to go through with this madness, and I don't know that anyone can stop him." Wren stopped her work and turned to face Ian, pushing hair back from her face with a dry forearm. "He made us promise not to tell our parents until he's had sufficient time to get away."

"And when will that be, exactly?"

"Tonight, I believe. Donnan's prepared to tell them at the first possible moment, but it will do nothing but break their hearts. I don't know that *they* can do anything, either. It's just a disaster, plain and simple."

"It *is* a disaster," she said, returning to her work. "It's heartbreaking."

"Indeed, it is," Ian said, choosing not to feel the heartbreak at the moment. But it hovered and grew inside of him while he helped Wren hang the wash. Then he dumped all of the wash water and cleaned out the tubs while Wren prepared supper. He chopped wood and took it into the house, and he ate with the family as if nothing were out of the ordinary. But when the day was finally done and he crawled into bed, Wren's arms came around him as if she knew how hard he'd been trying to hold back his anguish in regard to his brother. She only had to whisper a few words of compassion, and his heartache rushed out in childlike tears.

"He's my brother, for the love of heaven," Ian muttered, "and I may never see him again."

"Perhaps ye will," Wren said. "We don't know how all of this will turn out. Perhaps he'll follow yer example and come home disillusioned and a little wiser."

"Perhaps," Ian said. "And perhaps the Earl of Kentigern will have him hunted down and murdered in his bed before he has a chance to become a little wiser."

Wren said nothing, but she held him closer and pressed a kiss into his hair and then on his brow. He found her lips with his, then whispered, "Do you know how dear you are to me? How I ever managed without you, I cannot imagine!"

"I will always be here," she whispered, and he let go of his every worry while Wren held him. No burden or challenge was strong enough to withstand the power of Wren's love.

* * * * *

Ian slept little and woke early, overcome with an urgency that pushed him out of bed. Once he was dressed, he bent over to kiss Wren awake enough to hear him say, "Forgive me, but I feel like I need to go to Brierley." She became more alert. "If James left in the night and Donnan is breaking the news to my parents this morning, I just . . . need to be there."

"I understand," she said and kissed him again. "I'll say a pray for ye . . . for all of ye."

"Thank you. I don't know how long I'll be. If you need me, send a message with Blane's boy and I'll come straightaway."

"We'll be fine," she said. "Ye must see t' yer family."

"My *other* family," he said and kissed her once more before hurrying to Blane's livery to saddle his horse and ride to Brierley, accompanied by the sun coming over the east horizon, illuminating the beauty of spring that Ian didn't see. He wondered if they might be granted a miracle, and he would arrive to learn that James hadn't gone through with his mad plan. But a deep dread smoldered inside of him. Instinctively he knew this would not end well.

Ian arrived before breakfast but soon after Donnan had told their parents that James was gone. Donnan had first checked James's room to be certain, and he'd found the letter James had left. After delivering it into his father's hands, the drama had begun. Anya sat and cried while Gavin paced and ranted, expressing all of the same reasoning that Donnan and Ian had used in trying to convince their brother that this was madness.

When Anya became inconsolable and Gavin was consumed with coughing, Ian and Donnan both put their full effort into calming their parents down. They encouraged each of them to lie down and had breakfast brought up to their room. The day wore on with the atmosphere as heavy with grief as if James were dead. Ian's anger toward James was all consuming, and he knew Donnan felt the same way. Then it occurred to Ian that *he'd* done the same thing to his family. He'd not left here for the same reasons, but he'd still left, leaving only a note behind for his family. Had his parents been this upset? And his brothers? The fist Donnan had greeted him with upon his return took on new meaning, and he felt more penitent over his leaving than he ever had.

In the long hours of the afternoon, Gavin insisted that Ian needed to go home to his family. He considered that he probably should, but for reasons he couldn't explain, he felt the need to stay—at least a little longer. An hour later they all looked up to see James enter the room. Ian sat quietly with his brother while their parents embraced him and expressed extreme relief and astonishment. Ian and Donnan exchanged more than one discreet glance as they observed the reunion. They both knew James well enough to know that this wasn't over, and that something wasn't right. James didn't look glad to be home, and his countenance was completely absent of any of the arrogance or confidence he'd carried so proudly the previous day.

When James sunk into a chair, his parents began to grasp that something wasn't right. "What's happened?" Gavin asked, just before Ian said, "You're obviously very upset."

"Did she tell you no?" Donnan asked. "Did she come to her senses and decide to stay and solve her problems the right way?"

James growled with uncharacteristic anger, "She did *not* tell me no, and she did *not* decide to stay."

"Then why are you back?" Ian said. "Not that we're complaining, but . . ."

A heavy silence settled over the room. James rubbed his face, then pushed his hands into his hair as if he'd encountered the devil himself since he'd left home in the middle of the night. Gavin and Anya seemed to perceive that something was terribly wrong. They both sat down, watching James closely, waiting for an explanation. The silence continued until Ian wanted to yell at his brother and angrily demand that he tell them what was so grievous. Donnan spoke up with a more calm version of the demand. James cleared his throat but wouldn't meet the eyes of anyone in the room. He cleared his throat again and stared at the floor.

"The Earl found out," he said. "He . . . waited until he had . . . proof . . . that we were . . . running away." The silence in the room intensified, underscoring the horror that everyone wanted to express. "He . . . uh . . . he was . . . furious . . . naturally."

"Naturally," Gavin said. "For all that he's a man with abhorrent behavior, having someone steal his wife is an enormous affront to his honor."

"That's what *he* said," James went on. "That last part, anyway; almost word for word. He, uh . . ."

"He what?" Gavin demanded, and Ian felt sick to his stomach. He knew what was coming, and he felt sure the others did as well.

"He, uh . . ." James tried again. The words came reluctantly out of his throat with a stark tremor. "He . . . demanded . . . that I meet him at dawn . . . tomorrow, and . . ."

"A *duel*?" Gavin rumbled, shooting to his feet. James's complete lack of response made clear he had no argument, nothing to say. "I'll not lose my son to something so utterly . . . ludicrous! The very idea ought to be outlawed!" Gavin was overtaken with breathing difficulties, and the focus turned toward getting him to sit down and stay calm.

Once her husband was breathing normally, Anya turned toward James. "You can't go!" she insisted. "You just can't!"

"And what?" James finally had something to say. "Run and hide for the rest of my life?"

Ian couldn't believe what he was hearing. "Is that not *exactly* what you were prepared to do when you left here in the middle of the night?"

James turned toward him, enormously angry. "To run *with* her would be to defend her honor. To run *from* her . . . to leave her behind in the hands of that odious . . . brute would be to dishonor her in the worst way!"

"Stealing her from her husband is not dishonoring her?" Donnan countered. "Engaging in adultery is not dishonoring her?"

Ian rumbled, "You've got a lot of nerve talking about *honor* when you've been having an affair with the man's wife!"

"You do *not* understand!" James snarled. "Not one of you does."

"At least we agree on that," Ian said.

"You can*not* die for this, James," Anya pleaded. "You can't!"

"Better to die for this than to leave the woman I love believing that she is not *worthy* of love."

The argument ran round and round until all parties became exhausted and James left the room declaring firmly, "I'm going to face him tomorrow, and with any luck I'll have half a chance to kill him and this will all be over."

"James," Gavin said. He hesitated but didn't turn. "Everyone knows that the Earl of Kentigern is matchlessly skilled in shooting. You cannot face him with pistols and survive."

"Then I will face him and die," he said with an angry determination that had completely vanquished the apparent fear he'd had at the beginning of the conversation.

As James left the room, a hush remained in his wake that implied a death in the family had already occurred. The drama and emotion of the day had drained away Ian's strength, and he recognized the same exhaustion on the faces of his brother and parents. The grief they'd all been feeling earlier due to James's hasty departure and precarious safety was now amplified a hundredfold by the imminent doom hovering at the threshold of James's life. Ian didn't understand why James had become so rash and unreasonable. Through all his years of dallying with women, he'd been able to readily admit that it wasn't necessarily right or noble, even though he'd still chosen to indulge in his bad habits. But this! The very irrationality of his behavior was perhaps most frightening of all. How could there be any reasoning with him when he was so determined to carry through with this absurdity that could very well cost him his life?

Ian wanted to say something to console his parents, but he could think of nothing. He wanted to convince his brother to have another try at talking some sense into James, but he knew it would be pointless. He resisted the urge to find James and try himself to help him see reason, but he knew that if James was interested in seeing reason, he already would have. As helpless and drained of strength as he felt, he could only think of one thing.

"I need to go home," he said and came to his feet. "Please send me word if I'm needed, or if anything changes." He exchanged wordless farewells with his brother and parents and rode anxiously toward town, toward home, toward his sweet wife. He needed her, needed her reason, her strength, her ability to soothe and comfort him. And with any luck, his brother would survive until this time tomorrow.

* * * * *

It was after dark when a light knock sounded at the door and Ian knew it had to be someone in his family—or perhaps the delivery of a note from one of them. He glanced across the table at Wren, but neither of them rose to open the door, not wanting to face the possibility that James was still determined to go through with this madness. They'd been sitting there talking since Angus had gone to bed and Bethia had retired to the cellar. He'd spilled his every thought and feeling on the matter more than once while Wren had listened with compassion and perfect love. But the conclusion was always the same. No one could convince James he was wrong to do this if he had convinced himself otherwise. The knock at the door was repeated, and Ian rose to answer it, not surprised to see Donnan, but surprised to see James standing behind him.

"We need to speak with you," Donnan said. Ian motioned them inside and turned to see that Wren had stood up.

"Hello, Donnan," she said, and he kissed her cheek in a way that was typical of his affection for her.

"Hello," Donnan said with the tenderness of a brother, then she turned to face James.

Ian was struck with the irony of Wren's previous relationship with James when she said his name with an edge of heartache laced into her tone. He too kissed her cheek. She took hold of his arm and looked hard at him. "Please tell me ye've come with news that ye've changed yer mind."

The silence preceding James's answer felt eternal. Ian counted his own heartbeats, praying that this would be so. His heart dropped to his stomach with the certainty that James was signing his own death decree. "I have to do this," he said to Wren. "I don't expect anyone to understand, but that doesn't change what I know I have to do."

"Do ye not know the broken hearts ye'll leave behind?" Wren asked, her eyes filling with tears that Ian hoped might soften James.

But James only looked at the floor, as if to avoid them. "With any luck I'll be the one to come back alive. Maybe we'll get a miracle."

"God expects us to work for our miracles," Wren said, like a scolding mother now. "How can ye ask for God's blessing in this when ye're knowingly stepping into a trap that'll see ye dead?"

James glanced at Wren, then his gaze again fell to the floor before he looked briefly at each of his brothers. Wren picked up on the hint that the men needed some privacy. She hurried to kiss James's cheek. "I hope t' see ye again," she said in that saucy voice of hers. Then to Ian, "I'll give the three of ye some time."

She went into the bedroom and closed the door, and Ian knew she was probably crying. He also knew she could hear what was being said unless they spoke in whispers. But if she overheard the conversation he wouldn't have to repeat it to her after his brothers left.

The three of them sat down, and Ian asked, "Do you want something to eat? To drink?"

"No, thank you," they both said in nearly perfect unison.

Silence made it evident that James was expecting Donnan to do the talking. Donnan cleared his throat and said, "James wants us to go with him in the morning."

"To watch you die?" Ian snapped in a tone he'd learned from his wife.

"If that's the outcome," James said, "then . . . yes."

"That's a lot to ask," Ian said, "even for a brother."

"Or perhaps *especially* for a brother," Donnan clarified.

"Exactly," Ian added, then he leaned over the table and put a hand over James's and pleaded, "James . . . there must be another option. What good are you to this woman you love if you are dead? What can you do to help her?"

"That's what *I* asked him," Donnan said.

James stood up, his anger showing again. "I didn't come here to debate the situation any further. I just want my brothers to go with me. Whatever the outcome, I need the two of you there."

Ian imagined bringing James's body back from the dreadful event, and having to tell their parents that the worst had happened. But even if that were the case, who better to do it? He pondered his words a long moment before he said, "I completely disagree with this, James, and I don't want to be there. I don't want to have anything to do with it. But I'm your brother, and if you want me there, I will be there."

James sighed and sat back down. "Thank you." He forced a smile that was not at all convincing, and Ian wondered if James truly believed he would die tomorrow. "Perhaps the two of you will be my good luck."

"Not unless we actually get our own pistols," Donnan said, "but that's not how the rules work."

"I can't believe there are actually *rules* for such barbaric means of solving a dispute," Ian said. "Father is right. It ought to be outlawed."

"Enough with your opinions," James said. "Let's go have a drink together, and . . . since we have to leave very early, perhaps you should stay at Brierley tonight, Ian, or . . . if not, you'll need to meet us at the crossroads at—"

"Just give me a minute," Ian said and went into the bedroom to find Wren sitting on the edge of the bed, dabbing at her eyes with the hem of her apron.

"I heard," she said when he approached her. "Of course you should go; you should spend the night there." She stood and embraced him tightly. "I will be praying . . . very hard."

"I love you, Wren."

"Oh, I love ye too, Ian MacBrier." She kissed him. "Keep your brother safe."

"That's hard to do when he puts himself in front of a loaded pistol."

"Ye'll do yer best, I know," she said, "and that's all ye can do. He's made up his mind t' this. Ye can't change the course he's set himself upon."

Ian nodded, trying to hold her words close to his heart, wishing he *could* change the course. "I will see you . . . or send word . . . as soon as I can."

Wren nodded and kissed him again. Ian grabbed his coat and left with his brothers, knowing that anything else he might need was available in abundance at Brierley, even a wardrobe filled with his own clothes. He only wished that he could hope to get even a wink of sleep and that the fears destined to keep him awake would not come to pass.

Chapter Nine
Responsible

Ian could hardly bear observing the farewells between James and his parents before they all went to bed. Then their parents were up to see them off an hour before dawn, and the ritual was repeated with even more grief and drama. James kept trying to assure Gavin and Anya that he would be back, that this was all unnecessary. But Ian recognized his barely disguised lack of conviction, and he felt sure the others sensed it as well.

The three brothers set out on horseback, leaving their mother crying in the arms of their father as if their sons were going off to war. This was worse than war, Ian thought. At least war had a cause, or at least it was supposed to. Not one of them had much to say as they rode. James had made them promise to stop trying to talk him out of it. They'd both told him how they loved him, and he knew how they disagreed with this. They'd promised James they would not have a big funeral. They'd refused to promise that they wouldn't grieve too long or too deeply.

When they arrived at the designated place, Ian's panic set in. He'd managed to keep it from showing, and he'd even managed to hardly believe that he felt it. No one else was there yet, and Ian tried once again to convince James that this was madness.

"Let's go," Ian said. "Let's go right now. It's not too late. We'll help you leave the country. We'll do everything we can to—"

"Ian's right," Donnan said. "We'll help you. You don't have to do this."

Ian's hope was that with the moment actually at hand, James too would be blessed with some kind of panic that might help him see reason. But he only said, "He will cause trouble for the family . . .

for all of you . . . if I don't go through with this. I have to. There are reasons I can't tell you. I want you to know that I'm grateful for your support, for your love, for being the best brothers a man could ever have, and . . . I'm sorry for the grief I've caused, but . . ."

The approach of a carriage halted the conversation. Ian wanted to take James in his arms, to save him, to express his love, his fear, the full depth of the panic consuming him. But it was too late. The opponent had arrived in all his arrogant glory. The Earl of Kentigern stepped out of the carriage, dressed as if he were about to attend a ball. Three servants attended him, besides the driver who waited on the box seat. He seemed impatient to have this over, and in a matter of moments the weapons were presented, and the paces marked off. Ian stood close to Donnan, unable to speak, not daring to move, praying with every fiber of his soul that a miracle would intercede and save James's life. But while his heart prayed, his mind recalled Wren saying that God expected hard work in return for miracles. And in his deepest self, he knew that he and Donnan were here to witness the undoing of their brother.

The two loud pops of the pistols occurred almost simultaneously. It would have been impossible to know which of the guns had fired first, except that it was James who fell to the ground, while his opponent strode quickly away and stepped into his carriage before Ian and Donnan could even get to their brother. They both fell to their knees on either side of James, who was gasping for breath while a pool of red crept out from beneath him onto the ground. And the Earl of Kentigern's carriage disappeared, as if this business had been a minor inconvenience.

Donnan said nothing. He just held tightly to James's hand as if he could feed his own strength into him and save him. Ian shouted at James, telling him to hold on, demanding that he not leave them, insisting that it could not be the end. When a little voice in his head told him that it *was* the end, he listened for James to say something, to utter some final words that might assuage such insufferable grief. But he made no sound except for the rattle of a final breath, and then it was over.

"No!" Ian howled, touching his brother's face, searching for any sign of remaining life. "No, no, no!" he muttered, and the reality began to settle into him, starting in the pit of his stomach with a grinding sickness, then strangling his heart and constricting his chest. The physical pain erupted out of his throat as if it might explode through his chest otherwise. He pressed his face to that of his dead brother and cried in a way he'd never seen or imagined a man capable of crying. He'd cried over Greer's death, but he had learned about it when it was long over. What he'd just witnessed was too unspeakably horrible to believe that his mind could ever pass through thoughts of it without re-creating this unfathomable grief.

Ian's mournful cries startled Donnan from a stupor, and he too sobbed over his brother's dead body. The only indicator of time passing was the coldness spreading through James that could be felt in his hands and face. Ian and Donnan succumbed to shock and exhaustion, and both sat on the ground in a stupor, each holding one of James's hands, with nothing to say to each other. Ian finally shook himself out of his shock, as if some being he couldn't see or hear had nudged him, reminding him that they couldn't sit there on the ground all day; their parents and wives were waiting and wondering. Ian squeezed his eyes shut, wanting to block out the painful prospect of having to give the news to his parents. But then, he suspected they already knew. It would require no words. Still, they needed to get back.

Ian nudged Donnan the way he had been nudged. "We need to go," he said. "We must . . . take him back."

"Take him where?" Donnan asked as if his thinking was not capable of reaching beyond this moment.

Ian thought about it a moment. "Straight to the undertaker. Mother and Father should not see him like this; they shouldn't see him until he's cleaned up and dressed for burial."

Donnan nodded but didn't move. Ian forced himself to stand on stiff legs and took hold of Donnan's arm to force him to do the same. They both stared down at James while Ian wondered how they could do this. But they had to. Was this the real reason he'd asked his brothers to come with him? So he wouldn't have to die alone? So his body wouldn't be left in the middle of a meadow to rot?

"Let's just do this, Donnan," Ian said. "Don't think. Just do it. Help me get him onto his horse."

Donnan let out a sharp breath, and they lifted James's body and draped it over the saddle of his horse. Ian wondered how they could possibly transport him to the undertaker, exposed that way. It only seemed fitting that the dead should be covered. Then he noticed a blanket rolled up and tied to the back of James's saddle. Donnan noticed it at the same time, and their thoughts were the same. "Do you think he brought that with this intention?" Donnan asked.

"It seems he had everything carefully planned out," Ian said with dry bitterness as he untied the blanket. Donnan helped him cover James and tuck the blanket carefully around him, then they mounted their horses and slowly escorted James on his final journey.

They rode in silence for interminable minutes before Ian said, "We should have stopped him; we should have found a way."

"You have a short memory, brother. We *tried* to stop him—over and over. You can't blame yourself for this."

Ian heard the words in his head, but his heart didn't hear them. In his heart he believed that he could have and should have prevented this. He should have tied James up and hidden him in Bethia's cellar until the meeting time was over. And then he would have helped James leave the country in the dead of night, where he could have found a new life for himself—and at least he would have been alive. Yes, Ian knew there must have been some way to prevent this. He knew he was somehow responsible. And as Ian bathed in regret over James's death, his regrets over Greer's death also came rushing back to taunt him. He'd believed he'd made peace with that. He'd believed that he'd accepted Wren's explanations of all that Greer had done to bring his death upon himself. But Ian had still been too drunk to help him. He should have gotten him out. It should have been different. And Ian wondered how he would ever recover from the cumulative effect of the deaths of his best friend and his brother. It was just too much for any human being to endure!

As they approached town, Donnan suggested they take the long way around and arrive at the undertaker's discreetly. Ian agreed, but pointed out there was no way to actually get the body there without *someone* seeing them. Taking that into consideration, they made the decision for Ian to wait with the body while Donnan fetched the undertaker and his wagon, so that the body could be taken to his place of business with discretion and dignity, and no one would know the identity of the deceased until the gossip could be spread through other means. Of course word would get out; people would know the truth. Ian didn't care what people thought, but he didn't want James's body to be viewed this way by anyone but the man who made a living by caring for the dead. And Ian knew him to be a good and respectful man.

While Ian waited, his brain and his heart once again did battle over this outcome. He recounted all the efforts James's loved ones—himself included—had put into trying to talk James out of doing this, of considering other options. But he also imagined different conversations, different scenes, different outcomes—ways that Ian might have made a difference in order to avoid this fiery grief blazing in every aspect of his being.

Donnan returned with the undertaker and his wagon more quickly than Ian had expected. As much as he desperately wanted someone else to take responsibility for the body, he had a difficult time seeing the wagon roll away with James's body concealed in the back. Ian and Donnan stood there for a stretch of minutes, neither speaking. Ian turned to look at James's horse and cringed at the blood on the saddle. He felt that nudge again and covered the saddle with the blanket before he nodded at Donnan. Then they rode wordlessly home to Brierley. They were halfway there before it occurred to him that they'd just been at the edge of town. He should have gone home and told Wren the news. He immediately knew it wouldn't have been a good idea. Once he told Wren, he would likely collapse into the comfort and security of her boundless love and understanding, and he'd likely not be capable of functioning beyond that moment. He knew that grief could heal, and that time moved on. But right now he couldn't imagine any life at all beyond losing himself in Wren's embrace and never coming back.

Ian made no comment to Donnan about his dread of confronting their parents, or the grief consuming him. And Donnan made no comment to Ian. In the stable, one of the hands stepped forward to help with the horses. Ian and Donnan generally unsaddled their own horses and helped care for them, but today they just stood there a long moment before Ian found the voice to say to the servant, "Thank you, Gillis. There's . . . uh . . . blood on that saddle. It will . . . need to be cleaned." He heard himself say the words and wondered how he'd said them without once again releasing that explosive need he felt to cry and scream like a madman.

Gillis's expression was one of silent question and panic, but he just nodded in response, and Ian took hold of Donnan's arm to guide him to the house. Ian wanted to get this over with, and he wasn't going to do it alone. He was struck by the thought that if something had happened to him while he'd been away from home—or if he'd simply never found the good sense to return—Donnan *would* be doing this alone. For the thousandth time at least, Ian was grateful he'd had the good sense to come home, then he prayed that his parents would have the strength to get through this—that they *all* would have the strength to get through this.

While Ian was wondering where they might find their parents, he looked up to see both of them coming out of the door. It only took a moment for them to realize that Ian and Donnan had returned without James. One more moment allowed them to take in the grief and regret on their sons' faces. Then Anya collapsed against her husband, sobbing in unrestrained heaves. Ian and Donnan stopped to face their parents. But Anya didn't look up, and Gavin's eyes were squeezed closed, but not tightly enough to hold back a steady stream of tears. Ian and Donnan exchanged a helpless glance. Ian fought to keep his own emotions from crossing the border, holding them in control. Once they crossed the threshold, he knew he had no hope of keeping them restrained. The unnatural tightness in Donnan's face implied his similar struggle. But they both just stood there, allowing their parents time to take it in.

Gavin finally opened his eyes and exchanged a gaze of shared grief with each of his sons. "Did he . . . suffer?" he asked, his voice raspy.

"Only for . . . a minute," Donnan said.

"It was over quickly," Ian added, and Gavin gave a slight nod at the same time as he tightened his arms around his wife. Ian cleared his throat and added the most necessary information. "We took . . . him . . . to the undertaker. He will be visiting to make arrangements, but . . . not until tomorrow morning. He said he would give you time to . . ." Gavin nodded again and it didn't seem necessary to continue.

Gavin then said, "I'm going to see that your mother lies down. The two of you should be with your wives." He started to guide Anya toward the door and added, "Thank you . . . both of you . . . for being with him . . . for doing all that you could."

Ian and Donnan both nodded, but Ian felt that inevitable explosion of grief pressing closer to the surface. He quickly said to Donnan, "I'm going home. Send word if I'm needed."

Donnan nodded, then hugged Ian tightly. Ian took comfort in the bond of brotherhood he shared with Donnan, and the stark grief they also shared. But that too tempted his sorrow to become unleashed. He stepped back and said, "I need to go," and hurried away.

Back at the stable, he was glad to see that Gillis had left his horse to be unsaddled last, and he didn't need to resaddle it. "Thank you, Gillis," Ian muttered and rode away as if his grief might be running after him.

Ian tried to convince himself that he could hold his feelings in until he could be with Wren, but he wasn't halfway home before he had to ride into a patch of trees a short distance from the road and dismount, so overcome with heaving sobs that he could hardly stay in the saddle. He sunk to his knees and pressed his head to the ground, howling like a trapped and wounded animal. He wrapped his arms around his middle as if that might ease the gnawing, physical pain. His grieving transcended time, and he experienced a complete lack of awareness to anything around him until he found himself flat on his back, looking up through the trees, hunger growling in his stomach. The sun was high but easing toward the west, and he knew Wren would be waiting and worrying. He pulled himself together enough to mount and continue toward home, wondering how life could go on while his mind was continually clouded with the image of James bleeding to death on the ground.

Ian left his horse at Blane's livery, glad to find no one there so that he could be alone while he removed the saddle and saw to the horse's needs. He walked toward home with the dread of telling Wren, yet an urgent desperation to do so if only to know that she would share his grief and offer her unfailing strength and comfort. He stepped into the kitchen to find no one there. He then heard voices from the shop indicating that Angus and Bethia were there on the other side of the curtain. That suited him fine. He'd prefer having time alone in his bedroom before facing them or anyone else with what had happened.

But he wondered if Wren was there too, and he wondered how to get her attention without having to speak to anyone else. He closed the door, making certain it made a noise, and she didn't disappoint him. She stepped through the curtain into the kitchen, her expectant expression indicating that she'd been listening carefully for his return. She took one glance at his face and muttered, "No. Oh, no."

"Yes," Ian rasped. "He's dead." He felt the eruption of tears coming again and hurried to the bedroom, not willing to risk anyone seeing him like that, knowing that Wren would follow. He sunk onto the edge of the bed and hung his head. Wren closed the door and was there beside him, her arms around him, drawing him into the comfort he'd been seeking. She held him close, and they cried together. He wondered what he would ever do without her, but even with having Wren in his life, even with having so very many blessings at every turn, he didn't know how he would ever recover from this, how he would ever to be able to find peace and be whole again.

* * * * *

According to James's wishes, the family held no formal funeral in the church. He was buried quietly, surrounded by his family and a few of the townspeople who knew him personally. The minister said little, and Ian could well imagine him thinking that since James had died in such a sinful state and such a shameful way, he was lost eternally and there was nothing to be done and nothing to be said that could change it. Before that moment, Ian had never thought too deeply about how the choices of this life could affect the life to come. He'd grown up going to church and hearing sermons on the need to avoid sin, with the prospect of eternal damnation held high as an incentive to do so. But it had never felt personal to Ian—until now. He wondered if his brother *was* eternally damned. And what of Greer? Did he not also die a shameful death, crippled by the sin of gambling? But what of the people of this town who bore less obvious sins? The sins of judging and gossiping? The sins of coveting and quietly lusting? And yet they were good people at heart; imperfect, yes, but good. And Ian himself saw his own imperfections and shortcomings greatly magnified. Was redemption possible for a man like him—or a man like James? Or any man, for that matter?

In the days following the burial, Ian became consumed by the question, but he didn't want to talk about it. He hated being around his family, because no one had anything to say, and the silence among them was unnatural and brutal. He hated being around anyone else, certain that one more sincere offer of sympathy would provoke him to scream and curse at some unsuspecting, well-meaning friend of the family. He hated being alone because the memories haunted him mercilessly. He only felt comfortable and able to relax with Wren, and she was eager to offer her care and comfort. But they had a household to run and many chores to keep them busy. Ian was glad for wood to be chopped and laundry tubs to be emptied and cleaned. He was glad for the way Angus needed him more and more, even though that meant his arthritis was getting worse—and so was his pain. He was glad that Bethia needed to be watched over, and he was glad he had a wife that he was obligated to care for and look after. Without these things he felt certain he would go mad; even *with* them he sometimes wondered.

Late one evening after Angus and Bethia had gone to bed, Ian sat at the kitchen table and noticed that Angus had left a partially emptied glass of whiskey on the table. He kept a bottle in a nearby cupboard and had a little nip of it here and there. Ian had not consumed a drop of liquor in this house since the night he'd asked for Wren's hand in marriage and Angus had wanted to drink to it. Ian had enjoyed a single drink on occasion at the pub when he'd gone there with his brothers or with Angus. But not since he'd returned home had the idea of a good, stout drink appealed to him as it did in that moment. He so desperately wanted to dull the grief of losing James and the way it had intertwined into his ongoing grief over losing Greer. He wanted to drown out questions of damnation and redemption, and he wanted to blur the memory of James dying while Ian had helplessly looked on.

Ian knew Wren was in the bedroom, using the bed to fold clean linens that she'd taken down from the line just before supper. He quickly found Angus's bottle and a clean glass. He poured a fair amount and stared at it, pondering the boundary before him, and praying for strength not to cross it. Simultaneous with his prayer was a hypocritical desire to just get blindly drunk and block out anything

God might do on his behalf. He thought of leaving Angus's bottle as it was and just walking the short distance to the pub where he could get an unlimited supply of the sweet nectar of oblivion.

Wren's thoughts were wandering aimlessly until she felt a sudden uneasiness that prompted her to see what Ian was doing. She came quietly into the kitchen to see her husband looking into the glass of liquor in his hand, the bottle on the table within his reach. The flames from the grate cast strange shadows over his dark countenance. She felt sick at heart. As if the grief of losing James were not enough, she had to also fear that Ian would allow that grief to draw him back to his old and ugly habits. Recalling how thoroughly ugly his behavior had been following Greer's death, the thought of him turning heavily to his drinking made her sick to her stomach. Determined to make her concerns known, she stepped farther into the room, and he turned to look at her. He didn't look as guilty as she had expected—or perhaps hoped. But he quickly looked back at the golden liquid swirling in the glass as he methodically rotated it with his hand.

"I didn't take even a sip," he said.

Wren sat beside him and took his chin into her fingers to hold him steady while she kissed him, relieved not to taste any hint of liquor.

"You don't believe me?" he asked, sounding insulted.

"Should I not be concerned t' find ye sitting here this way? When it used t' be yer habit t' drown yer grief in a bottle of scotch, I have cause t' be concerned."

"Maybe you do," he rumbled and set the glass down. "But that doesn't mean I would lie to you." He looked at her hard. "I've never lied to you, Wren."

"I'm glad t' know that," she said. "I also know ye've held the truth back from me."

"That was years ago," he countered. "Will you never be able to trust me?"

"I've trusted ye with my life and the lives of my loved ones, Ian," she said. "I only want t' know why ye poured the drink if ye had no intention of drinking it."

Ian looked away and she saw the muscles of his face tighten. "I was praying for the will to not drink it," he said. "Perhaps that's why you came into the room."

"Perhaps," she said but sensed that his casual tone of voice was barely disguising the grief rumbling inside of him. A moment later he swept his arm across the table. The bottle and the glass flew and crashed.

"I should have been able to stop it," he growled. "I . . . should have been able to . . . to save him . . . just like Greer. It's just like Greer. I should have been able to stop it."

"Ye know that's not true," Wren said in a soft voice that she hoped would soothe him. She pressed her fingers gently into his hair. "In yer heart, ye know it, Ian."

"I don't know it, Wren. I don't." He dropped his face into her lap, heaving great sobs as if something vile and baleful had come gushing out of him. Wren just held him until he was exhausted enough that she insisted he go to bed. She wept while she cleaned up the splatter of liquor and broken glass in the kitchen. And while she wept she prayed. She prayed that her husband would find peace, that life could go on, that she could find the right moment to share with him the wonderful news she had—that life *would* go on. But she wanted news of her pregnancy to be received with joy, not swallowed by Ian's grief that presently had such a complete hold on him.

When she had finished cleaning up the mess, Wren found Ian sleeping. She undressed for bed and snuggled up close to him, continuing her prayer on his behalf until she too drifted off to sleep, pondering the miracle that she was going to give birth to Ian MacBrier's child. And she prayed for the miracle that this child might bring its father joy enough to compensate for the harsh losses in his life.

* * * * *

Ian awoke to a vague hint of morning light, and for a brief moment he felt the normalcy of life and the regular joy of an ordinary day before him. But that moment quickly vanished with the memories that taunted him and the grief he couldn't shake. He recalled with shame the way he'd left broken glass and spilled liquor for his wife to clean up. His regret was at least buffered by the very fact that he *could* remember it. He'd not given in to the temptation to drink away his sorrows, and he was grateful for that now when he knew his sorrows would only be amplified by a hangover. And contending with his wife would have been far worse than the hangover. He'd promised her, and breaking that promise would erode the only thing in his life that was stable and secure.

Ian turned to find Wren watching him. She offered a smile that confirmed her ongoing love for him and touched his face with fingers that echoed the sentiment.

"Sorry about the mess," he said. "I should have cleaned it up myself. Or better yet, I shouldn't have done such a childish thing."

"It doesn't matter," she said. "I only wish I could take away yer pain as easily as sweeping up the broken glass. However," she leaned up on one elbow, "ye'll be owing my father a bottle of whiskey, so ye'd best be going int' town t' get one before he notices."

"I'll do that," he said, returning a hint of a smile. "And I promise *not* to get one for myself."

"Thank ye, Ian."

"For what?"

"For keeping yer promises."

Ian wrapped her in his arms and held her tightly. "You are precious to me above all else, Wren. I don't know what I would do without your love . . . your patience."

"Ye would do the same for me," she said and kissed his brow.

They held each other in comfortable silence for many minutes before she added, "There's something I need t' tell ye, Ian."

Ian lifted his head, a bit panicked from the solemnity of her tone. "Is something wrong?"

"No, not at all," she said and pressed a hand to his face. "It's a good thing I need t' tell ye. I hope ye'll be happy about it. I hope it might ease some of yer grief."

"Just tell me," he said, not even bothering to consider the possibilities.

She sighed, she smiled, she let out a little chuckle. "We're going t' have a baby, Ian."

Wren saw a brief second of confusion, then Ian's eyes widened with enlightenment. He let out a joyful laugh the same moment he hugged her tightly. Then he looked at her face as if to see if she looked any different. "Are you certain?" he asked.

"I waited t' tell ye until I knew for sure," she said. "Are ye happy about this?"

Again he laughed. "More than I could ever say."

"I know it can't make up for what ye've lost, Ian, but I know a child will bring great joy int' our home . . . and t' our family."

"James would be pleased," he said, and it was the first time since his death that Ian had been able to say his name without having it wrench at his heart. "So would Greer."

"Yes, I believe they would."

* * * * *

The weather turned warmer while Ian did his best to go about his life in a normal way. He could see that his family members were trying very hard to go on living and find joy in their lives, and Ian felt it would be selfish not to be making that same effort himself. He felt a thrill each time he thought about having a child, and since Lilias was also pregnant, they would have two babies in the family, not too far apart in age. Gavin and Anya spoke frequently of their excitement at having grandchildren, and how joyous it would be to have little children in the house again. Gillian had a child and another on the way, which also gave them great joy, but they saw Gillian and her family rarely, and Gavin and Anya longed to be grandparents to children they could see and interact with frequently. Wren's pregnancy would be an occasion for further rejoicing once Ian and Wren decided it was appropriate to share their happy news with the family.

On a Sunday that was almost hot with the coming of summer, Ian and Wren attended church with the family, then went to Brierley for dinner and visiting. Angus and Bethia had come along, and it was a typical Sunday in every way except for the absence of James and the lingering pall left by his death. But no one talked about that, and Ian tried not to think about it. His efforts proved to be more difficult than usual, and his mind became stuck in the mire of wondering if James's spirit truly lived on, or if his shameful end was *the* end. And if he *did* live on, was it in some kind of eternal torment due to his poor choices?

After dinner everyone was lounging about in the main parlor, chatting and filling up the couches with pleasant relaxation. Ian felt a sudden restlessness and came to his feet, forcing Wren to readjust her comfortable position, since she'd been leaning on him. He casually paced the room, wondering if he should take a walk or perhaps go riding. He was about to ask anyone if they would like to join him when a thought came to him so suddenly that it almost took his breath away.

"Is something wrong?" Wren asked. Thankfully no one else had noticed his little gasp.

"No, I'm fine. I just . . . feel restless. I'll . . . be back shortly."

Wren moved to stand up as if she were willing to go with him, even though she was enjoying the opportunity to just put up her feet and relax.

"It's all right," he said. "You rest. I won't be long."

Ian calmly left the parlor, then bolted up the stairs, leaping over three or four at a time with his long legs. He entered his bedroom that hadn't changed a bit in his absence and closed the door behind him.

"Please let it still be there," he whispered to the silent room as he opened the wardrobe. He went to his knees and probed into the dark corners, sighing when his hands found the familiar haversack that he'd carried on his journey. He remembered purchasing it in Edinburgh, and carrying it carefully close to him each day and night. It had held a change of clothes and his minimal belongings. But just before returning from London it had become the resting place for that book he'd purchased. *That book!* Its existence had seemed to spur him to seek it out, as if the book itself had awakened him from a deep sleep and called to him through the long hallways and down the stairs to the parlor. Ian opened the bag and pulled out the dirty clothes in there. He tossed them aside, recalling how he'd come home in Greer's clothes, which he'd returned freshly laundered to Bethia a few days later. With the clothes out of the way, Ian saw nothing but the book. He tossed the bag and its few other contents back into the bottom of the wardrobe and closed it. The dirty clothes on the floor seemed to taunt him with difficult memories, and he threw them into the fireplace grate where kindling had been left ready to light. He watched them catch fire and disperse into ashes before he turned his back to the embers *and* the memories and took up the purpose of his quest in coming back to his room today.

Sitting on the floor, Ian thumbed through the book, surprised to find a piece of paper tucked between two pages that naturally made it fall open there. He recalled looking through the book a little in the carriage from London to Edinburgh, and he didn't recall seeing the paper there before. He must have missed it. He took up the handwritten note to read: *"How beautiful upon the mountains are the feet of those who shall hereafter publish peace." Never forget that you will be in my every prayer while you travel so far to serve the Lord, and to publish His peace. May your feet be guided in your journey, and may you come home safely to my arms when your work is done. Yours eternally, Beatrice.*

Ian recalled the two men preaching in London—Americans. Had they left wives and families behind? Had this note inadvertently gotten into one of the copies of the book they were selling? Obviously. Ian felt deeply touched for reasons that were difficult to grasp. He then noticed a passage on the page of the book that was underlined in pencil:

"And again, how beautiful upon the mountains are the feet of those who shall hereafter publish peace, yea, from this time henceforth and forever!"

Obviously the note had been in reference to this passage, and Ian wondered if this copy of the book *had* been the personal copy of the man he'd spoken to. Had selling it been a mistake? Whether or not it had been, there was no way to correct it now. Ian read the rest of what had been underlined. They were the words of a prophet named Abinadi:

"And behold, I say unto you, this is not all. For O how beautiful upon the mountains are the feet of him that bringeth good tidings, that is the founder of peace, yea, even the Lord, who has redeemed his people; yea, him who has granted salvation unto his people; For were it not for the redemption which he hath made for his people, which was prepared from the foundation of the world, I say unto you, were it not for this, all mankind must have perished. But behold, the bands of death shall be broken, and the Son reigneth, and hath power over the dead; therefore, he bringeth to pass the resurrection of the dead."

Ian found his breath difficult to come by as the words reached into his mind and tangled around his heart. Only then did he recall, as clearly as if it had happened only a moment ago, one of those men speaking to the crowd about the unwavering love of Jesus Christ for all men and women, and the possibility of redemption no matter the sins or mistakes that had been made in this mortal state. And Ian hadn't given the matter a second thought since that day, even with all of his wondering and pondering since James's death. And now, here in front of him, were words that gave him hope in a way that he hadn't fully imagined he'd needed. He felt an urgent desire to read the book, as if he could sit there on the floor of his room and read it from start to finish without anyone noticing his absence. For the moment he just thumbed through the pages, feeling an odd sense of destiny surrounding him like a warm blanket after coming in from a winter storm.

Compelled to stop on a particular page, he began to read the words of someone named Alma: "Now, as my mind caught hold upon this thought, I cried within my heart: O Jesus, thou Son of God, have mercy on me, who am in the gall of bitterness, and am encircled about by the everlasting chains of death. And now, behold, when I thought this, I could remember my pains no more; yea, I was harrowed up by the memory of my sins no more. And oh, what joy, and what marvelous light I did behold; yea, my soul was filled with joy as exceeding as was my pain! Yea, I say unto you, my son, that there could be nothing so exquisite and so bitter as were my pains. Yea, and again I say unto you, my son, that on the other hand, there can be nothing so exquisite and sweet as was my joy."

Ian reread the same words over and over, attempting to comprehend, feeling like he was peeking into a room with a bright light, and somewhere inside he had the hope of finding the kind of joy he was reading about. The prospect of stepping into that light felt intimidating and overwhelming, but at the same time, it felt compelling. Reminded of the passing of time, Ian closed the book and took it with him, counting the hours until he might be able to start reading it from the beginning.

Chapter Ten
Return to Brierley

That evening after Ian had helped get Angus settled into bed, he sat at the table and leaned toward the lamp to start reading from the book. Wren was finishing up some tidying in the kitchen and asked, "What have ye got there?"

"I bought it from a man preaching on the street in London," he said, and her attention was piqued. "You should be grateful to this man," he added with mild facetiousness. "For some reason the things these men said—there were two of them—went into my heart that day and I knew I needed to come home. They were selling these books, and I bought one."

Wren took it from him and looked it over as if it were spun from gold—likely the effect of her hearing it had something to do with bringing him home.

"Truthfully," he said, "once I was on my way home, I hardly gave the book a glance, and I left it in my bag after I returned. Today I just . . . remembered that it was there and . . . I felt a sudden desire to read it."

"The writing sounds like scripture," she said after having glanced over a few passages.

"Yes, it does," he said, "although I've not read much yet." He wanted to share with her how some thoughts and concepts had been stirring something inside of him, but it was difficult to explain—even to Wren—and he decided to wait until he'd read more. Perhaps with more information, the ability to explain how he felt would become easier.

Ian began to read at every possible opportunity, and when he wasn't reading he was thinking about what he'd read. He began to feel a subtle hope about some of the questions that had haunted him, but it all still felt too abstract to define. Occasionally Wren asked if he was enjoying the book and he told her that he was. For now, he preferred to keep the details to himself—at least until he could figure them out.

* * * * *

Wren was cleaning up supper when she heard a knock at the door. Ian had gone into the other room to help her father get ready for bed earlier than usual, since he'd admitted to feeling more poorly than usual. Wren opened the door while wiping her hands on her apron. In the remaining light of dusk, she saw a young woman dressed in attire much like that worn by the servants at Brierley who worked at the highest level of service, mostly interacting with the family. Against one hip she held a basket that appeared to be holding a pile of clean bed linens, and in the other hand she held a letter.

"Mrs. MacBrier?" the woman said, sounding nervous, possibly upset.

"Aye," Wren said.

"I was told the Earl's son lives here. I was not allowed to go anywhere near Brierley, but I was told that I could come here and get important news to the Earl."

"Aye, that can be done. Do ye wish t' speak t' my husband?"

"No!" the woman said abruptly, and Wren wondered from her nervousness if she preferred to speak to another woman. She held out the letter, and Wren took it. "Ye should read this . . . and yer husband too. And then ye'll know everything. My lady wrote the first part. It was me who finished it."

Wren wanted to ask questions but she'd just been told the letter would answer them. Instead she asked, "Are ye in trouble? Do ye need help? We can—"

"No," the woman said with contradictory tears in her eyes. "Just . . . get this letter t' the Earl and his wife . . . and . . . and this." She shoved the basket toward Wren, exhibiting both an urgency to get rid of it and a hesitancy to let it go. "The letter will tell ye everything."

The woman rushed away, leaving Wren standing in the doorway with the basket and the letter, stunned and not certain what to think. She set the basket on the table at the same moment that Ian came out of Angus's bedroom and closed the door, saying, "Was someone here?"

"A woman; she said we should read the letter and then give it t' yer parents. She said it would explain all we needed t' know."

"Strange," Ian said and broke the seal on the letter while Wren unfolded the linens to investigate the contents of the basket.

"Ian!" she muttered breathlessly and took hold of his arm.

"What in the world?" he muttered in the same way, and it took him a moment to steady himself with a hand on the back of a chair. Wren didn't know whether to laugh or cry to see a sleeping baby. She'd rarely seen a baby so tiny, and knew that it was very new.

"Read the letter!" Wren insisted.

Ian had trouble taking his eyes off the baby in order to concentrate on the page in his hand. He knew the implication before he'd read a word; the resemblance to James in that tiny little face was unquestionable. He cleared his throat and read aloud:

"To the parents of James MacBrier. It is pertinent that I inform you the child I will give birth to is the result of my relationship with your son. My husband, the Earl, is well aware that this is the case, and he has made me promise to get rid of the child by any means necessary once it is born. He has agreed that my doing so will guarantee his agreement to care well for me in spite of our many differences. I am therefore giving my child to you with all of my heart, knowing that it will be raised well and cared for in a way that would never take place here with me." Ian paused in his reading and looked again at the baby. "This is unbelievable!"

"Or perhaps not," Wren said, stroking the baby's blond, wispy hair with her gentle touch.

Ian returned his attention to the letter. "The rest is in a different hand."

"The woman said she had finished it herself. Go on."

"'I am sorry to report that my lady has passed on soon after the birth of her son. It was her last wish that I deliver the baby to the MacBrier family. Please care well for him.' There is no name, no signature." He sighed and shook his head. "I hardly know what to say . . . what to think."

"I think we need t' take the baby straightaway t' yer parents," Wren said. "The woman said the letter and the basket should be delivered t' them."

"Of course," Ian said and grabbed his coat. "I'll harness the trap."

Wren admired the beautiful little boy while she waited. A part of her wanted to take on his care herself. And she would have if there was no other way. But she knew they did not have the space nor the means to care for more than one baby at this time, and their own child was on the way. At Brierley, this child would be loved and cared for in the best possible way. For some families, the circumstances surrounding this child's birth would be considered a shame and an embarrassment, and the child would be forever affected by it. But the MacBriers were not that kind of people, and she knew this child would be loved. Wren thought of how this little one would be a cousin and friend to her own child. She felt as if she loved this little boy already, and they'd just barely had the opportunity to meet.

Wren heard the trap pull up beside the house and lightly covered the baby to protect him from the night air. She put on her coat and tucked the letter into the basket, knowing that her father and Bethia would not even know that she and Ian had left the house. Ian met her near the door and took the basket, setting it gently on the seat of the trap before he turned to help her. Once seated, she kept a hand on the edge of the basket during the entire drive to Brierley, occasionally peeking beneath the linen to be assured the baby was breathing evenly.

"He must have been fed just before she brought him t' us," Wren said. "He's sleeping so soundly."

"And let's hope that when we get there, someone will know how to feed him before he wakes up. I've not been around a baby . . . well . . . ever. How is feeding him possible when the mother isn't available?"

"A bottle with a nipple," Wren said, "or a wet nurse."

"Let's hope they have one or the other."

"With all the women serving in the household, I'm certain someone will know what t' do."

Ian kept his eyes mostly on the road ahead, occasionally glancing at the basket as if that might convince him of this newfound reality. *James had a son.* He wondered now if James had known of the pregnancy, and if that had contributed to his intense motivation to run away with this woman. He surely must have known, because it had not been so many weeks since James had left them so tragically. Ian couldn't figure how James felt his death would serve this woman and her child. Perhaps he had known of the agreement the Earl had entered into with his wife. But if he had, why hadn't he said anything? Such questions—and their answers—didn't matter anymore. What mattered was that something of James had been left behind. The irony was unbelievable!

"What are ye thinking?" Wren asked.

"I just . . . can't believe it. James has a son. It's all so very tragic, and yet . . ."

"And yet . . ." Wren echoed.

A few minutes later they arrived at Brierley. Before they got inside, the baby was wiggling and cooing, indicating that he was waking up. Wren lifted him out of the basket, keeping him wrapped up except for his little face. Ian kept hold of the basket in one hand and the letter in the other. They found Gavin and Anya sitting close to the fire in the parlor. Gavin was reading, and Anya was concentrating closely on some stitching. Wren hung back a little as Ian entered the room. His parents looked pleasantly surprised to see him.

"What brings you here this time of day?" Gavin asked.

"Funny you should ask . . ." Ian said.

"Not that we're complaining," Anya said. "It's always good to see you."

"And you," Ian said. "But you could never guess in a millennium my purpose for coming."

"Then you'd do well to tell us," Gavin said, setting his book aside.

"A woman came to our door just a while ago, with a letter and a gift. She said they were to be delivered to you." He held the letter toward his father.

"What does it say?" Gavin asked and hesitantly took it.

Ian heard a little squawk from the hall that made it clear the secret couldn't be held back any longer. "It says that James left something behind for you." He motioned Wren into the room.

Anya gasped as Gavin said, "What on earth . . ."

"It's a baby," Wren said with a smile and laid the infant in Anya's arms.

"I can see that!" Gavin said.

Anya said with a tremor in her voice, "He looks like our James." She glanced at Gavin then back at the infant as Gavin rose to look over her shoulder. Turning toward Ian and Wren she said, "James was born with dark hair like your father, but it lightened as he grew." She touched the infant's hint of blonde hair. "But his little face is so much like James."

Anya then purposefully pushed aside the baby's little gown to expose his tiny shoulder. She gasped, then met her husband's eyes. "He has the birthmark, Gavin," she said with a distinct tremor in her voice. "Just like you . . . and James."

"Unbelievable!" Ian said again, noting the silent agreement of the others.

"And what of the mother?" Gavin asked, the letter unread in his hand.

"She's dead," Ian said somberly. "Although it seems her intention was to give you the baby anyway. You need to read it."

Gavin opened the letter and read it aloud while both he and Anya were reduced to tears. Then they turned their full attention to the child, and Wren said to Anya, "I'm thinking he'll be wanting t' eat soon. Perhaps we should do something t' see that—"

"Oh, of course," Anya said and told Ian to call for a maid, who called for the head housekeeper, who ordered the houseboy to quickly milk one of the goats and bring the milk directly to her. The head cook dug out a bottle with a special nipple designed for this very purpose, and everything was seen to very efficiently. The baby had commenced howling to be fed before the bottle went into his mouth, and it immediately soothed him.

Anya was clearly in love with the baby already. Gavin was looking back and forth between the letter and the baby. Ian and Wren looked on. They exchanged a smile, and Ian knew her thoughts were the same as his. Ian's parents weren't too old to raise a baby, especially when they could afford to hire a nanny. This child had given something back to them that they'd lost at James's death. He could see it in their eyes. And he felt it too. James had gone about all of this completely backwards with everything all wrong. But that didn't mean this little life left behind wasn't precious and deserving of the best possible chance in all that the world might give him. There was no place on earth better than Brierley for that to be accomplished, and it occurred to Ian that in spite of the shortcomings and mistakes of human beings, God's mercy still showed its hand. Perhaps there was something of redemption in that.

"Did I hear a baby?" Lilias asked, coming into the parlor with Donnan at her heels.

It only took a minute to explain. Donnan and Lilias were as stunned and as delighted as the rest of the family, and they all sat together for a long while, admiring the infant and passing him around. Ian and Donnan were both nervous about holding him, but their wives insisted that they needed the practice. Gavin and Anya firmly decided they would call him James, and they would have their solicitor see to a proper adoption. The baby had not been born with the MacBrier name, but Gavin was determined that he would be adopted officially into the family in order to make it so. They also determined that they would simply be honest with others about the child's paternity, since the resemblance to James could never be disguised. And they could honestly say that the mother had died and her name was unknown. Even though they knew her to have been the Earl of Kentigan's wife, not one of the family actually knew her given name.

Ian and Wren were both hesitant to return home, but they knew that little James was in good hands and that they would visit him often. On the way home they speculated over what it would be like when their own baby came.

"Crowded," Wren said, but they laughed over it and made jokes about where the baby would sleep and play in their little home. The images in Ian's mind of their future with a child warmed his heart, and he had to admit that his pain over losing James had been soothed.

* * * * *

Only a few weeks after little James had joined the MacBrier family, Ian worked up a sweat chopping wood, even though the morning air was pleasant. He brought an armload of freshly cut firewood through the door to find Wren cooking breakfast at the stove. He deposited the wood in its place near the stove, then wrapped his arms around Wren from behind, kissing her neck as he did. She laughed softly and turned with a spatula in one hand, and he kissed her full on the lips, drawing her eagerly into his embrace.

"If ye're not careful, Ian MacBrier, breakfast will be burned."

"We can't have that, now can we," he said and set her free.

"The others are not up yet?" he asked, washing his hands. They'd had a late start due to staying up much longer than usual the previous night.

"Bethia can heat up her own breakfast when she wants it," Wren said. "But would ye see about Pa? He's much less embarrassed t' get help from ye when he needs it."

Ian knocked lightly on Angus's bedroom door and waited a few seconds before he pushed it open slightly and peered in to see that Angus was still in bed. "You're missing breakfast," he said, moving toward the bed. "Wren is cooking those sausages you love and . . ." Ian noticed his father-in-law's arm hanging out of the covers in an unnatural way, and he held his breath. He took a step closer and couldn't let his breath go. He didn't even have to touch Angus to know that he was dead. But he touched him anyway, needing to know for certain. The cold, waxy feel of the skin on his face left no doubt. Angus had been gone for hours. Tears stung Ian's eyes. He'd grown to love Angus Docherty through these months of living beneath his roof, and Ian would sorely miss him. Thankfully Angus looked at peace. He'd apparently gone in his sleep, with no obvious pain or distress. It would be easier for Wren and Bethia to see evidence of that. His own growing heartache exploded inside of him to think of how to break the news to his wife and how hard this would be for her to face. And there was no guessing how Bethia would respond. That would depend on which fragment of her personality was in domination when she got the news. Since she'd not yet come up from the cellar, perhaps Wren could have a few minutes to adjust to the news before there was a need to tell Bethia.

Ian uttered a quick prayer, drew in a determined breath, and returned to the kitchen. He moved the hot pan from the stove and took the spatula from Wren's hand, setting it aside.

"Leave this," he said gently and took both her hands into his. He made firm eye contact with her and saw the pieces come together by the way her expression changed from confused, to shocked, to mournful in the breadth of a long moment.

"What's happened?" she muttered, her voice raspy and trembling.

She turned to investigate for herself, but Ian took hold of her arms and forced her to stay. "Listen to me, Wren. You can go and see him, but you need to prepare yourself first." She looked up at him, and he knew she needed to hear it. "He's gone, Wren. It appears that he died in his sleep, likely hours ago."

Ian saw the news settle fully into her, then a sob came out before she pressed her face to his chest and took handfuls of his shirt into her fists, weeping with an intensity he'd never witnessed before. As much as he'd cared for Angus and would miss him, he couldn't comprehend Wren's grief. But he did fear it. Each time his father coughed or struggled to breathe, Ian feared this moment. Thinking of the possibility increased his own grief until it was difficult to distinguish his mourning for Angus's death from his fear of losing his own parents. He lost track of minutes while Wren cried, and he hoped that Bethia would remain in the cellar until Wren had been able to get past the initial shock enough to help soothe her unpredictable sister. He shifted from hoping to praying until Wren gathered some composure and looked up at him again.

"I'm ready t' see him now. Ye'll stay with me?"

"Of course," he said, and they walked together into Angus's bedroom. Wren held so tightly to his arm that he suspected bruises might appear later. But he didn't mind. Being her support and foundation in life had given his own life new meaning. Even the grief he felt over Angus's death felt good to him in knowing that he'd invested enough of his life into this family to genuinely mourn over this loss.

Wren's response to seeing her father's body was not a surprise. Ian just stayed with her and allowed her to grieve as much as she needed. He remained alert to any noises from the other room, and when he heard evidence that Bethia had opened the cellar door, he whispered to Wren, "Your sister is coming. You must help her."

Wren bolted into the kitchen, and Ian followed more slowly. He leaned in the doorway of Angus's bedroom, prepared to aid Bethia in any way she needed. He just listened while Wren gave her sister the news, and marveled at how Bethia's response was very much like Wren's—more like the response of a normal-minded person than he'd expected. He stayed close while Wren escorted her sister into their father's room, and they both wept over their father's body.

Ian knelt quietly next to Wren and whispered, "I'm going to send for my father. I think we could use his help . . . to make arrangements. I won't be long." She nodded and pressed a grateful kiss to his cheek.

Ian left only long enough to walk to the livery where he gave Blane the news but asked him to keep quiet about it until Wren and Bethia had had the opportunity to adjust a bit. Blane agreed with a nod and was overtaken by huge tears that he wiped away with his ample handkerchief. "He was a good ol' soul, Angus," Blane said. "He'll be missed; he'll surely be missed."

"Yes, he will," Ian said, then asked if he could get Blane's son to deliver a message to Brierley.

Blane found his composure and called his son away from tending the horses. Ian gave the boy a sealed note and a few coins for his efforts. "See that this is delivered to the Earl straightaway. Tell the servants you were ordered to deliver it personally."

"Aye, sir," he said and was quickly bridling a horse.

Ian returned home to find Wren and Bethia still sitting on either side of their deceased father. Wren cried silent tears. Bethia whimpered and sobbed with her face pressed into the bedcovers.

The women insisted they could not eat the breakfast Wren had prepared, so Ian dumped it out and put the kitchen in order, needing something to occupy himself while he allowed them the time they needed. Ian knew that once his father arrived, they would need to inform the undertaker and have the body removed from the house. Until then, he saw no reason to insist that Wren and Bethia leave their father's side for any reason. He sat on a chair at the edge of the room, offering silent support, making himself available if he was needed.

A knock at the door startled all three of them. The women wiped at their tears and attempted to appear more tranquil. Ian rose and told them he would get it, certain it was his father. He opened the door to see both of his parents, who entered and embraced him tightly, each in turn.

Ian shouldn't have been surprised at the way his mother offered sincere compassion to both Wren and Bethia, and how she gently guided them into being prepared for their father's body to be taken and made ready for his burial. Ian went with his father to make arrangements with the undertaker and then to visit with the minister about arranging a proper funeral. Ian was grateful for his father's level head and familiar association with the people they needed to speak with.

The next few days were especially difficult for Wren and Bethia, and Ian was grieving just enough to have empathy for their pain, but not so much that he couldn't help them through their own grieving as the funeral approached and was carried out. There were few people from town who did *not* attend, and it was evident that Angus Docherty had left a warm and pleasant mark on this community. Bethia was calm and quiet during all that transpired in public associated with the funeral and burial, then she went home and went to the cellar and hardly came out except to eat and see to her own basic needs. Wren expressed concern to Ian over her behavior, but he suggested that perhaps this was simply Bethia's way of grieving, and they needed to allow her some time to do so. He wanted to believe that she would adjust with time and return to her normal self, and he tried to convince Wren of the same.

The tailor's shop remained closed to give the family time to mourn, but Wren admitted that with her father gone and Bethia apparently not up to any sewing, perhaps it was best. She knew there was at least one other competent seamstress in town who might appreciate more business and that there were also excellent tailors in the neighboring towns. She was tired of being responsible for the business, and without her father's desperate need to hold on to his profession, everything in that regard had changed. They agreed that unless Bethia came around to wanting to be actively involved in making clothes for paying customers, they would likely leave the shop closed, and perhaps eventually sell the house and shop, depending on Bethia's needs. For now, they agreed that she needed the security of her precious cellar. But they also agreed that her dependence on being there left them uneasy, and that perhaps a day would come when moving her to Brierley—for all that it might upset her initially—might be the best thing. Ian couldn't deny that living at Brierley had its appeal and advantages, the greatest of which for him would be the daily closeness and interaction with his family. He had no problem with doing the work required to care for himself and his family. It wasn't the elegance of Brierley or the presence of servants he missed.

And he had to admit—if only to himself—that he worried about Bethia, and that maybe his parents had been right. Perhaps she *would* be more protected at Brierley. The idea persisted in his mind enough that he began to think he should discuss it with Wren, but while her father's death was so fresh, he decided to wait until the time was right.

* * * * *

Ian was hovering pleasantly close to sleep when he heard a strange sound from the other room. His eyes opened wide the same moment Wren grabbed hold of his arm, the tightness of her grip expressing fear.

"What was that?" he asked. She didn't answer, and he knew she was listening, as he was, to see if they heard it again.

A moment later Bethia's crying became undeniably evident, and Wren bolted from the bed and had the door open before Ian could even grab his breeches. He pulled them on and followed his wife. In the kitchen he froze, aware that Wren had done the same. He didn't even have to ask to know that she'd been seized and silenced by the same hand of terror that constricted his throat and twisted his stomach. Bethia was kneeling on the floor, rocking back and forth, crying with a sound he'd never heard from any human being. It came from a troubled and harrowed place he couldn't begin to understand. The back door was open, with cold air rushing into the room. The lamp on the kitchen table was lit, as it often was when one of them went out after dark and they would need light to be able to get back in. On the floor in front of Bethia was a familiar paring knife that was used frequently here in the kitchen. Except that now it was covered with rich, red blood. The same redness completely coated the palms of Bethia's hands, which she held out in front of her. They were shaking violently, while her strange howling continued—as if the devil himself might devour her this very instant.

Wren finally moved, going to her knees beside Bethia, at first attempting to calm her down, and then seeking answers as to what horrible thing had happened. Ian closed the door and put a blanket around Bethia's shoulders. He put Wren's robe around *her* shoulders and she gave him a brief, appreciative glance. He met her eyes barely long enough to see a terror she'd never experienced. Ian paced while Wren continued her efforts to soothe her sister and get information, but Bethia kept rocking, kept crying, had nothing to say that made any sense. Ian prayed silently and considered the possibilities—and the ramifications of those possibilities. They knew nothing except that Bethia was *not* hurt. It wasn't her blood all over her hands and staining her nightgown. Somebody was hurt—or worse—and Bethia was responsible. And the only thought that he could take hold of was an urgency to get Wren and Bethia away from here, before daylight, before incriminating evidence could be found. The evidence of whatever had happened would surely be forthcoming—along with the consequences. But he would not have the people of this town taking matters into their own hands and threatening the safety of these women he loved.

Ian went to one knee in order to face his wife and speak to her firmly, in a quiet voice that he hoped Bethia would not notice through her ongoing stupor of senseless crying. "I'm going to get the trap, Wren, as quietly as possible. I'm taking both of you to Brierley. We must hurry." He was relieved that she didn't question him or argue. She only nodded. "I want you to hurry and pack a few things, make certain the fires are out, and . . ." He stood up and reached for a towel, which he used to pick up the bloody knife. Then he pointed to the blood on the floor where the knife had been. "I want you to clean that up so there's no sign of blood in this house. Do you understand?"

Wren nodded with stout courage, but it didn't disguise her growing horror. He could visibly see his reasoning coming to light in her mind, and she was terrified. So was he. But they had to deal with that later. Ian hurried to finish getting dressed, then he made the bed so it would look like they'd left in the evening, rather than in the middle of the night. The thought of someone actually *searching* the house to analyze such evidence tightened his stomach further, but he focused on just getting out of here—quickly and quietly.

He saw no lights on in any neighboring windows, no hint of human activity as he went back and forth to the livery, where he quietly harnessed the horse to his trap and got it out with hardly a sound. He went into the house to find Wren dressed, with a bag packed and waiting near the door. The blood had been cleaned up from the floor, and Bethia's hands were also clean.

"Where are the rags you used?" Ian asked. "And the water?"

"I dumped the water in the weeds. I've got the rags in my bag, wrapped in a towel. The knife is there too. I've not left a trace."

"Very good," he said, noting that Bethia seemed oblivious to anything but what might be going on in her head. She hadn't moved and hadn't stopped her ongoing reverie. Ian doused the lamp on the table and scooped Bethia into his arms, keeping the blanket around her. He carried her to the trap, and Wren followed with her bag, locking the door behind her. He was grateful Bethia didn't protest at being moved. An outburst from her now could be disastrous. She was apparently oblivious to *anything* going on around her, and he thanked God that she was—at least for the moment. *Please God,* he prayed over and over, *help me keep them safe. Help me know what to do.* Interspersed with his prayers on behalf of Wren and Bethia, he prayed that Bethia had not hurt anyone too badly, that the results of this would not be too hideous to be undone.

Driving the trap away from the house and out of town, Ian went quietly and carefully, alert to any possibility of being seen. He saw no evidence of any onlookers, but how could he ever know if someone might be having trouble sleeping and happen to glance out his window at the worst possible moment, and get suspicious. He tried to believe that nothing terrible had happened, and that even if someone saw him leaving with the women in the middle of the night, he would never connect it to any problem at all. But his deepest self knew that the results of whatever it was that had happened would change their lives irrevocably. And if he could begin to imagine *what* those changes would entail, he might be able to put together some kind of plan as to how they might endure the future and survive it.

Once beyond the town, Ian was able to gain speed. With the horse firm and steady on the road to Brierley, he turned his attention to Wren, who was sitting between him and Bethia, her arms wrapped around her sister. Bethia had become quiet, but she was still caught up in a subtle rocking motion, and she emitted a continual whimpering in a monotone cadence.

"What's going t' happen now?" Wren asked in a voice that betrayed how much she'd been crying, and how she'd been trying to hold it back so as not to further upset her sister.

"I don't know, Wren. How can we know what will happen now when we have no idea what Bethia's done?" He shifted the reins to one hand and put his arm around her shoulders. "I can promise you, however, that I will do everything I can to protect Bethia and take good care of her—*and* you. We will be safer at Brierley."

"Being that it's practically a castle, I'm certain we will," Wren said. "I just wonder how Bethia will . . ."

"One hour at a time, Wren," Ian said when she couldn't finish, overcome by her emotion.

It seemed to take longer than usual to get to Brierley, but that was surely due to Bethia's unending cries that were evidence of the nightmare taking place. They only stopped once, just long enough for Ian to take the knife that had apparently become some kind of weapon and toss it so far out into an obscure meadow that it would never be found. And even if someone came across it at some time in the future, it would never be connected to whatever had happened this night.

Ian parked the trap near a servant's entrance that he knew was closest to his own room. He knew there was an empty guest room directly next to it. He also knew the entire staff would be asleep at this hour, and he knew exactly where to find a lamp and matches just inside the door. He'd come home this way many times when he'd been out late.

"I'll take Bethia," he said and jumped down. "You get the bag and open the door. Just inside on the left is a little table where you'll find a lamp and matches."

Ian helped Wren down, then went around the trap to lift Bethia into his arms. She curled up against him, almost like an infant instinctively seeking parental comfort. Once inside the door, Wren found the lamp and lit it. Ian told her in whispers the direction to go, down a hall and up the stairs, around two corners and through the door to a guest room that was always kept ready for potential overnight visitors. Wren set the lamp on the bedside table and turned down the bed.

"This is right next to my old room," Ian said to Wren and pointed. "There's an adjoining door. You stay right there with her. I'm going to take care of the horse and the trap. Get her out of that nightgown and into something clean." He paused for consideration. "Did you bring something she can wear?"

"I did. I brought plenty of my own things to share with her."

Ian said nothing more as he lit a fire, glad that each room always had kindling in the grate and wood stacked nearby so that the chill could be taken off without delay if necessary. He squatted in front of the fire long enough to make certain that it was burning well, and he added some wood. He brushed off his hands as he stood up straight.

"You need to burn everything with blood on it," he said to Wren, "before I get back."

Wren nodded again, the courage in her countenance battling with the terror in her eyes. Ian knew exactly how she felt. He managed to park the trap in a discreet area of the carriage house where it wouldn't be noticed right off by the servants. He cared for his horse and left it in the stall where it had resided for many years. He doubted the stablemaster would give much thought to seeing it there; he would just believe Ian had come for a visit and decided to stay. On the way back to the house, Ian wondered exactly what to do now. He didn't want to alarm his family, but he needed their help. His little family could not be at Brierley without the entire staff knowing about it before breakfast. There had to be a good reason for it. By the time he'd entered the house he knew that the reason was obvious. Wren's sister was ill and was not doing well. Since Bethia had hardly gone out in years, Ian felt confident that he could convince others that she had a chronic health issue—which was true. No one needed to know that it was her mind that ailed, rather than her body. With Angus's recent death, it was logical to say that his daughters no longer wanted to remain where they had stayed in order to please him up until this point. These two facts together had pushed them to an impulsive decision. Bethia could be more comfortable and be better cared for here.

With his story becoming more firm in his mind, Ian got some water from the pump in the kitchen and took it upstairs so they'd have some for drinking or cleaning up if needed before the servants were available in the morning. He went quietly into the room that would now be Bethia's and found his sister-in-law curled up beneath the bedcovers, her glazed eyes staring at nothing. But she was quiet and seemed more calm. Wren lay near her sister, a hand on Bethia's arm, her eyes showing thankfulness just to see Ian enter the room. He wondered what might have transpired for Wren and Bethia if he'd not come back. Without their father—and with Bethia's illness creating such horrors—what would Wren have done? He felt chilled at the thought, and was immensely grateful that he'd had the sense to come back and be here for her.

Chapter Eleven
Protection

Ian noted that while he'd been seeing to the horse and the trap, the fire had warmed the room. Now that they were here and settled, he breathed a tentative sigh of relief. He moved a chair close to the side of the bed where Wren was lying. She rolled toward him and reached for his hand. He took it and pressed it to his lips before he spoke with a tenderness that he hoped would help calm her fears. "Everything will be all right."

"Ye can't promise that," she said.

"I can promise that I will do everything in my power to make everything all right," he said and she nodded, thankfulness showing again in her eyes. He told her the ideas he'd come up with for their reasoning in coming to Brierley in the night, and how he believed they could keep Bethia safe and secure in this room, bring meals to her, and help her be content here once she'd adjusted.

"But we don't know what's happened t' her, Ian. Look at her. I've never seen her like this before."

"We will just have to take it one day at a time. If one of us needs to be with her all the time, then we will."

"And if the story is that she's ill—and we want people t' believe it's not an illness of the mind—how do we explain why she's never seen one of the doctors around here?"

"If someone actually asks that question, we will say that she saw a doctor while on her honeymoon with Greer who diagnosed her and told her how to treat it, and she's had no reason to see another one since."

Wren shook her head and sighed. "Your efforts are noble, Ian, and I'm more grateful than I could ever say, but . . . it's such a big basket of lies. I fear the lies will just keep getting deeper and bigger until we don't know what's true and what isn't."

"I can assure you that my parents are not going to support us in being deceitful—especially if it comes to something illegal. If Bethia has hurt someone . . . if she has committed a crime . . . I don't know what will happen, Wren." Tears welled in her eyes, and she tightened her hold on his hand. "But I do know my parents will do what they can to help protect her as far as it's possible." Wren nodded and gnawed at her lip. "My parents are very wise and compassionate. They will help us know what's best. There are some things we can't solve until we know exactly what the problem is. We have no choice but to take it one day at a time—one hour at a time, if need be."

Ian stroked Wren's dark hair and pressed a kiss to her brow. "Right now we need to try to get some rest." He glanced at Bethia. "I don't think she's going anywhere. You stay with her and try to sleep. I will be in the next room, and I'll keep the door open." He stood up and added, "I'll need to speak to my parents very early, before anyone else realizes we're here." He bent over and kissed her brow again. "Try not to worry."

"I'll try," she said, and Ian went into the other room, feeling as if the world had gone topsy-turvy in the preceding hours, when he'd barely begun to get his balance following the previous horrors that had occurred for him—and for Wren. It was just too much!

Wren knew there was little point in trying to sleep. She could only stare at her sister, who was staring at nothing. She had to force her mind completely away from the blood Bethia had come home with, and the evidence that implied she'd done something horrible. She knew that Ian was right; they could not lie to the point of avoiding the consequences of the law if a crime had been committed and Bethia was at fault. But what possible alternative could there be? If not the punishment of the law, then it would be some dreadful asylum for certain. Wren had devoted years to protecting her sister so as to avoid any such thing. And now it had come to this! How could it possibly be?

Wren realized she had slept when she came awake with a start to see Ian dousing the lamp on the bedside table. The light of dawn filled the room, and a quick glance revealed that Bethia was sleeping soundly. Wren took in her surroundings, and a portion of her fears and concerns melted beneath the warmth of being safe and secure within the walls of Brierley. Wren had always found comfort in Ian's home, but she'd never been upstairs before. The room was comfortable and spacious, and it seemed a secure distance from the world—especially with servants to help meet their needs and Ian's family to help protect them. She wished then that they'd come to Brierley sooner, certain her father would have adapted, and Bethia likely would have as well. Perhaps they could have prevented this tragedy if Bethia had not been living in the center of town. Wren wondered who had been hurt and how badly, and her stomach knotted. She shifted her thinking with great force to the comfort of her surroundings, and turned toward her husband as he sat on the edge of the bed and bent over to kiss her.

"I didn't mean to wake you," he said. "I just wanted to be certain you were all right."

"Ye're very good at that, Ian MacBrier. I cannot imagine where we'd be without ye." She sat up to hug him tightly, making no effort to conceal her tears.

"I know it's difficult, my darling, but you must try not to worry."

"I know," she muttered and continued to cry.

Ian took her face into his hands, wiping at her tears with his thumbs. "We will find a solution, Wren; we will! If I have to take you and Bethia *far* away from here to keep both of you safe, I will! I will! I'll not let anyone take her away from you! I'll do whatever it takes! Do you understand?"

Wren nodded, apparently comforted by his conviction. But Ian could hardly breathe. The words had rushed out of his mouth without any thought or premeditation. Hearing them audibly penetrate the air and then settle back onto his own ears, their meaning rushed from his brain to his soul. He was glad to note that Wren hadn't noticed how the words affected him, nor had she picked up on the connection to his words and a lifetime of feelings he'd never been able to come to terms with. He stood and took a step back, as if she *might* sense the sudden warm rush of thoughts and feelings consuming him. "I need to speak with my parents," he said, "as soon as they're awake. I'll come back to check on you as soon as I'm finished."

Wren lay back down and Ian returned to his own room, where he slumped onto the edge of the bed and tried to make sense of the thoughts that had overtaken him, seemingly in an instant. *Could it be possible?* Could it *truly* be possible, to believe something one moment that had not even been an idea the moment before? To not only believe it but to know that it was somehow meant to be? Destiny—a part of some kind of greater plan maneuvered by a higher power to bring to pass purposes beyond mortal comprehension. For the first time in his life, he had the tiniest inkling that all of the feelings he'd struggled with from his very infancy were not in vain and senseless. Perhaps they had been leading him to this moment, to this time when *leaving* might be the only viable option in order to keep his family safe. He had to ask himself if he had simply attached himself to the idea because he *wanted* it to be the answer, because he wanted so desperately to make sense out of his senseless feelings. But he knew that was not the case. He also knew that for all of the clarity of the answer he'd just been given, he needed to give the matter time; he needed to be cautious. He needed to keep praying and listening and trust that God would guide him. His confidence on that count had just been strengthened immensely. He was on the path God had meant for him. He knew it!

A distant noise in the house startled him to the realization that the servants were up and about, and he needed to speak with his parents before anyone else became aware of his being there with his little family. He hurried into the hall after looking both ways, proceeded around the corner, down another long hall, and to the door of his parents' room. He uttered a silent prayer for strength and guidance and lifted his hand to knock lightly, hoping he wouldn't wake them, but hoping also that they would both be here.

"Come," he heard Gavin say immediately, his voice alert.

Ian opened the door to see his father in a dressing gown, sitting near the window, reading a newspaper; his mother was leaning against pillows in bed, reading a book. The first rays of morning sun were streaming into the room. They both turned in the same moment, surprised to see him, each setting aside their reading.

"Ian?" Anya said. "What on earth are you doing here so early?"

Ian closed the door. "I need your help . . . your advice; both."

"Well, sit down," Gavin said, motioning to a chair. Anya slipped out of bed and put a wrapper over her nightgown to take a chair as well so that they could all sit close together.

Ian took a deep breath and just said what he'd been lying in bed planning to say. "I arrived hours ago, actually . . . with Wren and Bethia. Something happened last night. I brought them here for protection."

He saw their concern. Gavin asked, "*What* happened?"

"That's the crux of the problem, I'm afraid," Ian said. "We don't know *what.* We only know that it's likely very serious, and ramifications are sure to follow. But Bethia is apparently incapable of telling us anything."

"I'm *very* confused, Ian," Anya said. "Please start at the beginning."

"Bethia came into the house late last night—and we had not known that she was *out* of the house, mind you—with blood on her hands, and a knife covered in blood."

Anya gasped and put a hand over her mouth as the implication sunk in quickly. Gavin showed less emotion, but he said gravely, "This could be very serious, indeed."

"Precisely," Ian said. "We cleaned everything up and came straightaway. Bethia was horribly upset, but so lost inside her own mind that we know absolutely nothing. My fear is that by now the constable knows that someone was hurt last night—or worse—and that this person may know it was Bethia who was responsible. Of course, I realize we cannot be dishonest or avoid the consequences of the law. The problem is that Bethia is not fit to face such consequences. The law does not allow for such situations beyond sending someone like her to some kind of frightful institution that would be worse than prison. I brought them here. I didn't know what else to do. But now that we *are* here, I don't know how I could possibly turn Bethia over to the authorities. I wonder if it might just be best if I leave here . . . and take my family with me."

"Let's not get too hasty," Gavin said, belying the utter panic in Anya's expression. "I can certainly see that this is a difficult dilemma, at best. But until we know what exactly happened and who it happened to—and why—we'll not have you running away with no hope of ever coming back if it's truly the commission of a crime you're running from."

"Are you saying that you would support me in leaving for the purpose of running from the commission of a crime?" Ian asked.

"It would break our hearts to have you leave, Ian," Gavin said. Anya's tears echoed this. "But Bethia's situation is unique, and I can understand why it might be necessary. After what happened to James . . ." Gavin's voice cracked slightly, and he took a moment to regain his composure. Anya hung her head and dabbed at her eyes with the corner of her wrapper. "I believe we would far prefer to know that you are living elsewhere and are at least alive and well. However, for the moment, we will not leap headlong to any conclusions without more information. I'm certain that whatever's happened will be known throughout the entire town—and consequently by every servant here—before the day is out. And perhaps Bethia will come around and be able to tell you. She has her lucid moments."

"Perhaps."

"What if someone was trying to hurt her and what she did was in defense of her own safety?"

Ian was ashamed to admit, "I hadn't even thought of that."

"Therefore, we will give the matter some time and see what happens," Gavin said.

"Except for the two of you, I would prefer that everyone believe we've come here because Bethia is ill and she can be more comfortable and get better care here. This will justify keeping her secluded in her room, where Wren or I will look out for her. We're going to say that it's a chronic condition that was diagnosed while she was on her honeymoon with Greer, and there's no need for a doctor to see her further. The timing of our coming here can be explained with their father's recent death. Beyond that, as you say, we should just . . . see what happens."

"Of course," Gavin said. "Now, is there anything we can do for you right now? Do you have what you need?"

"I need *you* to tell the servants the story I just told you. It will sound better coming from you, I'm certain . . . if that's all right."

"Of course," Gavin said again.

"Beyond that . . . I just need everyone to behave as normally as possible, and I will certainly keep you apprised if Bethia offers any information. I will speak to Donnan later."

"Is Wren all right?" Anya asked as Ian stood.

"She's very concerned," Ian said, coming to his feet. His parents did the same.

"I'll have breakfast sent up for them," Anya said. "Perhaps *you* should join us downstairs . . . for the sake of normal appearances."

"I'll be there," Ian said and received embraces of love and support from each of his parents. He expressed his humble appreciation for all they did for him, then he returned to find Bethia still sleeping and Wren pacing the room. He wrapped her in his arms and just held her for long minutes, hoping to pass on some of the support his parents had given to him, and wishing he could begin to explain the peace and hope he'd felt a short while ago.

When their embrace seemed sufficient, he urged her to sit close to him, and he repeated the conversation he'd had with his parents. She was calmed by Gavin's practical approach and agreed that for now they would just wait and see what transpired.

"I do hope no one was hurt badly," Wren said, a hand pressed to her heart. "The very idea of Bethia doing harm t' someone just . . ." She couldn't finish.

"I know," he said. "Right now I'm concerned about her getting upset when she wakes up. The servants will quickly be gossiping about her mental state if we can't keep her under control."

"I thought of that before we left," she said. "I still have a fair amount of the medicine the doctor gave my father. I admit that I've given it t' Bethia a time or two when she had an especially bad fit."

Ian didn't like the idea of using laudanum to control Bethia's problem, but he felt some relief to know that it was an option if needed. He only hoped she would be more lucid when she awoke, and be able to offer some insight as to what had happened.

Ian touched Wren's face and gave her a smile that he hoped would offer encouragement. "Breakfast will be brought up for you later. Perhaps you should try to get some more rest in the meantime."

"I'm all right," she insisted.

"I can sit with her whenever you need to get out," he said. "Perhaps you should go and get some fresh air while she's still sleeping."

"Thank ye, no. I need t' be with her. If I need t' get out, I'll be letting ye know. What will ye tell Donnan?"

"The truth if I hope to have his help . . . which I'm certain we will need."

"Of course," Wren said, but she hated the idea of bringing such a burden to Ian's family. She didn't want to admit how Ian's suggestion earlier of possibly leaving here had clung to her mind. If they went away from here, this nightmare could all be left behind. Yesterday she never would have thought she'd want to leave this fair valley that she'd never left before. But everything had changed since yesterday. Now, being safe—and keeping Bethia safe—was more important than anything. And keeping Ian's family from trouble was equally important, if not more so. She wanted to ask Ian if he'd really meant it, if he would leave everything behind to take them away—if that's what it came to. But she didn't want to bring it up, fearing what the answer might be if he were pressed for complete honesty. For now, she chose to consider it as a possible option that gave her the tiniest reason to hope that they could get beyond this.

* * * * *

Ian hurried to get cleaned up and change his clothes before breakfast. He checked on the women once more. Bethia was awake but had that glazed look in her eyes again. Wren assured Ian that they would be fine while he shared breakfast with his family and helped make their presence in the house appear normal. The way she said it, Ian felt as if she believed his doing so might be tantamount to going out into the world to slay a dragon on their behalf. He assured her that it was just breakfast, and he would return soon to be sure all was well. He pointed out the bellpull in the room and said, "If you pull that, a maid will be here in a few minutes. You can meet her at the door if you don't want to let her inside. You can ask her for anything you need: food, water, preparations for a bath. Anything. If you need her to find me, she will."

Wren nodded and said nothing, but Ian could tell she'd never fully comprehended the nature of the life he'd lived here. He kissed her and added, "I'll come back right after breakfast."

"We will be fine," Wren said.

Bethia turned toward the sound of their voices, her eyes focusing on them as if she'd just come back from some faraway place. Wren quickly moved to her side and stroked her hair. "Are ye well, darling?"

"Well enough," Bethia said, almost like herself. Then she took in her surroundings, and panic edged her voice. "Where are we?"

"We're at Brierley, my dear," Ian said. He exchanged a discreet glance with Wren and recognized the message. In dealing with Bethia, he had learned to be sensitive to Wren's signals. Right now, she was telling him to be forthright but not push for any information from her. Allowing her to become comfortable in new surroundings was clearly most important at the moment. He remained silent and allowed Wren to take the lead.

"Ye were not well last night, my darling," she said to Bethia, her voice soothing. "We thought it would be best t' bring ye here, that ye would be more comfortable, that we could care for ye better here."

Bethia's expression showed alarm, and Ian steeled himself for an outburst that might require drastic measures to keep her quiet. "What if Greer can't find me?" she asked with self-possessed tears.

Ian took a deep breath and went along, pushing away the sting he felt at the very mention of Greer's name. "He grew up at Brierley, Bethia. You lived here with him. Of course he would know where to find you." Bethia nodded and seemed reassured.

"And what of Jinty and Selma?" Ian asked, knowing that the presence of these two imaginary beings always sparked discord in Bethia's head as the two of them argued and took opposing views on Bethia's behavior and actions.

"They're here," Bethia said as if he should already know. Of course they would have come with her. She was never free of them.

Wren took her sister's hand and said, "I must talk t' ye about being here at Brierley. At home we knew that if Jinty and Selma were too loud . . . the neighbors might hear and become suspicious."

"And I had t' speak quietly t' them, so that no one would hear."

"That's right, Bethia," Wren said. "It's the same here, sister. There are many servants in the house, and Ian's family. His family loves us both, and they will help us. The servants will help us, as well, but they would not understand how things are for ye . . . and Jinty and Selma. Do ye understand what I'm saying?"

"Aye," Bethia said.

"The household believes ye're not well. They'll be told ye've got an illness that affects yer health. That way ye can stay here safe in this room and no one will ever come in here that ye don't want t' come in. Do ye understand?" Bethia nodded. "Meals can be brought here. Ye can bathe here. We can lock the doors." She pointed at the adjoining door. "That is Ian's room, and that's where he and I will be sleeping. Ye can always knock on that door in the night and we will be here in just a minute." Bethia nodded again. "It will take us a little time t' adjust, but we can be well here."

Bethia considered all of this for more than a minute. Wren and Ian exchanged concerned glances and allowed her the time to take it in. She then looked at Ian and asked, "Is there a cellar at Brierley?"

Ian felt as confused as ever over Bethia's need for damp, dark places, but he answered her honestly. "There are many cellars, Bethia, and I can show you how to find them and avoid the servants, but you can't sleep down there. People will become suspicious. You must sleep and eat in this room . . . unless you ever might feel well enough to eat with the family. You can read here and sew as much as you like. There's a wonderful library here, and Wren can bring you books. Or we can take you there and you can choose them for yourself."

"Ye remember the library at Brierley, sister? We came here when we were younger."

"Greer was here," Bethia said and smiled. "I remember."

"Do ye think we can be happy here, my darling?" Wren asked.

Bethia didn't answer but her expression implied nothing to the contrary. She asked Ian, "Will ye show me the cellars?"

"Later," he said. "Right now it's time for breakfast. A maid will bring your meal here, unless you would like to get dressed and come with me to eat with the family."

Bethia recoiled slightly. "I want t' eat here."

"I'll stay with ye, sister," Wren said, "until ye can get adjusted. Ian's going t' spend some time with his family, so that no one will think our being here is very strange."

"We don't want anyone t' know about Jinty and Selma," Bethia said. "They cause so much trouble." She started to whimper and became agitated, as if some remembrance of the previous night were creeping into her mind.

Wren eased closer to Bethia and whispered gently, "It's all right, sister. It's going t' be all right. We'll work t'gether t' keep Jinty and Selma calm and happy, and everything will be all right."

Ian was relieved that Bethia was quickly soothed, but he feared they would never be able to get her to unleash her memories of what happened last night without pushing her to a place where they would not be able to control her. For now, keeping her calm and secure was most important.

At breakfast Ian greeted Donnan and Lilias the same as he might when coming for Sunday dinner. It was evident they'd been given a simple version of the story when they inquired over Bethia and Wren, and Donnan offered to help in any way needed. A little wink and a small, firm nod came with his offer, and Ian knew that he meant it—even considering Bethia's bizarre and sometimes overwhelming needs.

Ian found breakfast with his family enjoyable as long as he could push the present dilemma from his mind. Near the end of the meal, the newly hired nanny brought little James into the dining room, according to Anya's instructions. Ian was glad to see the baby being so well cared for and to observe how easily and quickly the entire family had taken to him. He saw his parents laugh and smile as they observed their new little grandson, and everyone passed him around, teasing Lilias about how she always got to hold him the most. Ian enjoyed holding him a minute or two himself, trying to remember his brother fondly, and trying to imagine the day he would have his own child.

After the family gathering broke up so that little James could be fed, Ian went upstairs to find that Wren and Bethia had just finished eating. Wren reported that Bethia had a healthy appetite and had eaten a good meal, but since the maid had come to bring fresh water and collect the dishes, Bethia had become agitated and was now pacing and mumbling indiscernible phrases. When Wren's attempt to soothe Bethia only agitated her further, she asked Bethia if she would like some of their father's medicine to help her relax.

"Will it make Jinty and Selma go away?" Bethia asked with such pleading that Ian felt heartbroken to think of the inner torment that plagued her continually.

"I don't know, my darling," Wren said. "But I think it will help ye rest."

Bethia eagerly took a cautious spoonful and agreed to lie down. Wren stayed close to her sister while Ian sat on the far side of the room, hoping that his presence at least offered silent support in letting Wren know that he was there for her—even if he felt helpless to do anything. Bethia was soon asleep and Wren sat close beside Ian, resting her head on his shoulder. But neither of them had anything to say. Ian was glad to see Bethia sleeping soundly, and he was grateful for the laudanum that had calmed her down. But he knew they couldn't rely on it as a permanent solution. He knew enough about it to know that long-term use had the potential to cause other problems. Even Angus had admitted to Wren and Ian that while he was grateful for the way it eased the pain of his arthritis and helped him sleep, he knew he'd become dependent on it, and his body could not get by without the regular dose.

A light knock at the door startled both him and Wren, but Bethia didn't even flinch in her sleep. Ian rose to answer the door. Wren stood a short distance behind him, then moved closer when she heard Ian say, "Father, what is it?"

"The constable is here, son," Gavin said gravely.

Wren took hold of Ian's arm as if they might be eternally torn apart otherwise.

Ian tried to subdue the pounding of his heart and take this on with dignified self-composure. "Did he say what happened—"

"I haven't spoken to him. I was simply told he was here and wished to speak with you, your wife, and your sister-in-law. I suggest that you and I go speak with him together. Bethia is ill, and Wren needs to be with her." Gavin put a hand on Ian's shoulder and looked at him squarely. "God will be with you in your desire to protect your family. You will know what to say; we both will. Take a deep breath and come along."

Ian nodded firmly. He kissed Wren and smiled at her with the hope of counteracting some of the terror she made no effort to conceal. "Everything will be all right," he said. "You mustn't worry."

Ian left with his father before she could give him even one of all the many reasons they had for worrying. He was going on faith here, relying mostly on his father's faith in God to get them through this. Then he recalled the powerful feelings he'd had last night, as if God had spoken directly to *him* through those feelings. Now, the thoughts he'd had came to back to him with comfort. It was as if he'd been shown the possibility of taking his family from here was reassurance that there was a back-up plan. Perhaps it wouldn't become necessary, but if it did, he knew that he could do it and all would be well.

Slowly descending the stairs by his son's side, Gavin said, "I assume you've thought this through, that you have a plan."

"Of sorts," Ian said. "But that might depend on what the constable has to tell us."

"Which means we should listen and answer questions but not try to explain any more than absolutely necessary."

"That makes so much sense that I have to wonder if you have experience at this sort of thing."

"Not exactly," Gavin said. "Just experience at . . . dealing with difficult situations."

They came to the door of the drawing room. Ian took a deep breath, and Gavin opened the door. Ian felt proud of himself for the way he entered the room with perfect confidence, as if he had no idea what this could be about. The constable turned when the two men appeared. Ian stepped forward first with an outstretched hand and a smile.

"Hello," they both said at the same time, then Gavin shook the constable's hand as well, offering a kind inquiry over his well-being.

"I'm fine, thank ye."

"And what is it that we can do for you?" Gavin asked, motioning the constable toward a chair as they were all seated.

"It was Ian here I wished t' speak with," the constable said. "It's about his sister-in-law."

"Truly?" Ian asked and chuckled with perfectly pretended astonishment.

"I wonder if I might speak t' Miss Docherty," the constable said.

"She's very ill, Constable. My wife is with her. I would be happy to give you any information that I can, although I cannot begin to imagine what this might be about."

Ian forced the air in and out of his lungs in a steady rhythm, fighting to resist holding his breath. He was prepared to hear that a citizen of their fair village had been badly hurt in the night—or murdered. And he had no idea how he would respond to such news or what he would say. He couldn't imagine boldly lying any more than he already had. He couldn't imagine his father allowing him to do so. He uttered a silent prayer that simply amounted to, *Please, God.* He figured God knew the problem and his present unfathomable dilemma, and He could figure out well enough what help might be needed.

"We had a report this morning," the constable said, "from someone who saw Miss Docherty out very late last night, arguing with a man; a rather violent argument." Ian feigned ignorance and the constable added, *"Did* your sister-in-law go out last night, Mr. MacBrier?"

"Yes, Bethia *did* go out late last night. She came in chilled and not feeling well, but said nothing about where she'd been. She's sometimes prone to walking at night; her illness can make it difficult for her to sleep."

"Her illness?"

"Yes, Constable. I'm sure you're aware that beyond her attendance at church she's hardly been seen in public for years. She saw a doctor about it while abroad on her honeymoon. His diagnosis concluded there was nothing to be done but to be easy on herself and live with the symptoms. But she rarely feels well and has trouble sleeping. I can tell you nothing more about it, except that she's very vulnerable to becoming ill from any little germ or exposure."

"I see, yes," the constable said, taking a few notes with paper and pencil he'd drawn from his pocket. "And I understand that ye left yer house in the night. The neighbors say ye were there when they went t' bed, and not there in the morning."

"You spoke with the neighbors?" Ian asked as if it were a huge affront.

"Just doing m' job, sir," the constable said, unaffected. "Can ye tell me why ye left in the night?"

"Since my sister-in-law is prone to illness, we made the decision to bring her here straightaway rather than waiting until morning when we had planned to move our residence here, anyway. Since Mr. Docherty's funeral was seen to only a few days ago, my wife and her sister had decided that it was time to let go of the tailor's shop and live here with my family."

The constable scribbled more notes and Gavin said, "Forgive me, Constable, but . . . you say that someone saw Miss Docherty arguing with a man. Is such a thing considered criminal?"

"Not at all. The witness—who shall remain anonymous—was concerned that one or both of them might have been hurt." The constable looked straight at Ian. "Ye're certain Miss Docherty's not hurt? She's only ill?"

"I'm certain," Ian said. "I thank you for your concern." He didn't want to say it, but he had to know, and he thought it was better to bring it up himself. "Was someone else hurt?"

"Not as far as we can tell. There have been no injuries reported, if that's what ye mean."

"I'm glad to hear it," Ian said, sounding more nonchalant than he could believe with the relief prickling his every nerve. "But I must admit to some confusion. If no one was hurt . . . then why this visit, Constable? Is there a problem we are not aware of?"

"It's a small town, Mr. MacBrier," the constable said as if he were bored. "People get up in arms over anything out of the ordinary. Perhaps people just want t' know that all is well with ye and yer family. Perhaps they're just hoping for a little excitement."

"I think I would far prefer the tranquility of knowing that everyone is safe and well," Gavin said.

"Amen t' that," the constable said and stood. "Makes m' job a lot easier, t' be certain." He nodded at both men. "I'm sorry t' bother ye this way."

"Not at all," Gavin said. "Anything to help keep the peace."

To Ian the constable added, "Give my well wishes t' yer good wife and her sister."

"I will, thank you," Ian said, and the constable was shown out.

The moment Ian was alone with his father and the door to the room closed, he slumped into a chair with inexpressible relief. Gavin put a hand to his shoulder. "I doubt we could hope for any better outcome than that," he said.

"I agree with you with all my soul," Ian said, and Gavin sat down across from him. "But this does *not* give us any insight into what happened last night. Bethia doesn't seem to remember. We're afraid if we push her too hard to *try* to remember, she'll . . ."

"You don't have to explain."

"She came home with blood on her hands, Father; a lot of it! And a knife. A knife covered in blood. *Someone* got hurt last night."

"Perhaps it was animal's blood."

Ian winced. "Perhaps; perish the thought. I can't imagine Bethia hurting any living creature for any reason. She loves animals! Why would she do something so . . . ludicrous?"

"Because she's not herself more often than she is," Gavin reminded him—as if he needed to be reminded.

"Yes, and if one of the other pieces of herself was in control last night, who knows *what* she might have done. And that might explain why she can't remember . . . or won't remember." He thought a long moment. "Hurting an animal would not explain the argument that was witnessed. What did he say? A rather violent argument . . . with a man?"

"If it was someone trying to hurt Bethia, and she was defending herself, perhaps that person is just hiding and nursing his wounds, not wanting to come forward."

Ian sighed. "That makes more sense than anything else. But I hate the thought of Bethia sneaking out at night and being vulnerable to such a thing."

"Which is why it's best for you to be here. She *will* be safer here, Ian."

"I'm sure you're right. Given that no one died last night and Bethia's not being arrested, I think my biggest concern is that she can't live here for long without the servants realizing that her illness is more of the mind than the body. Word will spread, and I fear that some people will become frightened or superstitious, and the problem will only escalate."

"And if that happens, we will discuss it and deal with it the best way that we can."

"And if that means our leaving?" Ian asked, once again recalling the power of his feelings in regard to that possibility.

"It would break your mother's heart."

"Only my mother's?"

"And mine," Gavin said. "But as I said earlier, we would far prefer to know that you are safe and happy, than to . . ." He didn't finish, but Ian knew he was thinking of James and the trouble he'd gotten into that had cost him his life. "We will do our best to work together to care for Wren and Bethia, and we hope that it doesn't come to that. Let's not borrow trouble before it appears."

"Very good advice," Ian said and took a deep breath, once again feeling relief in knowing that his worst fears were not a reality. Recalling that Wren would likely be pacing, waiting to hear what had happened, he thanked his father and excused himself. He took the stairs three at a time and hurried to his room as opposed to knocking on Bethia's door and disturbing her if she was sleeping. He found Wren there, pacing as he'd predicted, with the door open between the two rooms, and Bethia sleeping.

"Tell me," Wren said. "Tell me everything!"

Ian carefully closed both doors so there was no chance of Bethia overhearing if she came awake.

"According to the constable he does not know of anyone who's been hurt."

"Praise be t' God!" Wren said breathily and put a hand to her heart.

He repeated the gist of the conversation with the constable, and also his conversation with his father. When there was nothing more to say, Wren urged herself into Ian's embrace and cried. He knew the exhaustion and stress had been too much when she had trouble stopping. He scooped her into his arms and laid her on his bed, sitting beside her.

"I want you to get some rest," he said. "I will sit with Bethia, so there's nothing to worry about. I promise."

"Ye're very good t' us, Ian," she said.

"Being good to you, sweet wife, is the best and easiest thing I've ever done."

He kissed her lips, then her brow, and covered her with an extra blanket that was always left folded neatly at the foot of the bed.

"I will check on you later," he said. "You know where to find me if you need anything."

Wren was nearly asleep before he had even closed the drapes to darken the room.

Chapter Twelve
Bethia's Ghost

Bethia slept deeply while Ian dozed here and there in a comfortable chair situated near the window to take advantage of the light so that he could read when he wasn't napping. Both women slept through lunch, and since Ian had given clear instructions that he was not to be disturbed—that he would ring if they needed something—no lunch was brought to their rooms. Hunger didn't tempt him to ask that lunch be brought up until a couple of minutes before he looked up to see Wren standing beside him, looking more rested—and less upset—than she'd looked since Bethia had shown up covered in blood last night. She kissed him in greeting, and he reported that Bethia was still sleeping like a baby. They went back into his room, leaving the door open so they could hear her when she awoke. He rang for a maid, asked for lunch to be brought up, and ten minutes later a tray was delivered with cold beef, cheese, bread and butter, and a variety of beautiful fruits.

"Your sister's not the only one with a healthy appetite," Ian commented with a chuckle when he noted how much Wren was enjoying the meal. She just smiled and kept eating. But at least she was smiling, he thought.

* * * * *

That evening Ian went back to the house in town with explicit instructions and a written list from his wife on exactly what needed to be packed and brought to Brierley, and some things he needed to do to make certain the home and shop were secure until they could be cleaned out and sold. Donnan offered to go with him, and Ian was glad for the company *and* the help.

At the house, Ian tore the list in half and gave Donnan the half that mostly included boxing up the fabrics and notions in the tailor's shop so that they could keep Bethia busy sewing, and so that Wren would also have something to occupy her time while she kept an eye on her sister. The men had brought many empty crates and boxes with them, and it wasn't difficult to fill them with the things Wren had requested. Ian left Donnan busy in the shop and went down to the cellar to gather Bethia's things. He and Wren had both been surprised to hear Bethia give permission for Ian to do so, and she'd particularly asked him to get some books and her hairbrush, along with her clothes. With all of Bethia's things in the wagon, along with the majority of the contents from the shop, Donnan gathered some of Angus Docherty's things that Wren had put on the list as keepsakes that she wanted to have. Ian gathered his own belongings as well as Wren's from the bedroom they'd shared. He concluded that living a simple life made it simple to move to a new residence. They left very little behind beyond the furnishings and some dishes and linens. Ian would hire someone to oversee selling it and see that the money was given exclusively to Wren and Bethia to use however they pleased.

On the way back to Brierley, Donnan asked, "How are you doing, little brother?"

"Now that I'm fairly certain Bethia didn't murder someone last night, I'm doing all right. You?"

"As good as could be expected," Donnan said, "as long as I pretend that James is simply away in some exotic locale, living the good life."

"I pretend that as well," Ian admitted. "If not for the memories of that terrible day, perhaps we could be better at it."

"Perhaps," Donnan said, and minutes of silence passed. "I'm glad to have you back at Brierley, if you must know. I completely understood your reasons for living with Wren and her family, but now that it's come to this, I'm glad you're there with us."

"With any luck," Ian said, "Bethia's condition won't cause too much of an uproar and we'll be able to stay."

"What are you saying?" Donnan asked. "That you're thinking of leaving?"

"If I have to . . . in order to keep them safe. For now, we're staying."

"Good. I hope you stay forever. I might be the one to officially inherit all the responsibility, but—"

"And the title and the power," Ian said facetiously.

"Yes, yes. The title and the power. But I like the idea of you being around to assist in the running of the estate. It would all surely run more smoothly if we were to do it together."

"Perhaps," Ian said, not wanting to admit to the growing feeling inside of him that his time at Brierley would be brief. His lifetime of wanderlust had collided with the need to keep Wren and her sister safe. And the collision smacked of destiny. His heart was growing comfortable with the idea that leaving was the right thing to do—even if he had no idea where he would go or what he would do. He found it strange that previously the idea of leaving had been utterly negative and unfavorable for him and those he loved, yet since last night it had turned upside down and now felt like a glowing light before him, leading him to his purpose in this world. His thoughts felt so absurd that he'd never dare voice them—not to anyone; not yet, anyway. He needed to give the matter time, but he felt as if he were being prepared for something inevitable and life altering.

With the help of some able-bodied servants, the wagon was unloaded and all of its contents taken upstairs in practically no time at all. Even though it was getting late, Wren and Bethia enjoyed unpacking the boxes and seeing their own things bring familiarity to their new surroundings. Bethia seemed more like herself, but Ian noticed that Wren had a dark mood around her even though she was pretending to be cheerful and caught up in Bethia's present happiness. He asked her quietly if something was wrong, but she only said, "Nothing I can talk about right now."

The project came to an abrupt halt when Bethia's mood suddenly altered. She became agitated and begged Ian to show her where the cellars were. He only agreed when she promised that she would never try to sleep down there and that she would avoid the servants if she felt the need to be there. Wren went along with them, and Bethia quietly inspected a few empty rooms in what seemed like endless caverns beneath Brierley. Bethia was quickly appeased and declared the need to get some sleep. Back in her bedroom she became agitated again and asked Wren for some more of that medicine. Wren gave her a scant dose and asked Ian to hide the bottle. He did so and prepared for bed himself, hoping that Bethia slept long and well so that he could do the same. He'd rarely felt so exhausted!

He was drifting to sleep and waiting for his wife to join him when he heard her whisper, "Forgive me, Ian, but . . . Bethia's sound asleep now, and there's something I must show ye before ye go t' sleep."

Ian shook his head to rid himself of the sleepiness and sat up. He grabbed a dressing gown he'd left at the foot of the bed and followed Wren into Bethia's room, wondering what could be so urgent. He then recalled Wren's dark mood earlier, and how she'd implied they would talk about it later. He wondered if that was the purpose of whatever she wanted to show him. He was surprised when she crept quietly close to Bethia, who was sleeping on her side, looking as content and at peace as a child. Wren handed Ian the lamp she was holding, threw back the bedcovers and whispered, "Last night when I helped Bethia change her nightgown, I must have been too upset t' notice. T'day when I helped her bathe, it was impossible *not* t' notice."

"What?" he whispered in response, and Wren carefully pressed Bethia's nightgown over her belly, revealing that it had a definite outward curve. She was pregnant! Ian sucked in his breath but couldn't speak. Wren quickly put the covers back over Bethia and left her to sleep. She took the lamp from Ian and headed back to their room. He had no choice but to follow, quietly closing the door behind him. He sat weakly on the edge of the bed. Wren set down the lamp and sat beside him.

"Greer really is dead, isn't he?" Ian asked, knowing the question was absurd.

"Of course he's dead!" Wren countered. "Thinking otherwise is ridiculous, and ye know it."

"Yes, I know it," Ian growled, his exhaustion making him more prone to sounding upset. "So tell me what other explanation there is!"

"Apparently last night is not the first time Bethia has gone out of the house without our knowing."

"Apparently," Ian snapped, wondering what they would do now, how they would handle this. A baby? An illegitimate baby born to a woman who couldn't even take care of herself, who had to live in hiding in order to avoid utter disaster? The family was adjusting well to having James's son living in the house, but this was an entirely different matter.

"There are only two possibilities," Wren said. "Either she has been secretly involved with someone of her own free will, or—"

"Her own free will?" Ian snarled. "Or the free will of Jinty or Selma? God cannot possibly judge her for whatever she's done when she doesn't have control of her own mind."

"I don't think it's God's judgments we have to be concerned about," Wren said.

Ian sighed. "No, of course not."

"Ian," Wren said, "it's possible that if she's been going out at night that . . . that someone has hurt her. That this did *not* happen with her approval." Ian looked hard at Wren and felt sick to his stomach at the very idea. From Wren's expression he knew she felt the same. "What if . . ."

He finished for her. "Her coming home with that bloody knife was the result of trying to protect herself from such a thing happening again." He snapped to his feet and began to pace. "Which means . . . there is a man out there who might be wounded *and* guilty of hurting Bethia."

"And what are we to do about that?" Wren asked. "We can hardly report such a crime to the constable without alerting him to Bethia's illness and creating the very problem we are trying to avoid." Wren sighed and hung her head. "I don't know how I could have missed it. She's not been ill. She takes care of herself enough that I wouldn't have noticed a change in her cycles, but still . . . I'm her sister. I'm with her every day. How could I not have known?"

"Either she didn't want you to know," Ian said, "or she doesn't even realize what's changed in her. Perhaps she's completely blocked from her mind what happened to cause this." Ian shook his head and let out a burdened sigh.

"I needed ye t' see the evidence while she was sleeping, but now ye need t' sleep yerself."

Ian didn't argue. He removed the dressing gown and crawled back into bed. Wren extinguished the lamp and did the same, snuggling close to his back. "Forgive me," she said.

"For what?" he asked, turning toward her even though he couldn't see her face.

"Taking care of Bethia has not been easy for ye."

"If you think I might be regretting our marriage, you're wrong. I'll do whatever it takes to care for Bethia, so long as I have you in the bargain."

He wrapped her in his arms and tried to relax while his mind swam with recent events that seemed more out of a novel than something unfolding in his own life. He finally slept with the security of knowing that in spite of all else, they were safe within the walls of Brierley, surrounded by family who would help them through whatever might come.

* * * * *

Over the next week, Bethia settled well into the new routine of living at Brierley. She took to wandering the halls at night, and likely going down to the cellar. But she was always found sleeping in her bed in the morning, and she'd had no fits or outbursts. She'd taken to interacting a little with a couple of the maids, and she'd even come down to share a meal with the family a few times.

Ian was glad to be back at Brierley, even though there were aspects of the simple life he'd lived in town that he missed. It was nice to be with his family, especially since they all had enough space to spread out and not get in each other's way—or on each other's nerves. Wren quickly meshed herself into the household as if she'd lived there all along. He saw evidence of her thriving on her interaction with Lilias and his mother, and the family's kindness toward her and Bethia quickly strengthened bonds that had been growing since their marriage.

Neither Ian nor Wren said a word to anyone about Bethia's pregnancy, but they both knew it had to be revealed soon. Bethia's figure would certainly give it away before long. She was obviously farther along than Wren, and not as far along as Lilias, but it was impossible to know for certain when the baby would come. It seemed they had no choice but to accept that a baby was coming, and Wren and Ian would simply have to do what was necessary to care for the child, even though it would not be much older than their own.

Ian was about to get undressed for bed when a frantic knock sounded at the door. He pulled it open with Wren standing at his shoulder.

"Bethia!" Wren said when she saw her sister there, holding a lamp in one hand; her panic was evident. "Whatever is wrong?"

Bethia grabbed Ian's arm. "Ye must come, Ian; ye must. Ye must come right now. Right now." She dragged him out of the room and down the hall, and Wren followed, demanding to know what was wrong. But Bethia just kept walking, insisting that she needed Ian, repeating over and over that she needed him to come with her. They went down the back staircase, past the kitchens, and down more stairs into a storage cellar that was long unused. For all of their knowing that Bethia wandered freely through such areas of the house, Ian was still stunned by her avid fascination with cellars—in this case, the darkest, dampest one. He took the lamp from Bethia and held it high to try to see his way, but it was still challenging. He could feel Wren holding on to the back of his coat, and Bethia was still clinging to his arm.

"Tell me what this is about, Bethia," he said in a firm, directive tone that he hoped would hurry them along with this adventure.

"Greer needs ye," she said and started to cry. "I've been trying t' tell him that he needed ye a long time ago, but he wouldn't listen. He didn't want ye t' know his secrets." She cried harder as they pressed on down the stairs. "I didn't mean t' hurt him . . . that night . . . that night . . . Jinty was so angry and . . . she thought that Greer would hurt her. I tried t' tell her that he never would, but she wouldn't listen." Bethia's words became barely discernible through her sobbing. "Jinty told me t' hurt Greer before he hurt me. I didn't want t' do it. I didn't mean t' do it. But now he's so sick. So sick. So sick. I told him he needed ye a long time ago . . . before we came back t' Brierley . . . he needed ye . . . before we came back. But he wouldn't listen. Now, I'm so scared, Ian; I'm so scared. I can't lose him again. I can't. I can't."

"I'll do everything I can to help," Ian said, entirely unruffled by Bethia's outburst, but not certain how he might convince her that he was unable to help a man who was already dead.

At the bottom of the stairs, they turned two corners and entered a room that was empty and dark, except for what appeared to be some blankets rolled up in one corner, and some dirty dishes and a flask on the floor nearby. Ian held the lamp high as Bethia rushed to the mound of blankets, calling out Greer's name. Ian's breath took a long pause on its way out of his throat when the mound moved and groaned.

"What in the world . . ." Wren muttered. Ian couldn't begin to put a logical explanation to Bethia hiding a *real* person in such a place as this. He wondered if his sister-in-law was guilty of kidnapping. But if someone had gone missing, surely they would have heard about it. Had Bethia truly hurt someone as she'd been claiming? He felt nauseous at the thought, but determined to rectify the problem.

The human form on the floor rolled over and one word came gruffly out of his mouth. "Ian."

Ian set the lamp carefully on the floor, his mind frantically working through the possibilities of who this might be, why he knew Ian, why the voice sounded vaguely familiar. And *why* Bethia had taken on the delusion that this person was her husband. She was kneeling beside him, calling him Greer, cooing with worry over his illness. Wren apparently put the pieces together before Ian did. His heart began to thud when she muttered, "Dear Lord of heaven and earth, save us all." She dropped to her knees, breathing sharply. Ian took a step closer, and the air was strangled out of his lungs at the same moment his heart started pounding hard enough that he feared it would kill him. Unlike Wren, he couldn't get a word out of his mouth; not a single sound or syllable. He stumbled backward as if he'd been struck and found a cold wall behind him that he clung to in order to remain standing. He stood there suffocated by shock and keenly aware of his own pulse. Seconds ticked in his mind, each one recounting an unanswered question, each one attempting to piece together information and give this moment any kind of sense or logic.

Wren scrambled across the floor, startling Ian to his senses and the need to address the moment and ignore the questions. And one word finally wormed its way through his constricted throat and into the open. *"Greer,"* he muttered and scrambled to his knees, next to Wren, who was checking his face for fever. The little astonished noise that came out of her mouth indicated that she'd found him excessively warm.

Ian leaned over his friend and made firm eye contact, as if that might confirm the reality. Greer, long believed dead, was here, real, alive—and very, very ill. "Greer," Ian said again. "How . . . why . . ." They were the only words he could get out. He saw tears gather in Greer's eyes, but he was as incapable of answering a question as Ian was of asking one.

"We've got to get you out of here and get you some help," Ian muttered, finding motivation in doing something that needed to be done. With a strength beyond what he knew he possessed, Ian scooped Greer into his arms and carried him toward the stairs. Wren went just ahead with the lamp, too stunned to make a sound. Bethia came behind, crying like a child.

"You . . . mustn't tell . . . anyone . . ." Greer mumbled.

Anger rushed in to smother Ian's shock. "I'm in no mood to hear about your secrets . . . whatever they may be. You need help." He found it difficult to breathe as he carried a grown man—more husky than himself—up a long flight of stairs. "We'll talk about this later," he managed to say through the burning in his lungs. Having survived the ascent, Ian set his burden carefully on the floor of the hallway and knelt beside him, gasping for breath and willing the ache in his arms and legs to settle. He breathlessly said to Wren, "Find my parents . . . my brother . . . either, both." And to Bethia, "You stay here with me . . . and try to stay quiet."

Bethia nodded and put a hand over her mouth, her eyes filling with terror as she knelt beside her ailing husband. Ian hung his head and squeezed his eyes closed, wishing this might be a dream. A freakishly bizarre and frightful dream.

Ian's breathing settled while he took in Greer's pallor and the evidence of his pain. Since Greer's delirium made him barely aware of his surroundings, Ian looked hard at Bethia. "What happened? I need you to tell me, Bethia. I can't help him if you don't tell me. Do you understand?"

She nodded and whimpered behind her hand, still heeding his order to remain quiet. Ian added firmly, "Please try to be calm, Bethia, and tell me what happened."

Bethia started repeating things that she'd said before, but Ian listened, realizing now that her references to Greer had been real. He was glad to know that Jinty and Selma were *not* real. "I tried . . . I tried t' tell him he needed ye . . . a long time ago. But he wouldn't listen, Ian. He wouldn't listen. He didn't want ye t' know his secrets, and—"

"We'll worry about the secrets later," Ian said, wondering what could *possibly* constitute such an appalling and complex web of lies and deceit. "I need to know what happened to him."

"That night," Bethia said. "That night. Jinty was so angry and . . . she believed Greer would hurt her. I told her he never would, but she wouldn't listen. It was Jinty who told me t' hurt him. I didn't want t' do it. I didn't mean t' do it. But now he's so sick. So sick. I told him he needed ye . . . before we came back t' Brierley."

"How exactly did you hurt him, Bethia? I understand that you didn't mean to do it, but I need to know how you hurt him."

Bethia pushed Greer's shirt aside to reveal a festering wound in his shoulder that also explained the wretched smell Ian hadn't thought about until then. "Heaven be merciful!" Ian muttered, certain his discovery that Greer was living would only precede his actual death. He couldn't imagine how such an infection could ever be reversed. The night Bethia had come home with blood on her hands made sense now. But more than three years of believing Greer was dead certainly didn't.

Ian looked up and was both surprised and alarmed to see his father hurrying up the hall with Wren near his side and his mother coming behind. Gavin stopped breathlessly beside them and looked down. "It's true. I can't believe it."

"Exactly," Ian said. "I don't know what to do."

Anya arrived to stand beside her husband and gasped. Gavin miraculously gained control of his breathing faster than he had in weeks.

"Apparently there must be an important reason he wants everyone to believe he's dead," Ian said, "but the wound is . . . very bad." He looked up at his father. "Tell me what to do."

"We must get a doctor," Gavin said.

Anya added, "His life is more important than anything else."

"We will contend with the rest later," Gavin added. "Your mother is right. We can trust Dr. Craig." He turned to his wife. "Have the doctor sent for, and get Donnan to help Ian move Greer up to Bethia's room. As far as the servants know, it's she who is ill."

Ian liked that plan, but he said, "There's no need to disturb Donnan. I can manage."

"I wish I had the strength to help," Gavin said, holding the lamp to lead the way as Ian exerted all his strength to move Greer upstairs and into Bethia's bed. And thankfully they didn't pass any servants on the way.

"I'll get some water," Wren said to her sister, "and some clean linens. Ye must get him clean, Bethia, before the doctor comes. Do ye understand?" Bethia nodded. Gavin left with Wren to help her. Ian helped Bethia get Greer out of clothes he'd obviously been wearing for many days. Nothing was said between them, but she could hardly stop crying for a moment. Ian's thoughts swung like a pendulum between shock and anger. He was angry with Bethia, even though he knew she had no control of the limitations of her mind. He was angry with Greer for keeping his existence concealed all this time. All of the grief and anguish Ian had experienced made it difficult to keep from shouting at him, here and now. But Greer was barely conscious and nearly dead—an irony Ian could scarcely consider.

Wren and Gavin returned, and Ian was glad for Wren's suggestion that she take Bethia elsewhere until after the doctor had come and gone. With the women out of the room, the men rolled up their sleeves and worked together to bathe Greer with tepid water, not only to clean him but to hopefully lower the fever.

"Are you all right, son?" Gavin asked while they worked together with controlled efficiency. And again Ian noticed that his father was doing unusually well. A miracle, no doubt. Ian needed his father's strength and assistance right now.

"No, I'm not all right," Ian said. "I can*not* believe this is happening. I cannot even *fathom* how this is happening. And if he dies now . . ." Ian couldn't finish.

When their task was finished and Greer was covered with a clean sheet, Gavin put a hand on Ian's arm. "It's just not right to have to grieve *twice* for someone you love."

"No, it's *not* right," Ian said. "It is grossly horrifying and unfair. If he weren't so ill, I would . . . I would . . ."

"What?" Gavin asked with compassion.

"I would give him a bloody lip," Ian snarled, then he staggered into a chair, consumed with shock and grief. Gavin just sat beside him, offering silent support while they waited for the doctor.

Gavin rose to answer a knock at the door, and Ian did his best to appear composed. Anya stepped into the room to report that the doctor had been sent for, but in the meantime she was going to put a poultice on the wound; she'd learned how to make one in her youth. She declared that she'd seen it work before in drawing out infection, and with any luck it would make at least a bit of difference.

With the poultice in place, all they could do was wait for the doctor. Ian wanted to speak to Greer, he wanted answers to the innumerable questions swimming in his head. But his friend was delirious with pain and fever, barely aware of his surroundings—if at all.

Ian interrupted the grueling minutes of silence. "Is Donnan . . ."

"He'd already gone to bed," Anya said. "You can talk to him in the morning."

"It's really not necessary for both of you to sit here with me," Ian added. "I can—"

"We'll at least stay until the doctor comes," Gavin said.

Ian nodded, and they settled into more silence—haunting, unspeakable silence.

* * * * *

Wren guided her sister into her own bedroom and closed the door. They sat close together on a little sofa. She resisted the urge to badger Bethia with questions, fearing she would upset her to the point of never being able to conceal her outburst from the servants. Bethia's crying gradually subsided into a shocked silence, until she spoke without warning.

"Greer has been living in our cellar," Bethia said, her eyes glazed and distant.

"So it would seem," Wren said, fighting to keep her voice steady and conceal her anger at being deceived so thoroughly. "I understand that he asked ye t' keep his being there a secret, sister, but ye should have trusted me. I would never do anything t' hurt ye, or t' hurt Greer. But he's very sick now. Do ye understand? He's very, very sick."

"I understand," Bethia said and whimpered. "Is he going t' die?"

"I don't know," Wren said. "But it's very bad."

Bethia collapsed into sobs once again and buried her face in her sister's lap. Through her tears she muttered over and over, "I'm so sorry. I'm so, so sorry."

Wren's compassion for her sister softened her own anger, but in lieu of anger she was overcome with her own tears. Never would she have imagined such tragedy! And she had devoted a great deal of effort to imagining the problems that might be caused as a result of her sister's illness and Greer's death—his *supposed* death, she now realized. How could it be? How could this have possibly gone on so long with no one being the wiser? And what would happen now? She couldn't even begin to imagine how this might affect their lives from this day forward.

* * * * *

Ian hovered anxiously at the edge of the room in the shadows absent of the reaching glow of the lamps burning on either side of the bed where Greer lay while the doctor checked his symptoms and surveyed the wound. His examination was surprisingly brief, and his conclusion grim. "I'm sorry," he said as if Greer were already dead. *An atrocious irony,* Ian thought, not for the first time in the last hour. "The wound is gangrenous, and it's already spreading. His fever, his breathing, the heart rate . . . are all evidence that the infection has overtaken him. There's nothing to be done now but give him high doses of laudanum to ease the pain so that he can go peacefully." The doctor glanced toward Greer once more, shook his head, and sighed. "If it had been caught sooner . . . if the wound had been properly cleaned . . . it might have been avoided. It's tragic." He offered a compassionate gaze toward Ian's parents, who were standing close together. "Again, I'm sorry."

Ian didn't hear the rest of the conversation, and he was barely aware of the doctor being escorted out of the room. Alone with the dying ghost of his friend, he moved with trepidation toward the bed, as if he might see evidence to convince him that this was not real. If he couldn't even grasp the actuality that Greer was alive, how could he accept that he was dying? Ian knew that Wren and Bethia needed to be found and informed of the doctor's report. He knew that Bethia needed to be with her husband. But Greer had been an integral part of Ian's life for *most* of his life. He needed some time alone with his friend. He wished that Greer was conscious enough to carry on some semblance of a conversation. He needed answers! He needed to know why this ridiculous ruse had been necessary! Ian glanced at the bottle of laudanum on the bedside table, and knew that the doctor hadn't actually given any to Greer. Maybe, just maybe, before the pain became too much for him, before it became necessary to keep him in a drugged state, Ian might at least be able to get something out of him, some kind of explanation, some reason to find peace over this dire mockery.

Ian sat on the edge of the bed and took tight hold of Greer's hand. Greer groaned and shifted. Ian recalled the way Greer had spoken his name, how tears had shown in his eyes before the strain of being moved had pushed him deeper into delirium. Ian reached inside himself with his strongest hope and his deepest faith. He knew he couldn't expect miracle enough for Greer's life to be saved, but he needed the miracle of a conversation before Greer left him *again.* "Please God," Ian muttered, figuring if God were truly God, He would know Ian's thoughts enough to know what he was pleading for.

Ian was still there praying when he felt a hand on his shoulder and looked up to see his father. "I've sent your mother to bed. I told Wren what the doctor said. She said that Bethia is asleep and she will stay with her. I told her to try to get some sleep. We agreed that you likely needed some time alone with Greer."

"I do, yes," Ian said, grateful beyond words for his father's calm insight. "Thank you," was all he could manage to say.

"Is there anything else you need?" Gavin asked.

"No," Ian muttered. "Get some rest."

"I'm not far if you need me," Gavin added.

"I . . . know. Thank you. I . . . I'll get you . . . if I need you."

"If he comes around and he's in pain, give him a spoonful of that stuff the doctor left." Ian glanced again at the bottle, and the spoon and glass of water beside it that his father must have put there before Ian realized he was in the room.

"I will," Ian said. Gavin squeezed his shoulder once again and left the room.

Ian was grateful for the time alone with Greer, knowing that everyone else who was aware of the situation was either asleep or in bed attempting to sleep. He slid to his knees beside the bed and prayed more fervently, still keeping Greer's hand in his. Greer's delirium had slipped into what appeared to be a complete loss of consciousness. He seemed to be sleeping; if not for the labored rise and fall of his chest, he would have looked already dead. *Already dead.* The irony once again rushed into Ian's thoughts and strangled his breath. His prayers became audible as his pleading became more acute. A subtle calm settled over him slowly with the idea that he needed to speak to Greer, regardless of any response from him—or lack of it. Almost unconsciously the words began spilling out of Ian's mouth. He spoke with composure at first, quietly expressing his shock at the realization that Greer had been alive all this time, and his need to understand why he would keep such a secret from his dearest and closest friend. Ian's composure was swallowed by anger before he even realized he was spewing words that expressed all Ian had suffered in regard to Greer's supposed death. He had to get up and pace by the side of the bed to aid in releasing the sheer volume of his erupting emotions. He forced himself to calm down enough to return to the edge of the bed, where he sat with Greer's hand in his, repeating phrases he'd already spoken multiple times.

"I don't know how to face this, Greer; I don't know what to make of it. I don't understand why . . . why you would do this to me . . . to Bethia."

Ian held his breath as Greer's deathlike state eased into a writhing delirium indicative of his pain. He wanted to give him the medicine but didn't know how to do it unless Greer was conscious enough to be somewhat cooperative. He prayed silently while he said Greer's name, over and over, trying to reach him as if through a fog in which he was lost and being consumed by unseen beasts of prey. When Greer's eyes shifted and focused on Ian, he actually sobbed with a tearless relief.

"Are you with me, my friend?" Ian asked.

"Aye," Greer muttered in a huskiness that was barely audible. "The pain . . ."

"The doctor left something. Will you let me help you take some?"

"Aye," Greer said again with desperate eagerness.

Ian gave Greer a spoonful of the bitter liquid, followed by a few swallows of water. He gently laid Greer's head back on the pillow, knowing that the medicine would soon take its effect, and this might be the very final opportunity for any exchange between them. In that moment his anger and grief were replaced by a tiny sense of gratitude. How often was it possible to speak to a friend after long believing him to be dead? He only wished it could be under any other circumstances.

Mindful of the urgency of seconds ticking away, Ian leaned close to Greer and said, "Why didn't you tell me . . . that you were alive . . . all this time? Why?"

"How could I," Greer rasped, "when ye were gone?"

Ian's heart constricted with new pain. Had it truly been Greer's intention to make himself known to Ian? He felt a subtle squeeze from Greer's hand.

"Forgive me, my friend. Forgive me."

"Of course," Ian said, not willing to cast any stones in light of his own many mistakes. "I just . . . want to understand." He saw Greer's eyelids growing heavy again. "Why, Greer?"

"Bethia . . . understands," Greer said, and Ian wanted to protest. Even if Bethia *did* understand, getting her to tell all she knew with any amount of lucidity could be nigh to impossible. Greer forced his eyes open somewhat, as if there was something he felt the need to say. Ian hoped that it would offer more explanation. "This is . . . the end for me."

Ian wanted to protest. He wanted to offer some hope, to tell him to hang on and to fight this infection. But the doctor's words had not left any room for doubt or question. Ian could only say, "It appears that way."

Greer closed his eyes. "It's not . . . so hard to die . . . when I've been dead . . . for years now."

"Hard for whom?" Ian rumbled.

"I had no choice," Greer said, his eyes closed. "No choice." He relaxed more fully, and his voice softened to a whisper. "God forgive me."

Chapter Thirteen
An Extraordinary Quandary

Greer didn't come close to coherency again through the remainder of the night. Ian dozed off and on while he stayed near enough to be aware of his friend's every sound and movement. When morning came, Bethia burst into the room full of anxiety, immediately going to her husband's side, begging him in his unconsciousness not to leave her. Ian stood looking helplessly on the pathetic scene. Then his own unbearable heartache was soothed when he looked up to see Wren enter the room. She said nothing, but there was no need for words. Her expressive eyes and loving countenance let him know that she perfectly understood every niche of his sorrow. She crossed the room and wrapped him tightly in her familiar embrace. She settled her head against his chest, and he knew she was weeping. He held her as close as humanly possible and allowed tears to bathe his face and relieve him of some small amount of his confusion and aching.

Wren looked up at his face as if it might help her better understand how he was feeling, or perhaps to silently offer a more abundant outpouring of her love. Most likely both. She wiped at his tears, then glanced toward Greer, who was hovering on the threshold of death, with Bethia crying like a child beside him.

"It's impossible t' believe," Wren said.

"Indeed it is," Ian replied.

"Bethia told me he's been living in the cellar of the house all this time. I can't imagine all the times he must have sneaked in and out of the kitchen door, and not one of us had an inkling of what was going on." She looked up at Ian again. "Are ye well, my darling?"

"I don't know what I am. Astonished. Angry. Terrified . . . of losing him *again.* And I don't know how we're going to handle this. When the world believes he's already dead . . . what do we do?"

Wren couldn't answer. She just tightened her embrace and basked in the comfort and strength her husband offered in return.

Greer died again that afternoon, with Bethia lying on the bed beside him, and Ian and Wren sitting next to the opposite side of the bed. Ian felt Greer's hand start to go cold before he could bring himself to let go. He left Wren to try to comfort her sister and went in search of his parents. He found them in his mother's sitting room; Donnan was with them. The somber quiet of the room implied that they were all keenly aware of the tragedy at hand. He didn't have to wonder if his parents had informed Donnan of the situation. He'd clearly not wanted to intrude upon Bethia's privacy—or his own—but his expression declared his compassion for Ian the moment their eyes met. Ian then looked at each of his parents as he announced, "It's over. He's gone." He sunk onto a sofa, utterly depleted by grief and exhaustion. He pressed his hands brutally into his hair. "At least he's not suffering. At least the secrecy and the hiding are over for him."

"Were you able to speak to him?" Donnan asked. "Do you have any idea why—"

"No," Ian said. "He asked my forgiveness; he told me he'd had no choice. I have to assume it's for the same reasons that we believed he was dead; that it had something to do with his gambling. He told me that Bethia knew everything. Whether or not she is willing or capable of explaining remains to be seen."

"Are you going to be all right, son?" Gavin asked.

Ian sighed and rubbed a hand over his face. "I'm sure I will be . . . eventually. Right now, I . . ." He couldn't finish. He shook his head, attempting to think coherently. "I don't know what to do. How do we give him a proper burial without revealing that he's been alive all this time? And if he's been alive, who died in that fire? I fear this will put the townspeople in an uproar and only make everything in regard to Bethia more complicated . . . more difficult." Only silence followed the admission of his dilemma. "I'm open to suggestions," he added. "Do we just . . . sneak the body out in the dead of night like a bunch of vagabonds and bury it in the forest?"

"I think that's exactly what we will do," Gavin said. "The household believes Bethia is ill; even Lilias was told nothing more. She's visiting a friend in town today. I explained the situation to Dr. Craig. I'm absolutely certain he will not betray my confidence. We've been friends for years."

"I agree," Donnan said to his father, "so long as you only come along for moral support and allow us to do the work. You've been feeling better and we don't want to have you doing anything that will change that."

Ian took all of this in, grateful that his father and brother could actually think. He had to admit it was the most logical and least complicated solution. But it all just felt so awful. He had to say, "I'm sorry to have dragged all of you into this."

"We're family," Anya said. "There is no need to apologize, I assure you."

"And why should you apologize when you've done nothing wrong?" Donnan said.

"Your brother is right," Gavin said. "You're just doing your best to take care of your family, and your family is our family."

Warmth tingled in Ian's chest in response to such perfect and absolute love and support. The feeling enticed the full extent of his grief to the surface and he hung his head. A moment later his parents were sitting on either side of him. Anya guided his head to her shoulder, and Gavin put a hand on his back. He was overcome with gratitude for his family. He knew they loved him, and he wondered how he had ever believed he could manage without them.

* * * * *

Bethia became so upset by Greer's *actual* death that Anya suggested they give her a dose of the medicine the doctor had left for Greer. Wren got her to agree to take it with the promise that she could rest. Bethia fell into a deep sleep, which aided the family's story that Bethia was ill. Ian was able to take a nap, surprised that he was able to sleep, but glad to get some rest when he knew he would be digging a grave that night.

For the sake of appearances with the household staff, every member of the family did well at behaving as if everything was normal, except for a mild concern for Bethia. Even Lilias remained ignorant of the situation when she returned from town. Wren stayed with her sister, and someone in the family took meals to the room and took dishes out so that none of the servants would see that Bethia was actually sleeping in the same bed as her dead husband. Bethia came around in the evening, and Wren managed to keep her distracted enough to see that she ate some supper. Then she succumbed to grief all over again, and Wren resorted to the laudanum once more.

With Bethia in a medicated sleep, and Wren staying near her, Ian and his brother worked together to discreetly remove Greer's body from the house and put it into a wagon that Gavin had harnessed and moved near a rarely used side door. They went quietly and without light into the forest. Once far enough from the house to escape notice, they lit lanterns, and Ian and Donnan set to work digging an adequate grave. They lowered Greer's body into the hole, and the three men shared a prayer and some kind words over the grave. Ian felt eerily disturbed over having done this once before—although Greer's previous burial had been more formal and public. Gavin commented that only God knew for certain who was in the grave with Greer's stone marker over it, but he felt certain that God would work it all out in the life after this one. Ian felt some comfort in his own belief of life after death, but being left behind in this one was difficult at such moments.

The grave was filled in, packed down, and covered with leaves and pine needles in an attempt to make the ground appear undisturbed. They used pine branches to brush away their footsteps, and even to cover the wagon tracks until they were far enough away from the grave site that it didn't matter. Once back at the house, the three men got the wagon quietly back into its place and cared for the horses, eliminating any signs that they'd been used in the night. The men all returned quietly to their rooms to clean up and try to get some sleep. Donnan felt confident that Lilias would have slept soundly through his absence, since he was occasionally restless and left the room to read in the night without her noticing. Ian hated all the sneaking around. He was glad to have it over. Now he just had to contend with all that had been going on for years without his awareness, and how to accept and come to terms with the tragic results.

When Ian climbed into bed, he was grateful to find Wren awake. She turned toward him and eased him fully into her arms.

"It's done?" she asked.

"Yes, it's done." He hated the way he felt like some kind of criminal, burying a body in the forest in the dead of night. "Is Bethia all right?"

"I checked on her just a bit ago and she was sleeping well, but I can hardly get her t' stay calm without that tonic. I do hope she can get beyond this."

"As do I."

"And I hope ye can get beyond it as well," she said.

"We can only hope," he said and tightened his hold on her. His tears came without warning, but he didn't cry long before exhaustion lured him to sleep, knowing that he had to face another day of attempting to behave as if his friend had died nearly three years earlier, and not the previous day.

* * * * *

Wren woke Ian and told him that Bethia was starting to stir and she needed him to be with them when her sister came fully awake. She knew they shouldn't keep relying on the medicine to keep her calm. And she also knew that Ian was hoping to get some answers from Bethia, on the chance that she might actually have a lucid moment and be able to fully comprehend all that had happened and why.

Ian hurried to get dressed and found Wren sitting on the edge of Bethia's bed. He made brief eye contact with Bethia and took a seat on the far side of the room. Bethia came fully awake and said to Wren, "Is it real, sister? Is he really gone?"

"He really is," Wren said, "but I need t' speak with ye, and I need ye t' try t' stay composed so that we don't cause any more trouble for Ian or his family. Do ye understand?"

Bethia nodded with tears in her eyes, but she was managing to remain composed.

"Are Jinty and Selma here?" Wren asked, and Ian knew that the absence of Bethia's imaginary companions was always an indication of her being closer to what was real and normal in her mind.

"No," Bethia said. "They're hiding in the cellar. They're afraid of what will happen to them, now that . . . now that . . . Greer is . . ." Bethia bit her lip, fighting visibly to remain composed. Ian felt touched by Bethia's sincere desire not to let her sister down—or him. She had a good heart, and the state of her mind was eerily tragic in contrast.

"We will talk about Jinty and Selma later," Wren said. "I'm glad they're not here right now, because I want t' speak t' ye in confidence. Ye need t' let me know if they come, so that I won't say anything t' upset them."

"I'll tell ye," Bethia said with a firm nod.

"I need t' ask ye some questions, Bethia; questions about Greer. I need ye t' do yer best t' stay calm and answer them. I know how very sad ye are, and ye have a right t' be. There'll be time for crying all ye need, but right now I need t' ask ye some questions. Is that all right with ye?"

Again Bethia nodded with firm resolve, and Wren forged ahead. "When we all believed Greer t' be dead . . . ye knew he was alive?" Bethia nodded. "Did ye know right away?"

"It was a few days . . . after the funeral. At first," her voice broke, "I did not believe he was real. I kept telling him that . . . my mind was playing tricks on me, but . . . he wasn't the same as Jinty and Selma."

"He asked ye t' keep him hidden?" Wren asked. Bethia nodded again. Ian was amazed at her lucidity and felt certain that hours of sincere prayer were being answered. Greer had said that Bethia understood; there was nowhere else to go for answers. Perhaps God, in His mercy, was giving them an opportunity for the understanding they needed to go forward; him especially. No one had suffered more over Greer's death than he had. Until Greer had turned up alive again, he would have said that Bethia had suffered most. Now he knew that Greer had been keeping her company and keeping her happy.

Wren leaned closer to Bethia and put a comforting hand on her arm. "Bethia . . . we need ye t' help us know why; why did he want ye t' keep him hidden? Why did he want people t' believe he was dead?"

"It was those terrible men," Bethia said. "Greer owed them so much money. He knew the gambling was wrong. He was trying t' stop. But they were such terrible men. He knew they would come after him. He was afraid they would kill him. When the fight broke out and the fire started, he thought he would not survive. But then he did. He got out alive, and he hid in the woods thinking those men would come after him. Then he realized that everyone believed he was dead, and he thought it was the best way t' make those men forget about him." Bethia turned to look at Ian and repeated what Greer had said, what disturbed him most of all. "He'd intended t' tell ye, Ian. But by the time he'd gotten up the courage, ye'd left. And he felt it was best that Pa and Wren not know; he feared he might put them in danger. For me, it was different." She looked down with mild shame. "He knew my mind better than even I did, it seems. And he knew that even Wren and Pa wouldn't think too much of my talking about him. I knew he didn't want me t' talk about him to anyone, but sometimes Selma told me I should tell Wren. I did tell Wren, but she . . . she believed he was like Jinty and Selma. But he wasn't." She looked at Wren. "He wasn't dead." New tears came to Bethia's eyes. "But he's dead now. Now he's gone, and he's not coming back."

"I'm afraid that's true, my darling," Wren said. "And ye must understand that no one but us—and Ian's parents and brother—know that he wasn't dead all along. We mustn't talk about it t' anyone. Their suspicions and misunderstandings could cause a great deal of trouble for us. Do ye understand, Bethia?"

"I understand," she said, then a flood of tears rushed out of her. She wrapped her arms around herself and began rocking back and forth, but it wasn't in the stupor of insanity that Ian had sometimes seen. This was raw, simple grief. The kind of grief he'd felt when James had died, and Greer—both times. Wren wrapped her arms around her sister and allowed her to grieve, overcome with her own tears. Ian watched the women, and his own grief consumed him. He couldn't believe it! How could this have happened? What had gone wrong? And worst of all was the raw, gnawing question that haunted him: What could he have done to prevent this? What had he missed? Shouldn't he have figured it out? Shouldn't he have known that Greer was still alive? Or, as Greer had implied, if Ian hadn't run off like a coward he would have been here to be a friend to Greer when he'd needed one. He tried to tell himself that he'd believed Greer was dead. Why would he have believed otherwise when there had been a funeral and a burial? His logic told him he could have done no differently, but the heart of him refused to believe it. He wanted to leave the room so that he could be alone with his grief and regret. But his desire to get up and leave was outweighed by his inability to move.

Ian was glad to still be there when Bethia looked up at her sister, visibly forcing composure as if there was something she needed to say. "Everyone believes that Greer is dead," she said.

"That's right," Wren agreed.

"Then how will we explain . . . the baby?" Bethia said it as if she expected them to both already know, as if some part of her believed she'd told them and they were fully aware of the situaion. Ian was glad now that Wren had already figured it out, which kept this moment from getting lost in a shocked response from Wren and Ian that likely would have catapulted Bethia back into the furthest caverns of her lunacy.

"I don't know, sister," Wren said with her usual serenity and compassion. Ian didn't know how she could do it when he was barely holding himself together. At least now they knew *why* Bethia was pregnant, and he was glad to know that no one had hurt her. But this was *Greer's* baby. Beyond everyone believing that the child was illegitimate, how would they explain its likely resemblance to a man who had been dead more than three years? Thankfully they had some time before the baby came in order to make some decisions about the best way to proceed, but there was no easy solution. He still hadn't informed his family of Bethia's pregnancy. There had been far too many other issues to contend with.

"We will take care of you, Bethia," Wren said gently. "You and the baby. There's no need to worry. Ian has promised to do whatever is necessary to take care of us."

Bethia looked in his direction, silently asking for his assurance that this was true. "I will do everything in my power, Bethia, to keep you and the baby safe. I promise you." He was proud of himself for the steady voice with which he'd spoken. Bethia seemed assured and put her head on her sister's shoulder. Ian hurried into his own room and closed the door, unable to hold back his grief any longer, unable to sit there with the evidence of Bethia's situation, and Bethia's mourning. He knew that Wren was mourning too, but she always put her sister first. He wondered how she could possibly be holding herself together in light of all that had happened, and all the uncertainty of their future. He concluded that Wren was a stronger person than he was. And yet she often looked to him for strength, for protection, for comfort. They needed each other, and together they needed to care for Bethia. He could only hope that their combined strength would be sufficient.

* * * * *

Once Ian was able to come to his senses and get cleaned up, he checked on the women to find Bethia busily sewing, which he knew had a calming effect on her. It seemed to keep her from thinking, or perhaps from indulging in the strangeness that her mind forced upon her so much of the time. Wren was also sewing, but with less intensity, and less enthusiasm. Ian bent to kiss her and saw her eyes brighten, but not even a hint of a smile had the strength to come through the clouds in her countenance.

"It's almost time for breakfast," Ian said. "I could have breakfast brought here for the three of us, and—"

"No, no," she said. "Ye should see yer family. We'll be fine. The maids have been so kind."

"Perhaps we should leave one of the maids to look after Bethia so you can get out of this room. She's taken well to Shona, has she not?"

"Yes, I do believe Shona has a tender spot for Bethia, but . . ." Wren forced that smile through the clouds, but it lacked conviction. "Perhaps when Bethia's grief is not so new and she's more settled, that will be a possibility. For now, I should be with her."

"I understand, Wren, but you've got to take care of yourself if you're going to be strong enough to care for your sister. And she is not the only one who is pregnant. After I have breakfast with my family, I'm going to sit with Bethia so that you can get some fresh air and then lie down."

Wren sighed, and her smile was a *little* more convincing. "Thank ye, Ian. Ye're very good to me." She took his hand. "If I need fresh air or a nap, I'll tell ye. I promise." She kissed him again. "Now go. Behave as if everything is normal, and perhaps it will become so."

"If only that could be true," Ian said with light sarcasm.

He took a step toward the door, and Wren said, "And perhaps ye should be talking t' yer parents about Bethia's condition. Perhaps . . ." She looked down with hesitation, then looked up at him again with darker clouds in her eyes. "Perhaps . . . it would be best . . . as ye brought up before, that we . . . leave here, and . . . find a new life for ourselves . . . . somewhere else; a place where people don't know . . ."

Ian returned to her side and went to his knees beside her, assuring himself with a glance toward Bethia that she was apparently oblivious.

And whether or not she overheard—or cared about what they were saying—was irrelevant. The matter involved her as much as it did them.

"If it comes to that, we'll do whatever is necessary. But we need to give the matter some time . . . we need to see what happens. Perhaps it *won't* become necessary." Ian recalled his own feelings about leaving here—those he had struggled with throughout his life, and the more recent impression he'd had that had stayed with him strongly—and he found it ironic that he was trying to convince his wife that perhaps there was no need to leave, that perhaps it would all work out. A thought occurred to him that made sense and was worth sharing. "If we do leave here, Wren, we need to know that we did everything we possibly could to stay. We might face new and different challenges as a result of leaving the security of Brierley. When those challenges arise, we need to know there was no other way. Do you understand?"

"I do," she said, and her voice quavered. "I don't want t' leave, Ian. I feel . . . safe here. I feel . . . comfortable. But I don't want t' bring hardship upon yer family. They've always been so good t' us, and . . ."

"I know," he said. "I feel the same. I will speak with my parents after breakfast. They're very wise; they'll help us know what to do."

Wren nodded, and he kissed her again. Her smile, however faint, was more genuine this time. He rose to his feet and rubbed a gentle hand over the back of Bethia's head. She stopped stitching for just a moment, as some kind of acknowledgment of his expression of care and concern for her. Then she returned to her stitching, and Ian left the room.

Breakfast was surprisingly normal, and Ian realized that he came from a family of very good actors. There was no indication that the three men sitting at the table had been out in the night secretly digging a grave to bury a body. When the meal was finished, Ian looked toward his parents and said, "May I speak with the two of you . . . privately, if you will?"

"Of course," Gavin said, and a few minutes later Ian was seated in the study, facing their concerned expressions.

"Is Bethia all right?" Anya asked. "And Wren?"

"Wren is holding up," Ian said. "But I worry about her. She's a strong woman, but perhaps not as strong as she would like to think she is at times."

"Which is why it's such a blessing that she has you," Anya said.

"And the other way around," Ian pointed out. He then felt compelled to add, "You should also know that Wren is pregnant. We haven't known very long, and . . . there's been so much going on."

"Oh, that's wonderful news!" Anya said and Gavin smiled. "But it's all the more reason Wren needs to take care of herself."

"And how is Bethia?" Gavin asked.

"For the moment she seems fine . . . or she did when I came down to breakfast. Her sewing keeps her engaged. It's impossible to know when she might cause an uproar. I've offered to sit with Bethia so that Wren can rest or get some fresh air, but she's hesitant to leave her at all. I've been wondering if we should confide in one of the maids so that this might not be so difficult for Wren. Shona has taken to Bethia—and vice versa, I believe. But I don't know how trustworthy she is. If there was any question about her loyalty . . . any possibility that she might gossip, I don't know if we'd dare. If the servants gossip, it will inevitably reach the townspeople, and we have no way of predicting how that might affect Bethia—or the rest of us."

"I have no reason to believe that Shona isn't trustworthy," Anya said. "I will discreetly ask Mrs. Boyle her opinion on the matter. Since she's in charge of the household, she knows everything about every one of the servants. I think we *do* need someone to help care for Bethia. It's been too great of a burden for Wren all along. With the baby coming, Wren needs someone she can rely on to help with her sister."

"I agree," Ian said, "as long as they're trustworthy, and both Bethia and Wren can feel comfortable."

"You must consider, son," Gavin said, "that the servants are likely to gossip regardless. It's something we don't have control over. It's a fact of living the way we live. It's not always pleasant having people working right and left in our home. But it has to be done to keep up this monstrous place, and it simply comes with the responsibility of being the Earl. While you were living in town, you were concerned about the neighbors and townspeople gossiping. It's just the nature of people. It may simply be something that we'll have to contend with, regardless of how carefully we choose someone to help with Bethia. In spite of all that, I agree that Wren does need help with her sister. If Shona has taken to Bethia, that would be a good place to start."

"Thank you," Ian said, "but there is another matter I must discuss with you. It's all the more reason that Bethia needs someone she can rely on, but it complicates the situation in ways that I cannot begin to imagine." He rubbed a hand over his face and sighed, searching for the right words.

"What is it, Ian?" Anya asked. "Whatever it is, you know we'll do everything we can to help you."

"I know that," Ian said. "I don't know what people do who don't have family to help them get through their struggles. And of all the families in the world, I'm certain mine is among the best."

"You're very kind," Gavin said. "We feel the same way, but I believe you're avoiding whatever it is you need to say to us."

Ian sighed again. "Given that Greer is dead—and has been believed to be dead for years now—I have no idea how we are going to explain the fact that Bethia is pregnant." Gavin and Anya were both unusually silent, their mouths hanging open slightly. "Yes," Ian said, "I know exactly how you feel. Except that I knew she was pregnant *before* I realized Greer was actually alive. I'm glad to know now that there isn't some other . . . . mysterious . . . horrible . . . possibility for such a thing."

"Yes, we can be glad for that," Anya said with complete resolve and dignity. "But this certainly does create an extraordinary quandary."

Ian rose abruptly and stood at the window. "That is a polite understatement. There is no way that every servant in the house won't know about the baby, and that means everyone in town will know. With everyone believing that Greer has long been dead, a possible explanation would be that she was promiscuous, or that she was raped. Or we have to admit that Bethia is not of sound mind, and therefore subject her to that which we've feared all along—that the people will misunderstand, be afraid, and create problems, perhaps even insisting that she be sent to an asylum. Either explanation brings public shame and ridicule. And you . . ." Ian motioned to his father, "the Earl of Brierley, are housing this mad, pregnant woman beneath your roof, which implies your endorsement of any possible number of ridiculous notions that will be the result of grossly distorted gossip."

"I do *not* care what people say, *or* what they think," Gavin said firmly. "And you know that."

"Yes, I know that," Ian said. "But I must admit that my fears are not rooted in what people think or say, but what they might do." He forced out the idea he knew he needed to share, knowing they would not take it well. "Perhaps," he added ruefully, "it would be better if I take my family and . . . . leave."

"Leave?" Anya echoed in a high pitch of panic.

Gavin added, "There is no reason to think that this problem can't be handled without resorting to such drastic measures. We've already lost one son. We're not losing you as well—especially over something so . . . ridiculous and trivial."

Ian said nothing more beyond agreeing to give the matter some time. But in his heart he felt the idea of leaving gathering strength inside of him. He didn't understand why; he just knew it was inevitable. In his heart he knew that the outcome of this dilemma would likely be scandalous, but certainly not trivial. Rather than focusing on the uncertainty and fear, he chose to embrace the undeniable warmth and comfort he felt within his deepest self, a seeming voice from within that spoke to him without words, letting him know that when all was said and done, he would be guided to the path that God would have him take, and that he would blessed to be able to care for his family, no matter what that path entailed. But he wasn't ready to share such feelings with his parents, not even with Wren. Not yet. He *would* give the matter some time. And perhaps the present dilemma would resolve itself, and the need to move on would be delayed for years. Either way, he was prepared.

* * * * *

Ian was pleasantly surprised, after all his worrying, to see Wren and Bethia both settle comfortably into life at Brierley. Bethia's grief over Greer's death seemed swallowed up in her madness, as if it buffered her from remembering or feeling the reality of what had happened. She spoke of the baby moving inside of her, and was very matter-of-fact about it being Greer's baby—something that Ian and Wren both hoped no one beyond those closest to her ever overheard. She also talked about Jinty and Selma, making it clear that her imaginary companions were still making themselves known. Apparently Jinty and Selma each had their opinions on Greer's death, Bethia's pregnancy, and life at Brierley. Jinty was angry and cynical; Selma was more quiet and passive, and could usually talk sense into Jinty enough to keep Bethia behaving herself when others were around.

After Anya got a good report from Mrs. Boyle concerning Shona, they spoke to her in confidence about Bethia needing someone who could give her more personal care, and that she had some challenges that needed to be kept in confidence. Shona was eager to take on the responsibility. She would receive a raise in her pay and be excused from her other duties, mostly becoming a personal maid to Wren and Bethia, with her focus being on her care of Bethia so that Wren could get the rest she needed with her pregnancy, allowing her to have somewhat of a normal life. Shona settled quickly into a routine that had been agreed on between her and Wren, and Bethia enjoyed Shona's company. Wren began to share meals with the family and interact with them more, which Ian enjoyed very much. They were able to take walks together, spend time in the library, and even go on an occasional picnic. Sometimes Bethia went with them and did well on those occasions, but mostly she preferred to stay in the security of her comfortable room, where everything she needed or wanted was brought to her without trouble or delay. She didn't expect much and expressed gratitude for every meal and every bit of help she was given. All in all, the situation was working, and Ian felt somewhat relieved. For all that a part of him still wondered if leaving Brierley would become necessary—and he was prepared to do so—he certainly didn't want to be traveling with two pregnant women, and have to face the uncertainty of them giving birth and caring for infants in unknown circumstances. Leaving on his own had been entirely different. His care of these women was now his most important responsibility.

Ian felt relatively happy unless he allowed himself to think about the deaths of his brother and his best friend. No matter which perspective he chose in order to examine the situations surrounding their deaths, he always came out feeling somehow responsible. He took some time each day to study the book he'd bought in London. He found passages that tugged at him, luring him to believe that there was hope for redemption for him *and* for James and Greer. But it all felt complicated and difficult to understand, especially in personal application to himself and those he loved. He only knew that he felt compelled to keep reading, and he took in the stories and messages with eager expectation. He shared a little here and there with Wren about what he was reading, and she showed a genuine interest, but he'd not yet told her the full depth of how this book seemed to have some inexplicable power over him, as if his spirit believed it held the answers to his life, even if his mind couldn't begin to comprehend such an idea.

At the warmest point of summer, Lilias gave birth to a healthy boy, and everyone in the household shared in the joy of this new little life. With James's baby in the house, and the prospect of two more on the way, there was much talk of how lively and colorful the household would become. Gavin and Anya enjoyed the babies thoroughly and were nothing but pleased with the beginning of the next generation of MacBriers in their home.

Ian and Wren were both surprised when Bethia expressed a desire to go to church. They'd been going without her since Shona had become comfortable with watching out for her. In spite of their nervousness about taking Bethia into public, they had asked her if she'd wanted to go, but she had expressed a fear of going beyond the borders of Brierley, having come to feel a great security there. Now, seemingly out of nowhere, Bethia wanted to go to church, and she wanted Shona to come along. Shona admitted that she'd never held much to religion, but she'd be more than happy to attend with Bethia and perhaps be able to help keep her calm. Ian and Wren talked about it privately, and they even discussed it with his parents, wanting to handle the situation in the best possible way. It was tempting to tell Bethia that she just couldn't be seen in public until after the baby was born, because people wouldn't understand. And Bethia probably would have understood and been all right with that. But Gavin boldly declared Ian's own thoughts: of all places, a person ought to be able to go to church if she wanted to. If Bethia wanted to go, she would attend with the family, and together they would take on any repercussions. Since Bethia was visibly pregnant, those repercussions were inevitable. But Ian felt good about the decision, even strangely calm and at peace over it, as if it might be an important step in the course of their lives, even if it didn't turn out to be an easy one.

Chapter Fourteen
Madness

Not many days after Donnan had become a father, Gavin's health suffered a sudden decline. His coughing and breathing difficulties were worse than ever, and it was terrifying at times to see him struggling to take in enough breath to even speak. The doctor reported that he had no way of knowing if it would improve or worsen, but Gavin needed to stay down for the time being and not exert himself at all. He continued taking the tonic for his cough that he'd been taking for a long time, but the doctor suggested increasing the dosage in order to calm the intense coughing fits that were sure to cause other problems if they couldn't be controlled.

Ian was grateful to be living under the same roof as his parents when he had a desire to spend as much time with his father as he possibly could; his mother also needed the support of her sons. They sent a letter to Gillian with the hope that she would be able to come and visit on the chance that Gavin's life was drawing to a close. Anya expressed worry that she might not be able to come—or even worse, that she might not make it in time if the worst happened. Gavin remained in good spirits and did not behave like a dying man. He assured Anya repeatedly that he did not feel like a man on the brink of death, and he would surely be able to manage with this illness for years to come. Still, Ian had great compassion for his mother's concerns. It was difficult to tell if Gavin sincerely believed the end was *not* near, or if he was simply trying to assuage the concerns of his family. Wren told Ian that she believed his father was not the kind of man to be dishonest about his feelings for the sake of placating others. She believed he would want to be prepared, and to know that his family was prepared. Ian thought about that and believed she was right. He felt some comfort to think that this was just a temporary setback, and that they would all have the sixth Earl of Brierley with them for many years to come.

One evening after supper, the family gathered in Gavin's room, a routine that was becoming typical. Donnan and Lilias were proud parents, and everyone enjoyed taking turns holding the baby. Little James was smiling and cooing, and everyone in the family loved to try to get smiles out of him. Wren loved holding both of the babies, and Ian loved imagining what it would be like when they had their own child. He too loved holding the babies, and he liked the practice it was giving him so that he wouldn't feel completely awkward when he became a father himself. Anya always sat on the bed next to her husband, leaning against the headboard so that she could be close enough to hold his hand while they visited as a family.

As the evening wore on, the family gradually dispersed. Lilias took the baby to change him and get him to sleep. Wren left to check on her sister and see that she got to bed so that Shona could be relieved of her duties. The nanny came to get little James to get him to bed. The two brothers remained a while longer, enjoying Gavin's recounting of stories from his youth. Donnan finally rose to leave and said, "Ian, could I talk with you before you go to bed?"

"Of course," Ian said and stood to bend over the bed to kiss each of his parents on the cheek. Donnan did the same, and the brothers left the room.

Ian followed his brother downstairs to the parlor, where Donnan made certain the doors were all closed before he sat down and motioned for Ian to do the same. Apparently he wanted to have a very serious—and private—conversation.

"Is something wrong?" Ian asked.

"Only that our father isn't going to live forever," Donnan said.

"I would think it's obvious that *no one* is going to live forever."

"And it's obvious that in the case of our father, his time here is growing shorter. Even if he's not at death's door right now, he's not going to live to be an old man."

"Yes," Ian agreed. "We've been discussing Father's health a great deal these last few days. I don't understand the point, Donnan."

"The point is that . . . I don't *want* to be the Earl of Brierley, Ian. Not now, not ever."

Ian chuckled, and Donnan glared at him, obviously not finding this humorous. "What do you expect me to say, Donnan? It's your obligation . . . your birthright."

"Not if I give it to you," Donnan said, and Ian almost choked. While he was coughing, Donnan added, "My being born a year ahead of you should not make me any more obligated or capable of being an Earl than you."

"You mean like Jacob and Esau in the Bible. They were *twins,* and yet it was still evident that the one being born before the other was *very* important in the inheritance they were meant to receive."

"I'm glad you brought up that story, because it was the younger brother—Jacob—who was destined to receive the birthright, in spite of the order of their birth."

Ian chuckled again, but only with irony. "That story has no bearing on us whatsoever!"

"You brought it up."

"Only to illustrate that the difference in our age is relevant," Ian said. "You're older, and the inheritance is meant to be yours. This is not a new concept. You inherit the title, the land, the estate, the—"

"I know what I'm to inherit," Donnan said. "The responsibility for many lives—in the household, and on the tenant farms. We've both worked with Father. We know what the responsibility entails, and we're both technically capable of seeing it through. The point is that . . . I don't want it. I don't want the title or anything that goes along with it. I think you're much better suited to the position, and I want to legally give it to you and—"

"Wait a minute," Ian said, holding up his hands. "You can't give it to me if I'm not willing to take it. I don't want it either."

"Then this will turn into a dispute?"

"A dispute?" Ian was astonished. "There's no dispute. You are the older brother. It's *your* responsibility, not mine."

Donnan sounded angry. "Well, I don't want it. I did not plan for this. I did not expect my brother to die and leave me to this. Sometimes I think I'm most angry with him for that."

"Considering the long list of reasons to be angry with James for dying, I'm assuming you're pretty angry with him."

"Indeed!" Donnan said. His voice softened. "How can I tell my father that I don't even want what he's devoted his life to leaving to me?"

"You shouldn't tell him. You should accept it graciously and devote yourself to filling the position to the best of your ability. I believe you're underestimating yourself. I think you will make an excellent Earl, and the people are in good hands."

Donnan made a dubious and disgusted noise. "I don't want to do this, Ian. How can I do it when my heart is not in it?"

"I don't know, but life is filled with doing things we don't want to do."

Donnan leaned forward and looked firmly at Ian. "I'm asking you to consider—to seriously consider—the possibility of taking this position. I would be here to help you, of course. We can do it together, but I believe the title should be yours."

"Then we disagree," Ian said.

"I just asked you to consider it. Are you not at least willing to give it some thought?"

Ian knew what his answer would be. He knew that his own destiny was not intertwined with Brierley. He wondered what Donnan would think to know Ian's thoughts in regard to eventually leaving here and taking his family with him. But since his decision to refuse Donnan's request needed to be made separate of any other issue, he nodded and agreed, "I will consider it. I will even pray over the matter."

"Thank you," Donnan said with such relief that Ian wondered if he really believed that Ian would take this burden from his shoulders.

"Do you believe that God answers such prayers, Donnan? Do you believe that He somehow . . . communicates His will to us . . . through our thoughts and feelings?"

Donnan considered the question a long moment. "I've never really thought about it exactly like that, but . . . hearing you put it that way . . . yes, I do believe that's true."

"Then let me assure you that I will give the matter some serious prayer, and I will base my decision on what I believe in my heart God wants me to do with my life. I don't think it's unfair for me to expect the same of you. Have you asked God what *He* wants you to do? Or is this attempt to trade away your birthright based on your own desires? Or your fears, perhaps?"

Donnan thought about *that* question even longer. "It certainly poses an interesting thought," he said. "We can talk about it some more in a few days."

"That will be fine," Ian said.

Donnan told him goodnight and quickly left the room. Ian sat there a few more minutes, then went upstairs to get ready for bed. He found Wren curled up in the chair near the bed, wearing her nightgown, reading a book. She smiled when she saw him, and he greeted her with a kiss.

"Is everything all right?" he asked, putting a hand to her pregnant belly that was just beginning to show the evidence of her condition.

"I'm feeling fine—albeit somewhat tired. Bethia is sound asleep. How is my husband?"

"Fine, I suppose. Donnan wanted to speak to me privately." He sat on the edge of the bed to pull off his boots. "He wants to relinquish his title—and all that's attached to it—to me."

"What exactly does that mean?"

"It means that when our father dies, *I* would become the Earl, and I would be entirely responsible for the estate. The title comes with an inheritance *much* larger than what I would be receiving now, but it also comes with a great deal of responsibility."

"It would mean staying at Brierley . . . forever."

"Yes, it would," he said, surprised that was the first thing she'd thought of. Did she too have feelings that they would eventually leave?

"What did ye tell him?"

"I told him that it was his birthright and he needed to honor his responsibility. He asked me to at least consider it, and I told him I would. I told him I would pray about it, as well, and I asked him to do the same."

"Do ye think God wants ye t' be the Earl, Ian?"

"No, I think Donnan just needs to become accustomed to the fact that with James dead, he is the one to rightfully inherit. I think God has other things in mind for me."

"Like what?" she asked with an intrigue that sparked the reminder in him that she, more than anyone else, was invested in him and his life. Perhaps he shouldn't have held back in sharing his feelings with her. On the other hand, what was there to share? He'd told her before that he'd continued to struggle with feelings of unrest and wanting to leave. Even though the motivation behind those feelings had shifted inside of him, it was difficult to explain, and he had nothing to go on. But Wren's expectancy prompted him to share something else that he'd been longing to talk to her about.

Ian leaned his forearms on his thighs and said, "That book I've been reading . . . is quite remarkable. It's left me thinking about things I've never thought of before and . . . there's a feeling I get sometimes when I read it that . . . well, it's difficult to explain."

"Try t' explain it anyway," she urged.

"It's as if . . . it holds the answers to what God wants me to do with my life. It's as if . . . when I read it I feel like I'm opening some magnificent treasure chest, and any moment I might get a glimpse of my own destiny."

The silence startled Ian out of somewhat of a stupor, and he looked at Wren to see that the intrigue in her eyes had deepened, but so had her expectancy. "What?" he asked.

"I've just never seen ye quite like that before."

"Like what?"

"I don't know. Talking about yer own destiny . . . as if it might be magnificent. And it's as if there was almost a glow about ye when ye said it."

Ian's first temptation was to scoff at her observation. A glow? But he couldn't deny that he felt something akin to a glow when he read from the book, and he wondered if there was something to her observation. When he didn't know what to say, he was glad to hear her ask him to tell her more about the book. They both climbed into bed and leaned against a fluffy pile of pillows while he showed her certain passages, told her some of the stories he'd read, and tried to explain how he had felt at times while reading. He was surprised at how speaking of it aloud had a way of cementing the ideas more firmly into his mind, and he was more surprised at how receptive Wren was to all that he shared—not in a diplomatic kind of way, just trying to be kind and polite to her husband's interests, but in a way that let him know she was genuinely intrigued with the book, and glad that he had bought it that fateful day in London.

Two days later, Ian was reading an especially fascinating story in the book about a man named Mosiah who had become king following the death of his father, Benjamin, who was a very good and wise man. When Mosiah's sons came of age, they all went through a miraculous change in their lives from living very wickedly to having a strong desire to serve the Lord. But none of Mosiah's sons wanted to be king. The story struck Ian deeply in light of the issue between him and Donnan at the moment. He knew that Donnan was waiting for a firm answer, and he'd made it a matter of prayer as he had promised Donnan he would. The outcome of the story Ian was reading had no relation to his own situation, but the dilemma itself stuck with Ian. He couldn't stop thinking of how the reason that Mosiah's sons didn't want to be king was due to their intense desire to leave their home and preach the word of God—just like those men Ian had met in London, he thought.

After pondering the implications of the story for nearly twenty-four hours, Ian read that chapter again, wondering why he felt so drawn to its concepts. He didn't understand all of why he felt the way he did, but he knew beyond any doubt that it was not his place to be the Earl of Brierley. Donnan needed to be willing to take on that responsibility, and Ian could only help him understand that, and support him as much as it was possible.

That evening Ian pulled his brother aside for a private conversation. Donnan was disappointed by Ian's answer, but admitted that in his heart he knew he needed to face this and honor their father by fulfilling the position well. With their father in such poor health, Donnan knew he needed to put more effort into taking on the responsibilities that Gavin was still overseeing from his bed.

Ian attempted to share with his brother the story he'd read and how it had affected him and helped him make this decision. Donnan listened politely but showed no inkling of interest in Ian's passion over the book. Ian was glad to return to his room and find his wife actually reading from the book. Since they only had one copy and they were both reading at different places, he went into town the following day to ask Mr. Munro at the book shop if he could order another copy. Mr. Munro looked at the book with dismay.

"I've never even heard of it," he said with excessive chagrin. "*The Book of Mormon?* How odd. It says here inside that it was printed in New York. I could write t' a book store there and inquire. Sometimes they can help me get American titles. That can be awfully slow, however."

"Thank you, no," Ian said, thinking in that moment it would be easier to just go to New York himself and not only find the book, but also the religion it represented. He stepped outside the book shop and had to stand there a long moment to allow the thought to settle into his brain—then it settled into his heart.

New York? Of all the places he'd thought of possibly going during all his wanderlust musings, his mind had never ventured as far as America. For some reason he'd preferred to think of remaining in the British Isles, or perhaps Europe. But America? It was *so* far away! Coming back to visit family would be extremely difficult, if not impossible. *New York?* He pushed the thought away, certain it was nonsense, knowing he could never take his pregnant wife and his pregnant sister-in-law across the Atlantic to try to find a home in such a raw country. Or even if he waited until the children were born, how could he take women *and* children on such a journey? It was so preposterous that he laughed out loud and headed home to tell Wren that they would just have to take turns reading the book, or they would have to read it together. And he was fine with that. Sharing such an adventure with her had its appeal. Uncovering the stories and messages of the book together felt like all the adventure he wanted right now. Funny how his wanderlust had been completely dispelled by the ridiculous thought of going to New York. Home suddenly felt very appealing. Home was comfortable, predictable, and safe.

* * * * *

Ian awoke earlier than usual to a gentle summer breeze teasing the curtains. The muted light in the room told him the sun had not yet come up, even though its rays had begun to offer their warmth. He watched Wren sleeping and counted the blessings she had brought into his life. He thought of the child they would have, and the joy they would share for many years to come in working together to raise a fine family. The challenges they faced in the present—and the potential challenges of the future—felt distant and irrelevant. He felt an inner warmth and a blanket of quiet peace that was impossible to ignore. Ian rolled over in search of the precious book that he'd left on the bedside table. But before he could pick it up, he had a sudden and urgent desire to go for a walk instead.

Ian dressed quietly and left a note for Wren. He stepped outside and lifted his face skyward, closing his eyes to breathe in the mixed fragrances of the morning. The dew, the grass, the flowers, the trees. He walked with purpose toward the forest that closely banked his home. He ambled for several minutes with no particular spot in mind, and no prominent thoughts in his head. He knew the sun had peered over the horizon when he saw the sparkle of its light between the trees to the east. He stopped walking to just look around at how the beams of light that sneaked past the barrier of trees had changed the appearance of everything around him. Then, with no warning, his thoughts changed so abruptly that he gasped and turned, as if he might see someone behind him, whispering to him. He immediately knew that was ludicrous. The words in his mind had not come through his ears; he'd not heard any actual voice. But he knew the words had been spoken to him. He absolutely knew it. Pondering how he knew, and what he knew, his heart quickened, and his lungs struggled to draw breath. He dropped to his knees and muttered, "Can this be real?"

An inexplicable warmth rushed over him from head to toe, chilling him with gooseflesh, while his heart became so hot he believed he could touch his chest and feel the heat. The immeasurable magnitude of the experience—and his physical response to it—overflowed in the form of tears that ran down his face and trickled onto his shirt. Now that he was completely still and paying close attention, the words came again, a perfect repetition of what he'd heard before. *You were not responsible. The worth of souls is great in the sight of God.*

Ian moaned and wrapped his arms around his middle, bending over them until his head nearly touched the ground. For a long moment he felt the pain of the responsibility he'd held on to in regard to Greer's death, and that of James. But only for a moment. A heartbeat later the huge and magnificent meaning of the words he'd heard extracted that pain from him, as if a festering splinter had been plucked out and the wound had immediately disappeared. And into his mind came a perfect memory of the words he'd heard proselyted in the streets of London, the words that had set him on his journey toward home: *Wherefore, redemption cometh in and through the Holy Messiah; for he is full of grace and truth. Behold, he offereth himself a sacrifice for sin, to answer the ends of the law, unto all those who have a broken heart and a contrite spirit.*

The meaning of those words consumed him body and soul. The perfect peace that replaced his pain caused a physical reaction in him beyond what he'd felt when he'd dropped to his knees. In that moment everything changed, everything was different. He knew that everything he'd read in that book was true, and he knew that encountering those men in London had not been coincidence. And it was a complete surprise to him to realize that even his seemingly senseless wandering had been prompted by the hand of God. He had needed to fall to such depths in order to understand who he really was, in order to be prepared for the work that God would have him do. The Book of Mormon had been destined to come into his hands, and he was destined to follow where it led him.

Ian put his hands to the ground and hung his head while his mind attempted to assess the enormous amount of information that had entered his mind—seemingly in an instant. And while his mind tried to catch up, the emotional impact of the experience had no trouble convincing him that what he'd felt was real, and that the information he'd been given was true. It was as if God had spoken to him—*to him*—directly, and with such force that he would never be able to doubt or question the message he'd been given. He'd been freed from his pain and sorrow, and utterly forgiven of his sins. He felt it as if he'd been drowning and had been miraculously lifted up out of swirling waters into perfect peace. And as surely as he felt the dampness of the dew on the ground and the brightness of the sun gleaming through the trees, he knew that God had planted in him the need and desire to wander. The feeling had been there from his childhood, not as a curse or a detriment to his life, but to lead him to this moment, and to prepare him for the path before him. He didn't know where that path would lead him, but he knew the next step, and he knew that all he needed was faith enough to take that step. And when he had taken that step, he would be guided to the next step, and the next. He'd been born to wander, but he knew with every fragment of his body and spirit combined that at the end of the journey was a destiny that would bless his posterity for generations to come. And he knew that as long as he remained true to the undeniable witness of the power of Jesus Christ, he would be guided and strengthened to face whatever challenge might arise.

Ian rolled onto his back and stared up through the trees, recounting every thought and feeling that had just occurred. He marveled that an experience so brief could be so undeniable, and so life altering. He would never be the same! His *life* would never be the same. The man who had walked into this forest was not the same man who would walk out. He weighed and measured the information he'd been given, even though he knew that it could take days, perhaps weeks—or longer—to fully sort out and understand what had happened. He felt perfectly at peace and prepared to go forward with determination. He knew where he needed to go, and he knew why.

Then a stone crashed into the still, glassy waters of his peace, sending out ripples of fear and concern. He immediately reminded himself that he'd just received an undeniable witness that God would be with him, no matter what. He had to hold to what he knew and trust that he would be blessed to be able to conquer any impediment. At the moment he was most concerned about how this would affect his family. To declare that he was leaving—likely never to return—would break the hearts of his loved ones who would remain. But his concern for Wren far outweighed that of his family. He'd once told her that he would never go anywhere without her. But would she be willing to go wherever he felt he needed to go? And wherever they went, Bethia was a part of their family and would need to go as well.

It occurred to Ian that leaving would solve the problem of having to explain Bethia's pregnancy. Once away from this valley, there would be no need to explain anything. Bethia's husband had died recently; that was a fact that anyone who didn't know of Greer's supposed death years ago would accept simply and with compassion. Ian's breath caught as he recounted the thoughts and feelings that had been showing up in his mind for weeks now, allowing him to become accustomed to the possibility of leaving—a possibility that he now knew must become a reality. It must! It was his destiny. God had healed him, heart and soul. And now he would devote his life to going wherever God wanted him to go, to doing whatever God wanted him to do.

But what of Wren? She was his dearest friend and closest confidant. Could he explain to her all that had just happened? Would she believe him? Would she truly be willing to leave everything behind? And how could he do it? How could he take two pregnant women into the unknown? He believed Bethia would be fine as long as her sister was at her side, wherever they might go. He simply needed to convince Wren of his reasons for needing to leave, and pray that she would understand. He prayed for it right then, certain God was listening, even though the intense feelings that had verified His presence earlier were no longer with Ian. He reminded himself that knowing the path he needed to take didn't mean he needed to leave tomorrow. He didn't know *when* it would be right to leave. He just needed to be ready, and he needed to keep listening for that voice, with the faith that he would know when the time was right.

The angle of the sun alerted Ian to a realization of how much time had passed, then a growl of his stomach alerted him to the fact that he'd likely been gone for hours. He'd left a note for Wren, but she wouldn't have expected him to be away for so long. He jumped to his feet and took another long moment to look around him, wanting his memories of this place and this time to remain clear and unobscured in his memory. With a light heart and a bright spirit, he walked back through the woods, across the lawn, and around the gardens. Once inside, he hurried up the stairs, hoping Wren would be there. In that moment he didn't worry about how to tell her what had happened, or whether or not she would believe him. He didn't worry about whether or not she would be agreeable to the prospect of a tremendous journey. He only wanted to see her and to hold her in his arms. He wanted to tell her how dearly he loved her and how very happy she had made him. He wanted her to know that he knew having her in his life had been an important piece of his destiny, and that wherever that destiny might lead him, he would be grateful to have her by his side.

Ian entered Bethia's room after knocking, knowing it was the most likely place to find his wife. Shona was there with Bethia, and they were happily engaged in some sewing project. Bethia saw him and said, "Wren went t' the gardens, hoping t' find ye. I think she was worried that ye missed breakfast."

"I'll find her," Ian said and hurried back down the stairs and outside, wondering why he hadn't seen her when he'd passed the gardens. Of course, they were huge, with many shrubberies and trees. He wandered through them for only a few minutes before he saw her sitting on a little stone bench, her brow furrowed with what he assumed to be concern over his absence.

"Hello, Mrs. MacBrier," he said, and she looked up, startled.

"Oh, there ye are," she said, putting a hand to her heart.

"You were worried?" he asked, stepping closer.

"Only a little," she said and stood. He embraced her tightly, then looked at her face, surprised to find evidence in her eyes that something was troubling her. "T' tell the truth, I wasn't worried at all. I knew ye must have needed some time t' yerself."

"How did you know that?" Ian asked, even more surprised to find tears pooling in her eyes.

Wren took both of his hands tightly into hers, and the tears spilled down her face. "Ian," she said, as if she might tell him that someone had died. His heart pounded. He wondered if something had happened to his father since he'd left—or in the night. He held his breath and waited. "Ian," she repeated, "please tell me that I don't need t' explain what I mean when I say that our lives are about t' change very much."

Ian's pounding heart prompted his breath to become shallow. He wanted to ask how she knew that, to ask why she was crying. He was glad to hear her give some explanation.

"I had a dream, Ian, but . . . it wasn't a dream. I was asleep, but it was too real and vivid and magnificent t' be a dream. When I awoke, each detail was clear in my mind, and it was as if the memory of what I'd dreamt had filled my heart . . . and I felt warm all over . . . but chilled." She chuckled softly and glanced down. "Ye must think I sound crazy."

"No, Wren," he said. "Not at all." His voice trembled. "What did you dream, Wren?"

They both sat down as if weakness had overtaken them in the same moment, but their hands remained tightly clasped.

"I saw us together . . . with our children. We were far from here, in a beautiful city next t' a river wider than I've imagined a river could be. We were happy there. God was with us. And when I awoke, I knew that it was our destiny t' be there . . . even though I don't know where it is." Wren tightened her grip on his hands and leaned toward him. She sobbed softly and uttered with a quiet conviction beyond anything he'd ever witnessed in her. "I don't know how I know it, Ian; I could never put t' words how I know it. But I *know* that we're not meant t' be here, Ian. I know that this feeling ye've had . . . that it was put there by God t' lead us to a place where the lives of those who come after us will be greatly blessed. I know that book we're reading is true, Ian. I don't know how that ties int' everything else I felt, but I know it's true. And I knew that ye'd left early and not come back because . . ." Something between a sob and a chuckle came through her lips. "It sounds so very strange, Ian, but I have t' say it. I felt as if . . . God had called ye away from yer bed t' tell ye the same thing that He'd told me. I knew that when ye came back ye would know the same as I know, and if ye tell me I'm wrong, I'll have t' believe that I'm losing my mind as surely as my sister has lost hers."

Ian felt incapable of speaking. The miracle was too astounding to believe without a complete admission that God was real and His hand was indeed in the lives of His children. He was startled to hear Wren say, "Ye're crying."

Only then did he become aware of the tears running down his face. But he made no attempt to wipe them away, unable to let go of Wren's hands. He struggled to connect his voice to all he wanted to say, but the words eluded him. All that came out was simply, "You've not lost your mind, Wren. It's all true."

"Oh!" she gasped and let go of his hands only to wrap him in her arms. She scooted closer to him on the bench and held him with strength. Ian returned her embrace, and for long minutes they allowed the silence to help them assess and accept all that had happened. The miracle of their separate experiences added strength and confirmation to the miracle of the message they had each received.

Wren pulled back and wiped the tears from Ian's face while he wiped them from hers. "Oh, my darling," she said, her eyes bright and her countenance gleaming with perfect peace. They sat there together, and Ian quietly shared his own experience with her. While it was difficult, if not impossible, to find words sufficient to explain, Wren seemed to know how he felt, and it was easy to share details of something he'd feared no one could ever understand. As Wren shared more details of her dream, and how it had made her feel, they realized that they'd both been given separate information with the same undeniable message: they needed to leave Brierley to start a new life, even though they had no idea where they were going. America was all they knew for certain, and New York seemed a good place to start, since the book that had contributed to these changes in their life had been printed there.

They agreed to keep details of these experiences between themselves, certain that others might misunderstand—or make light of—all they had seen and felt. They also agreed that they would give the matter some time, and that they would both surely know when it was right to take the next step and leave this place forever. When there seemed nothing more to say and they knew it was far past lunch time, they walked hand in hand into the house to find something to eat. Ian had never felt so happy, never felt so at peace. And it only took a glance at Wren to know that she felt the same. He held the feeling close to his heart, knowing it would carry them through the inevitable hardship they would endure upon leaving this place of comfort and security.

* * * * *

The negative result of Bethia showing herself at church occurred much more quickly than Ian had imagined. But he was stunned by the manner in which the problem became known, and the intensity of its manifestation. It began with the minister paying a visit, asking to speak with Gavin and Ian. Since Gavin's health had shown some improvement, he was able to get dressed and come down to the parlor to receive the minister's visit. Ian was stunned to hear this man who supposedly represented God—at least in this community—speaking boldly on the deep concern of many people in his congregation concerning the presence of a woman in the MacBrier household who was unwed and pregnant. He pointed out that when the baby was born, the matter would only be made worse by having an illegitimate child in their midst, and this would present an appalling example to the youth of the community. To allow Bethia to continue to attend church would be an insult to the good people in the area.

"I wonder if you've considered," Ian said, barely able to keep his anger in check, "the possibility that a woman could be pregnant for reasons beyond her own control."

Ian was stunned that the minister did not ask if Bethia might have been raped or abused. Even though that was not the case, Ian felt it was a legitimate point that the minister should at least have considered—especially when he had no knowledge of the circumstances surrounding the situation, and he'd made no effort to find out what they were. Instead the religious leader of the community stated firmly, "The means of conception are irrelevant. The woman is not married, and we cannot abide having her attend church under such circumstances."

"How very Christian your principles are, sir," Ian said with intense sarcasm, but the minister completely ignored the comment and went on with his diatribe.

"If you," the minister looked directly at Gavin, "as a respected person of nobility in this community continue to harbor this young woman, I can assure you that the effect on you and your family will be disastrous."

"Are you threatening me?" Gavin asked, advancing on the minister as if he might have him thrown out the door and kicked down the lane.

Ian paused to consider what this might mean in regard to little James. Had the community figured out that the MacBriers had this child in their home? Since the baby hadn't yet been taken to church, it was likely a situation that had not yet come to anyone's attention, but when it did, Ian knew it wouldn't be good. This was made even more evident as the minister countered hotly, "You cannot expect members of this community to abide such a thing!"

"I would expect the members of this community to mind their own business," Gavin said, "and to behave as Christians. If Jesus Himself were in charge of this congregation, He would *not* turn Bethia away from her sincere desire to attend church, and He would *not* condone such judgmental treatment by others."

The minister huffed away, uttering more threats on his way out as if he had the power to call down the wrath of God on the house of Brierley. Gavin didn't speak for a long minute after the drawing-room door had slammed. Ian could almost imagine him never attending church again, for whatever time he had left in this world. But whatever his father chose to do or not do, Ian felt astonishingly calm. He drew a deep breath and took advantage of the moment to open the door of his destiny, and do what he knew needed to be done. The time had come. His leaving here with his family would solve every problem.

"There's no need to concern yourself, Father," Ian said, and Gavin looked at him abruptly, perhaps startled by Ian's serenity. "I will be leaving Brierley, and taking my family with me." Before Gavin could utter even a syllable of protest, Ian added firmly, "I know in my heart it's what God wants for me, and Wren knows it too. We've just been waiting for the right time. Clearly, leaving now would be best for everyone."

Ian quietly listened to his father's every argument, and then his mother arrived to inquire over the reason for the minister's visit. She cried and repeated every reason that Gavin had given Ian as to why he should not leave Brierley, and she tearfully counseled him that this plan to go to America and find some obscure religion was madness.

"It's madness," Gavin said, not for the first time. "Madness!"

Ian recognized the breaking hearts of his parents beneath the surface, and tears came to his eyes as evidence of his compassion for them—even if they couldn't fully understand it. "Forgive me," he said, "for hurting you this way; it's not my intention. In my opinion, the real madness here is that a man who holds no actual authority on behalf of God, as far as I can see, is able to dictate who will and will not be a part of his congregation. I made this decision many days ago, and I know beyond any doubt that this is the path God wants for me. You always taught me to trust in God and to follow where He leads me. That's what I'm doing. It's not easy, but it's right. We must all find faith and comfort in that."

Ian looked directly at his mother and knew he was being inspired when he clearly recalled words she had said to him long ago. "You once told me," he said, "that you prayed I would find whatever I needed to find, and that when I found it, I would be happy. You said that above all else, you wanted me to be happy . . . wherever I might go, or whatever I might become. You said that my happiness was important to you above all else. I know this is difficult to face, but I'm telling you, Mother, with all of my heart, this is what I am meant to do."

Anya had nothing to say, but her silent tears expressed her sorrow. Ian felt the need to add, more to his father, "After what happened to James . . . I can understand why this is especially hard for me to ask of you . . . to let me go this way. But you told me you would far prefer knowing that I was living elsewhere, and for me to be alive and well." He sighed and concluded, "I know in my heart this is best, and Wren knows it too."

Ian left his parents crying silent tears and went upstairs to tell Wren that they needed to start packing. He was surprised, though he shouldn't have been, that Wren didn't feel at all angry toward the minister. She simply saw his visit as a sign that it was time to leave, and she felt more peace than trepidation.

"You know," Ian said, "in every logical way, my father's right. This *is* madness. If I were him, and my son were leaving under such circumstances, I would likely say the very same thing. You and Bethia are both pregnant. We'll probably never see these people we love again. And we have no idea what we're doing."

"Yes, we do," she said. "We're going t' Liverpool and getting passage on a ship t' New York." She talked about it as if she were referring to their attendance at a social function in town.

"And after that?"

"God will guide us, my darling."

"Your faith inspires me, Wren. And I love you for it."

She laughed with a happiness that was more complete than she'd ever expressed, as if the actual decision to leave had soothed something within her. He knew exactly how she felt. The unrest that had existed in him throughout the whole of his life, haunting him, leading him to believe that he was strange and different, had been replaced by perfect peace. He didn't know where God would lead him, but now that he knew he was being led to his destiny, he would press forward to that horizon with all the faith and conviction of his soul.

"You sound very happy, Mrs. MacBrier," he said, "for a woman about to tread into the unknown."

"It is not unknown to God," she said and threw her arms around him.

About the Author

Anita Stansfield began writing at the age of sixteen, and her first novel was published sixteen years later. Her novels range from historical to contemporary and cover a wide gamut of social and emotional issues that explore the human experience through memorable characters and unpredictable plots. She has received many awards, including a special award for pioneering new ground in LDS fiction, and the Lifetime Achievement Award from the Whitney Academy for LDS Literature. Anita is the mother of five, and has two adorable grandsons. Her husband, Vince, is her greatest hero.

To receive regular updates from Anita, go to anitastansfield.com and subscribe.